S0-BRT-113

Praise for the Witch of Empire Series

"There's a grungy punk-rock bite to it that tastes like subways and smoke and whiskey-filled nights."
—Cassandra Khaw, author of *Hammers on Bone*

"An addictive blend of magic and murder noir."
—Gareth L. Powell, BSFA award-winning author of *Ack-Ack Macaque*

"Penman writes with the wit and charm of a foul-mouthed Terry Pratchett. His Agent Sully is what Dirty Harry would be if he was a lesbian witch fighting demons alongside the cast of *Yes, Minister*. She can be my date to the Imperial Bureau of Investigation Ball anytime."
—Robyn Bennis, author of *The Guns Above*

"Vampires and demons. Monsters and magic. Forbidden love, in a mind-blowing adventure. 'Sully' Sullivan returns in a blaze of fury and might as the plucky, magic-wielding heroine who takes crap from no one, even when the odds are stacked infinitely against her. Good luck trying to put this one down; it'll leave your knuckles raw."
—Kyle Richardson, author of the Steambound Trilogy

"Agent Sully . . . is a kick ass heroine, a kind of adult Harry Potter meets Katniss Everdene and is the tour de force that drives this novel along . . . The writing is fast paced, imaginative with an underlying intelligence that gives credence to the infrastructure of the magical aspects of crime and policing."
—Gill Chedgey, NB Magazine (4 stars)

"A very entertaining and atmospheric alternative history fantasy novel . . . I would highly recommend The Wounded Ones to fans of the first novel in the series, and I would certainly recommend the author as a superbly creative fantasy writer."
—Readers' Favorites (5 stars)

"Penman has a knack for speculative fiction, especially involving magic, necromancy and, oddly enough, colonialism."
—TRL Reviews (4 stars)

Also by G.D. Penman

WITCH OF EMPIRE:

The Year of the Knife
The Last Days of Hong Kong

DEEPEST DUNGEON:

Dungeons of Strata
Masters of Strata

ROMANCE:

Lovers and Liches
Moonshine

THE WOUNDED ONES

G.D. PENMAN

Meerkat Press
Atlanta

THE WOUNDED ONES. Copyright © 2020 by G.D. PENMAN

All rights reserved. No part of this publication may be used, reproduced, distributed, or transmitted in any form or by any means without prior written permission from the publisher, except in the case of brief quotations embodied in critical reviews and certain other noncommercial uses permitted by copyright law. For information, contact Meerkat Press at *info@meerkatpress.com*.

ISBN-13 978-1-946154-19-4 (Paperback)
ISBN-13 978-1-946154-20-0 (eBook)

Library of Congress Control Number: 2020938591

This is a work of fiction. Names, characters, businesses, places, events and incidents are either the products of the author's imagination or used in a fictitious manner. Any resemblance to actual persons, living or dead, or actual events is purely coincidental.

Cover design by Tricia Reeks
Book design by Tricia Reeks

Printed in the United States of America

Published in the United States of America by
Meerkat Press, LLC, Atlanta, Georgia
www.meerkatpress.com

ACKNOWLEDGMENTS

All of my thanks to Tricia at Meerkat Press for her ceaseless hard work to bring this book into being. Thanks also to Margaret for her editing prowess, and to my darling wife for being very understanding about the whole "waking up at 2 a.m. to add just a little bit more to the gryphon scene" malarkey.

OCTOBER 31, 2015

Sully stubbed out her cigar like the ashtray was her mother's face. The last coils of smoke twisted in the air to join the geometric patterns that drifted in a blue cloud around her. There were three assassins this time, and three weren't nearly enough. Sully set her glass down on the bar and let the mouthful of gin clear her sinuses. After an hour of quietly sipping liquor in the stuffy walnut paneled comfort of the train's bar, Sully's patience had run thin. The young men in three-piece suits might have blended in perfectly back in jolly old England, but here in the Americas, their blandness made them stick out.

Sully swiveled on her stool to take in the lay of the room. "Are we doing this or not? Because I've got a thirsty vampire waiting for me back in my cabin and that sounds like a lot more fun than this bullshit."

The men had been studiously avoiding eye contact with Sully and with each other for the whole trip, but now they all looked up, as if they needed to confirm that their cover was blown before acting. *Amateurs.* Sully set off the concussion spell that she had been tracing in gin on the bar-top for the last ten minutes, spellfire racing over the liquor. The whole carriage rocked on its rails, and bottles and glasses flew through the air, a maelstrom of chaos that Sully's contingency shield turned into a whirling dervish of shattered glass around her. All three assassins were moving now, leaping up from their tables and casting their own spells, but they were two moves behind her.

Her next spell seared the broken glass around her, sending molten droplets across the red carpet on their way to scorch half of one assassin's face off. The other men switched to casting shields and that delay gave her enough time to cast a more complex incantation. The next lance looked like white fire, and while the blond killer managed to get a shield up, the white flames used that dense structured magic as fuel, expanding out to consume him, leaving nothing behind but a heap of ash.

The last one got an attack off before Sully could give him her undivided attention. A ray of moonlight was launched from his fingertip, refracting through the spinning glass to pepper the whole room with patches of frost.

Sully let out a bark of laughter. "You're trying to take me alive? They really didn't give you fair warning when you took this job."

A new spell exploded in a corona around him, a nova of silvery blades that shredded what was left of the upholstery as they flew at Sully. Apparently, this one wanted to live more than he wanted big cash prizes. Sully dove into a booth as the blades and glass collided in a deafening, stinging explosion all around her. He didn't let up. A roiling wave of green fire swept through the cabin, stripping the walls to bare metal, annihilating the furnishings and reducing the cowering bartender to a stripped skeleton. Sully did her best to ignore the strange absence of heat as the fire rolled over her shields and concentrated on the task at hand.

She rose to her feet on the bare metal of the hollowed-out cabin. The assassin wasn't smiling despite his change in fortune. Maybe he was a professional after all. She launched another white lance at him and he didn't bother with a shield. His duelist instincts took over and he cast a traveling spell to jerk him out of the missile's path. It didn't work. The white fire hit him square in the chest. He vanished in a flash of light as his own magic consumed him from the inside out.

Sully staggered to her feet and let her protective spells drop. She took a deep breath of the fresh air that was pouring in through the new ventilation that her would-be killers had provided to the cabin. If portals and traveling spells hadn't been blocked by the Magi of Manhattan, then why would she have been on a train to begin with? The British really needed to hire smarter help. The last few assassination attempts had been almost insultingly lackluster.

She paused on her way back to the sleeper cars to look out of the window. The marshland flew by, barely visible in the starlight, and Sully caught a glimpse of her own reflection. Her pupils were blown large and she was bleeding from a dozen tiny scratches all over her face. It was the most alive she had looked in months. Since before Prime Minister Pratt had started forcing her to attend cabinet meetings. Sully quite liked taking the train. Flying probably would have been quicker, but every plane in the new American Empire had been grounded for the week after a half-dozen Thunderbird sightings. Besides, it gave her six uninterrupted hours with Marie, probably the longest time they had spent together since war on the British had been officially declared.

Sully fully expected the beds to be folded down and Marie to be dozing by the time she got back to their compartment, but instead Marie was sitting with her legs tucked up underneath her on the seat, staring out the window and chewing absently on the tips of her hair. Sully had to wrestle the smile off her face before Marie turned around. She looked just like she had back when she was alive, waiting around for a call-back to some audition. With a glance, Marie took in the wild mess of Sully's hair, the rips in her clothes and the spattering of blood, then sighed. "Ugh, again?"

Sully shrugged and the tattered sleeve of her one nice shirt slithered to the floor.

"It wasn't bad. Just three of them. Kind of trashed the bar though."

Marie had already turned to stare back out at the night flying by, and Sully quickly kicked her bloodied sleeve under the seat. She slumped down beside Marie and leaned her head against her lover's shoulder, carefully, as if Marie were a wild animal that was likely to startle. Marie tolerated the touch, so she leaned in more heavily. Without adrenaline to carry her through, Sully was starting to feel tired now. "What is going on with you? I haven't seen you this twitchy since *The Khan and I*. Are you getting cold feet?"

Sully felt the movement on the top of her head when Marie smiled. "I ain't seen my parents since I left New Amsterdam all those years back. I'm worried about what they're going to say. What they're going to think. It's been a long, long time."

Marie started to lap at the little cuts on Sully's forehead absent-mindedly. Her tongue was cool, soothing. Sully grumbled. "What is it about me that you think they are going to hate the most? Is it the fact I'm a woman? No chance of grandkids. Or is it because I'm a witch? That is a fair thing to worry about. Maybe it's because I'm Irish. Nothing like some good old-fashioned racism. Or maybe is it just the whole traitor to the crown thing? Were they loyalists? Are they going to try to shoot me when I walk in the door?"

Marie paused her licking to pluck a piece of glass from a gash on Sully's cheek, drawing a little hiss of pain. "Not everything is about you, darlin'. You're a big step up from some of the boys I dated when I lived with them. Hells, the last boy I brought home was a carny. You're a general. You're a catch as far as they're concerned."

Sully twisted to meet Marie's eyes. "Then what are you freaking out about?"

"Last time they saw me, I was still breathin'."

That shut Sully up for a moment. Then, very cautiously, she pried. "They don't like vampires?"

"I ain't got a clue. Far as I know, they've never even met a vampire before. Georgia Province ain't like New Amsterdam. The most exotic people we got were the Dutch. Everybody is just . . . normal there."

Sully tried not to grit her teeth. "White. Straight. That kind of normal?"

Marie shoved her off. "Don't make this a politics thing. Please. What if they think I'm a monster?"

Sully turned to face Marie, took a hold of her hands and whispered, "Then fuck them."

Marie blinked. "Fuck them?"

Sully nodded sagely. "If they don't want you center stage in their life then that is their mistake, not any fault of yours. If they're too ignorant to realize that a person is more than just their pulse, then fuck them. You don't need them. You're already perfect."

Marie snorted. "Iona Sullivan, you certainly do have your moments."

"Does that mean you are going to stop worrying?"

"Oh hells no. I'll be worrying until we leave the plantation, then I'll spend the next three months going over every moment we spent with them in my head. Picking at it." She leaned in and planted a soft kiss on Sully's lips. "But thank you anyway."

They settled back onto the seat together, staring out at the darkness. Marie's fingers started smoothing down the tangle of red hair on top of Sully's head, brushing over the shaved sides and back and drawing a shiver from her. One of the few benefits of leaving the IBI was that she could have whatever haircut she damn well pleased, so one of her first stops once she was given her commission as general was the barber down by the Black Bay. The one where all the young southern artists used to go before Red Hook caught a fireball in the British bombardment and dropped the pretentiousness of the whole city by about twenty percent. Shaved back and sides. A splash of oil— when she remembered—to keep the curls smoothed back from her face. Marie said that it made Sully look too butch, but she also thought sundresses were the height of fashion, so Sully didn't worry about that too much. Besides, anything that distracted from the mess of freckles and scars that made up her face was a blessing in Sully's opinion. She had just started to drift off when Marie asked, "Are you going to take me to meet your parents, darlin'?"

"Nope."

"Because you're ashamed of me?"

Sully snuggled in closer. "Because I never met my dad and my mother is the most bitter and vicious creature on the planet earth. I wouldn't inflict her on my worst enemy, let alone you."

It seemed enough to placate Marie, even if the details were sparse.

They lay against each other in comfortable silence. Out of some unnecessary reflex, Marie still snored when she fell asleep, even though she didn't breathe. Sully wasn't the kind of person to use words like adorable, but the gentle snorts of the vampire were enough to curl her lips into a smile despite the way it tugged on her cuts. Somewhere between Virginia and Carolina, Sully slipped into a dreamless darkness of her own.

November 1, 2015

Sully hung around the train platform looking as awkward as she felt. Marie's parents had come to meet them and there was a great deal of crying and exclamations of love going on that she wouldn't have wanted any part of, even if she had been invited. Marie's mother resembled her daughter, but her hair was darker and straighter. She was older too, of course—something Marie would never be. Her father had Marie's blonde hair and curls. Marie had had his soft blue eyes when she was alive. The color had changed now to a red so deep it was almost brown.

Sully lurked while the train pulled away with a shriek and she slipped unobtrusively into the backseat of the car when they headed out, casting quick and quiet charms to keep the worst of the sunlight on the other side of the windows where it wouldn't do any harm. Marie's father's name was Jeremiah—Sully had managed to gather that much from the non-stop flurry of conversation. Her mother's was a little more difficult, but from one of the few words that Jeremiah managed to get in edgewise, Sully suspected her name was Clementine. Marie had a lifetime of local gossip to catch up on, and her mother seemed just as desperate for any news from New Amsterdam. Looking out the window at the endless uniform fields, Sully could understand why. They had been driving for a half hour when there was a brief moment of silence and Sully realized that a question had been directed at her. "Sorry?"

Marie giggled beside her. "Momma was asking about your job. They don't know who you are. At all."

"Really?" Sully's face split into a grin that she wiped away almost as quickly. She met Clementine's eyes in the rear-view mirror. "I'm a soldier nowadays."

Jeremiah chuckled tactlessly. "Uh . . . well at least you'll always have plenty of work."

Sully laughed despite herself, a harsh little bark that sounded more like her own mother than she would have liked. Clementine filled the expectant silence with another story about somebody that Sully had never heard of and she was happy to sink back into her seat. It was nice to be somewhere where nobody knew your name. Where you could speak, or not speak, freely.

They arrived at the plantation an hour later. The Culpeppers were one of the older families in the Province, so when the land was being parceled out they'd had first pick and had chosen relatively fertile soil close to town over more acreage farther afield. The buildings must have been riddled with spells to keep them so pristine and white in such a muddy place after a century or more. The main house, a guest house, and long, repurposed stables formed three sides of a square around a manicured garden with a fountain at its center. On the other side, beyond their private road, was an orchard and beyond its bowed and withered trees was the rest of the Culpepper land. Sully had caught a glimpse of it on the way in, wheat waving golden as far as the eye could see.

It would have been nice to let Marie come home to this place the way that she remembered it, blazing in the sunshine, but it would have been a very brief homecoming. Sully got out of the car as it rolled to a stop, calling up as much of a raincloud as she could muster on the spur of the moment. It looked a little out of place hanging in the otherwise empty sky, but it did the job. Marie was hustled into the house without so much as a blush, her mother's arms wrapped around her shoulders, rubbing at her bare arms as if she could be warmed up. Jeremiah held back to walk Sully in. He rolled his eyes at the Culpepper women and would probably have made some comment about women in general if Sully hadn't been one. "Surprised that they let you away from your post. I heard that the Brits are bombarding the whole East Coast."

"It is just a few cities and they've got more Magi than they know what to do with keeping the barrier up. They can spare me for a couple of days."

Sully stepped into the house, where Clementine's and Marie's voices filled the space, but conversation ground to a halt when Clementine led them into the kitchen, where the rich tang of something slow-cooked and smothered in barbecue sauce assaulted them. The dining table was old battered wood, polished smooth by generations, and it had been set with four places. Sully met Marie's wide eyes across the table and she felt her stomach drop. They didn't know. They couldn't tell Marie was a vampire just by looking at her. Sully opened her mouth to say something, but Marie's scowl snapped her mouth shut again before she could make a sound. Marie loudly declared, "That sure smells good, Momma, but, uh, I already ate on the train."

Technically it was true, she had cleaned Sully off after the assassination attempt and she hadn't been shy about drawing out a little extra blood when she found a decent sized cut.

Clementine shook her head. "Always watching her figure. Wouldn't you like to see a little more meat on her bones, Iona?"

Sully opened and shut her mouth a few more times while Jeremiah cackled at the look on her face.

"Come on, Marie, you can have a little bit, your mother made your favorite for you."

Sully wouldn't be the one to say something—it wasn't her place—but when Marie sank down into the seat without a word, Sully stayed standing. Clementine was bustling around the oven, but Jeremiah seemed to realize that something was going unspoken. Marie took a deep breath. "Before we eat, there's something we need to talk about."

Sully sank down into her seat and said nothing. Marie groaned at their expectant faces, then let her face drop into her hands.

"Not everything's been good since the last time I saw you," she said to the tabletop. "I had a shitty marriage. I went off the rails afterward and . . . I made some bad decisions. I made some really bad decisions."

Clementine hadn't made it to a seat; now she wrapped an arm around Marie's shoulders and forced a smile. "Darlin', we all make mistakes. The important thing is that you are all right. You are alive, and you are back here with your family, and that is all that matters."

Marie's shoulders heaved as she sobbed, and Clementine began to rub at her arms again. "No. I'm not. I . . . I died, Momma."

Clementine froze in her comforting, confusion written across her face. Jeremiah seemed to stop breathing too. Marie blurted out, "I'm a vampire."

There was always anger simmering just below Sully's surface, ready to rise up when it was needed, and she could feel it burning in her chest now, just waiting for either one of the Culpeppers to say the wrong thing.

Clementine opened her mouth and—like a sigh—"Oh my sweet girl. You've been through so much" came pouring out. Jeremiah was up and out of his chair, rushing over to wrap his daughter in what might have been the clumsiest hug Sully had ever witnessed. The freezing spell that had been coiling between her fingers beneath the table whispered away. There was a murmured conversation in that tangle of arms, and some sobbing that Sully didn't need to hear. She was here for Marie, not these strangers who shared her name. If hugs and tears were what Marie needed, then Sully would sit in silence, smelling barbecue ribs burning all day if she had to. After a few minutes, the Culpeppers seemed to pull themselves together and remembered she was in the room. Clementine hustled back over to the oven. Jeremiah tried to straighten out his suit. Marie looked up at Sully when she finally escaped her mother's furious hug, blood-tinted tears staining her cheeks. She was smiling.

Sully had a limited selection of stories that she could tell a girlfriend's parents. Marie had vetted that list and nixed the more scandalous ones. The list was trimmed even further when Sully decided she didn't necessarily want them to know that she was the witch who had thrown the whole continent into upheaval and war. She got them through the meal with a few laughs and no need for any more blubbering. ". . . so, there I am, eye to eye with this bartender who is swearing blind that their drinks are completely tamper proof. That the glasses have been enchanted and there is no way somebody could have slipped a love potion into one without it exploding. He's sweating, and I figure he is about two minutes from a nervous breakdown and admitting that he forged the papers on the glasses. So, I order a drink and sit down at the bar. Now the boys from the labs are going mad at the other end of the nightclub. A love potion that can't be detected by enchanted glass? It would cause chaos. The bartender pours me a gin and puts it down on the bar right next to this glass that I am meant to be examining. And it is a different glass. One of them is a half-inch taller than the other. The bas—uh, the perpetrator, had brought an unenchanted glass from home."

Jeremiah slapped his thigh, Clementine smiled at her indulgently, and Marie was watching her with that look of quiet adoration that would make Sully cry if she thought about it for too long. The food had been good, and after eating her own portion and a fair bit of the pork that had been meant for Marie, Sully was feeling sleepy.

She stepped out onto the porch for a smoke as Marie helped with the dishes and Jeremiah slunk out to bum a cigar off her once he was sure Clementine was distracted. They looked out at the yellowing trees in amicable silence for a moment before he said, "So you're a witch? That is handy."

"Let me guess, you've got a heating rune acting up?" Sully chuckled.

He at least had the good grace to look embarrassed. "I really ain't sure what it is. But when something weird happens, more often than not it's magic. Care to take a stroll with me?"

He led her through the orchards trailing a blue cloud of cigar smoke behind them. Sully's time looking for clues was meant to be over, but everywhere that she turned she could spot traces of Marie. A heart carved into the bark. The tattered remains of a rope swing. The rusted frame of a bicycle half swallowed into the roots of a pear tree. She could almost hear a child's laughter echoing among the trees as the last of the day's sunshine filtered through. On the far side was a solid wall of wheat, taller than Sully, although that wasn't hard. It parted for Jeremiah, so Sully dove right in behind him, tripping and cursing all the way.

They emerged into a clearing after a few minutes and Jeremiah turned to her. "Well, what do you think?"

The clearing was a perfect circle in the crops. For something to do while the wheels in her head spun into action, Sully walked into the center and turned around slowly, then she paced around the outside of the circle, counting her steps. While she walked, her arcane senses danced over the circle, searching for the tell-tale signs that a spell had been cast. She stopped in front of Jeremiah and shrugged. "Circles are used for summoning or to contain magic. Maybe this is like a blast radius? The crops aren't snapped, just bent over. If it was magic, it was weak enough to have faded already. I don't get the point of this. Could it be kids messing around?"

Jeremiah nodded along with her non-explanation. "Could be. Could be. We ain't the first to have one of these pop up. There's been a few other farms around here with circles appearing in their fields."

Sully felt like more was required so she said, "I'll ask around once I am back in the city, see if anyone has heard about this."

"I'd appreciate that."

Back in the house, Sully could hear Marie and her mother singing a duet over the dishes. Some old war song about trying on a redcoat's jacket. Jeremiah caught her smiling and grinned in return. Marie's suitcase was still by the door, with Sully's duffel bag laying on top of it. Jeremiah hoisted it onto his shoulder. "Listen, I know that you and Marie are, uh, involved but this is a Christian house."

Sully fists clenched but he rambled on. "And while I realize that your relations may not be completely orthodox, that doesn't mean that we can have our daughter and her, uh . . . partner sleeping in the same room. Out of wedlock. You are grown women, and you can do what-ever you like in your own lives, but under my roof—"

Sully put a hand on his shoulder. "I'll sleep wherever you put me, it isn't going to be a problem."

He huffed out a sigh of relief. "Well we ain't tossing you out in a barn. The guest house ain't been lived in much but it has a bed and a roof without any holes."

For all of Jeremiah's jokes, the guest house was as well appointed as anywhere that Sully had ever lived and smelled a lot better than most of her homes, despite the damp seeping into the foundations. She had a little kitchen of her own to make coffee and a bedroom that was almost the size of her old apartment in New Amsterdam. She swung her bag onto the bed and finally found her courage. "What you said before, about living in sin."

He spluttered, "I didn't mean no offense."

"That is part of the reason that I came down here to meet you. Marie was nervous to see you again after all this time, but I wanted to speak to you properly before . . ." She cleared her throat and turned to face him. "Mr. Culpepper, I would like to ask your permission to marry your daughter."

He looked like he had been hit with a hammer. "Marry Marie?"

"I love your daughter, sir. I've loved her since the first moment that I set eyes on her, and I will take good care of her for the rest of my life. With or without your permission."

He spluttered, "I don't . . . I need to speak to Clementine."

Sully nodded. "Take your time. You don't really know me yet and I'm not trying to make anyone uncomfortable. Just making my intentions clear."

"It is a lot to think on. Uh, sleep well, Iona, we'll talk in the morning."

Sully grinned, "Nobody calls me Iona except Marie when she is mad. I'm Sully."

"Uh, pleasure to meet you, Sully."

"Likewise."

The evening stretched out long and empty ahead of Sully. For farmers like the Culpeppers, early awakenings were normal, but for

Sully, the sunrise was a sign that it was past her bedtime. She had been working nights her entire adult life and—especially with Marie's issues with sunlight—it just made more sense to sleep during the day. After some digging in the drawers she found some paper and a pen, and with those in hand, she settled at the counter to write out from memory the long and complex equation to cast Dante's Inferno. It was an old hobby, tinkering with the spell to get it to work without killing its user, and it would fill a few hours until she was mentally exhausted enough to try to sleep. Sully was fairly confident that she had resolved the Inferno's main problem— instantaneously draining all the magic from the caster—by forcing the spell to collapse even as it was being cast, creating a momentary burst of fire so hot it could incinerate nearly anything, without turning the caster inside out. Still, she wanted to re-check all of her equations before trying it, Despite what many of her "on the job assessments" might have said, she didn't have a death wish.

MAY 3, 1971

Iona didn't know what she'd done wrong. Normally when she did something wrong the nuns were happy to tell her, usually with a great deal of yelling and the odd smack with a ruler. When they'd caught her kissing Katherine Horgan out by the bike shed it had been hard to get a single word in. There had been a couple of red lines across the back of her thighs after that one. Most of the time Mother didn't have much to say about her transgressions. It wasn't that she didn't care, it was just that her version of right and wrong sat a little bit distant from the nuns' version. As long as Sully was still top of the class, Mother didn't give a damn.

Saying *damn* had earned her a whack too, which wasn't fair because Mother said it all the time, and with some passion. Every time she burned her fingers on the pot or she read one of the letters her friends up north had sent her, you could hear her muttering, "Damn, damn, damn," along with a few other words that she'd had the kindness to warn Iona off from using before the nuns had to intervene.

Something had been up all week. There had been a tension in the air that the little girl wasn't able to understand. Mother watched her intently as she ate her porridge in the morning. She ground the bones in Iona's wrist with her grip when she was traveling them to the woods behind the schoolhouse. It was like she was waiting for something to happen. Something that kept on not happening. Iona had no clue what it was going to be until one day there was a man in the classroom when she arrived, standing right beside Sister Mary-Elizabeth with a beatific smile on his face and a fancy silk cravat. He spent the first morning sitting quietly in the corner reading a book, and the other children seemed to forget all about him. Iona did not. By lunchtime she had ascertained several facts about the strange man: He was not a priest and did not seem particularly in awe of the nuns like the village dads were. He had a funny accent that Iona suspected was English, but he hadn't spoken enough to confirm that. He smelled a little bit like damp paper and oranges. Iona thought that he used the latter smell to cover up the former, but again, more data was needed. He was reading a book that Mother also kept in the house, but that Iona hadn't been allowed to read yet. Which was to say, a book about magic. He was some sort of magician, and he was probably British. No wonder Mother had been acting strange.

After lunch he began taking children out of class, one by one, and returning them unharmed a half hour later. It was after some careful badgering of one of those children that Iona got to the bottom of things. The man was from the Imperial College in Cork and he had been sent out to test all the children their age for magical potential. If he had just been a visitor from the Empire then Iona was pretty sure she would have spent her days splashing about in the swamp in peace, maybe snaring a couple of rabbits for the stew or chasing after the cheeky otters in the sunshine. Mother was a bit strange about magic. She'd never made a secret about loathing the way that the British taught it, compared to the traditional Irish methods that had been passed down, but she still pushed Iona to read about the British way as much as she could. Iona wasn't called out to be tested on the first day, but she gave the man from the college a big smile on her way out and he smiled back.

She was still smiling when Mother fetched her from the woods. She didn't talk about the man from the college. Not yet. Mother obviously knew about him, otherwise she wouldn't be acting so strangely, so Iona wanted to see how long it would take for the old woman to break and ask her. Iona wasn't called on the second day of testing either, but she did start to get excited about the prospect. She knew that she was magical. Her mother was a witch after all. It would be absurd if she wasn't the best at magic in her whole class.

On the third day her name was called, and she went down to the Mother Superior's office, which had been commandeered. She didn't talk about Mother to the man from the college—she'd been trained well enough to keep anything about that subject well away from the Empire—but the man seemed to recognize the confidence in her immediately and he responded in kind. She could understand the simple equations that he offered to her and she handed him back a few more complex ones that would improve the efficiency of the textbook spells, impressing him.

There was a chalk circle drawn on the desk, and he asked her to put her finger on it and close it. Iona diligently placed one finger on the edge of the chalk and concentrated on that white circle with all of her might. It didn't look like anything had happened, but that was often how it went with Mother's spells, so she didn't fret too much. He made some fire come out of his fingers, pretty blues and greens all fluttering around. Iona tried to do the same thing. Pushed as hard as she could until her hands were shaking, but nothing happened. He smiled at her anyway and they spent a good while trying different things— breathing exercises and thinking hard about different pictures—to try to make some fire come out. With some reluctance and a pat on the shoulder he sent Iona back to her classroom where she sat and pouted for the rest of the day.

When Mother fetched her there was no way that she didn't see the anger on her daughter's face, but she still said nothing. Iona put herself to bed and stared into the fire instead of eating whatever stew was for dinner, and if she felt hungry, she didn't notice because it already felt like her insides were hollow.

The rest of the week had gone on much as the weeks before. Iona went to school. She came home and studied whatever Mother told her to. She slept. If some of the spring was out of her step on the first few days, it was back by the end of the week. The resilience of a child cannot be overestimated. The strange tension had seeped out of the cottage and Mother had stopped giving her the long lingering looks, had stopped looking at her at all, really. By the weekend it was as if everything were back to normal. They made their trip into town to collect Mother's bundle of letters and whatever bare essentials they couldn't make for themselves, then hopped back home from inside a mausoleum in the churchyard where Iona was pretty sure she had seen a real skeleton poking out of a hole in the wall.

They'd eaten well that night on a whole chicken roasted on a spit and a pair of potatoes wrapped up in sooty foil that stung Iona's fingers when she tried to peel it back. Mother had given her a kiss on the head before telling her to sleep and that was when a tiny snake of doubt coiled up in Iona's tummy. Mother didn't do things like that. She must have done something wrong. There was no other explanation. She flopped back and forth under the furs by the fireside until the flames had died down to embers, by which time that little snake had swollen up to fill her whole torso. Iona got up, even though it must have been close to midnight, and made her way to the outhouse.

Mother wasn't sleeping in her spot when Iona passed it, but she barely even noticed, completely lost in her own worries. She wandered barefoot out into the grass and did her business without even thinking of wasting a candle. The whole swamp had been her playground since she was old enough to crawl and it didn't hold any surprises for her now. Or so she'd thought until she saw the marsh-lights out by the standing stones flicker from their usual green to an enticing red.

She didn't go rushing straight up to the stones. She followed the path around the row of apple trees that Mother called an orchard and tottered up the slick slope until she could see what was happening. A deep red glow poured out and there was something within it. Something huge and too terrible for Iona to put into words. A face like three baboons spliced together. Tails like barbed whips, smashing back and forth against the invisible barrier between the stones. "THE PACT IS SEALED, GORMLAITH O'SULLIVAN. ALL SHALL BE AS YOU WILL IT, AND WHEN THE TIME COMES . . ."

"I know the deal."

The light snapped out, but the dark was more than just the absence of light. It was the absence of everything. Like there was a hole in the world, pressing against the circle. Mother turned to look out, staring down at her little moldy cottage in the middle of nowhere, then she sighed and let the darkness loose.

It rolled out from amidst the stones until everything ahead of Iona was black and the stars had blinked out. She ran from it. Ran straight out into the swamp screaming at the top of her lungs. The mud sucked at her legs and she fell on her face in the shallow water. She tried to breathe but her lungs filled with nothing but burning. The darkness swept over her where she lay in the water. It dragged at her. Pulled her down, deeper and deeper. Further and further from air and light and life until it was as if she had never been there at all.

NOVEMBER 2, 2015

Rewriting the Inferno must have worked eventually, because about an hour before dawn Sully woke up with her face stuck to her notes and an ache in her back screaming to remind her that she was heading toward fifty years old, even if magic was preserving her looks. Marie's fingers were in her hair, brushing out the tangles of yesterday. She leaned in close and whispered, "You really can't take care of yourself, darlin'."

Sully mumbled, "Good thing I've got you to take care of me then."

Marie's fingers tightened in her hair and Sully let out a grunt. "Darlin', do you have any idea why my daddy was acting so strange last night after he came back up to the main house?"

Sully yawned and peeled the paper off her face. "Probably because I asked him for permission to marry you."

Marie bit her lip as Sully tried to stretch the kink out of her back until finally she couldn't wait any more and she blurted out, "D'you think you could have asked me first?"

"You can't ask permission for something you've already done. Just forgiveness." Sully staggered to her feet and carefully placed a kiss on Marie's cheek. "I wanted to do things right this time around. Since it's going to be forever. I had to ask your dad first."

Marie was glowering at her. "Are you going to ask me now?"

"He hasn't given me permission yet," Sully smirked. Marie put a hand to her mouth to cover her involuntarily lengthening fangs.

Sully's smirks held promises. There was a knock on the guest house door before either of them could go any further. Marie whispered, "They were still asleep when I snuck out."

An angry Jeremiah on her doorstep would have been a relief compared to what Sully found. When she opened the door, Magus Ogden was waiting for her, sweeping off his hat and bowing. Sully scowled at him, hard, but her scowls never seemed to penetrate his aura of perfect confidence. "Good morning, Miss Sullivan."

"I know you've been away for a while, but *morning* traditionally starts when the sun is up there." Sully pointed at the purple darkness above them.

"Then I suppose that I have been traveling through the night to come and see you."

In his tricorn hat and overcoat, Ogden looked perfectly at home in the little courtyard. Places like this probably hadn't changed since he was around the first time, before his little trip to the far planes. Sully sighed, "Come in then. Before you scare the farmers."

"Why, thank you."

Sully fussed with the kettle while Marie stood in the doorway behind Ogden and scowled at the back of his head. Even Sully couldn't burn water, so eventually two cups of instant coffee found their way onto the breakfast bar. If Ogden could taste how bad it was, he was too polite to mention it. "You know that you caused quite a stir the other night, flouncing out of that diplomatic function. The ambassador was quite offended. The Prime Minister considered it to be pretty rude."

Sully growled, "I figured that melting that condescending prick's face off would probably have been a bigger diplomatic incident."

"What on earth did Ambassador Red Bear say to provoke such ire?" Ogden was grinning.

Sully bit back her first response and then took a long calming sip of the scalding, godawful coffee. "He was rude about my girlfriend."

Ogden threw back his head and laughed. "In all the time that I have been back I don't think that I have met this girl who is always getting you into trouble. I am starting to suspect that she is just an excuse for you to avoid late night meetings and yell at politicians. I am not sure that she even exists."

Sully put the cup down carefully, her scowl twisting into confusion. "Marie is standing right behind you."

He rolled his eyes. "Yes, of course she is."

"No. She really is."

Marie stepped forward. "What in the nine hells?"

Ogden was smiling at Sully indulgently. "I am sorry, Miss Sullivan, but we are the only people in the building."

Sully leaned back on her stool. The cogs of her mind whirred into action despite the ungodly earliness of the hour. "Marie, could you poke Magus Ogden in the back of the head?"

Ogden started to frown. "Miss Sullivan—"

He leapt out of his seat with a yelp when Marie prodded him, spinning around on the spot and knocking his coffee all over the floor. "What was that?"

"That was Marie." Sully snorted.

"Sullivan, I do not know what tricks you are playing, or how, but I am warning you—"

"Oh, shut up for a minute. This is fascinating."

Marie looked giddy. "He really can't see me? This is so weird!"

Sully was tapping her fingers on the counter, rattling out the rhythm of her thoughts. "This has to be a vampire thing. Demons can't sense vampires, can't really see them unless they are right on top of them. This must be the same. The Magi of Manhattan were exposed to much higher levels of ambient magic in the Far Realms than anyone here experiences and they adapted to the saturation. That is why they can store so much more of it, why it comes to them so much more naturally."

Marie was dancing in a circle waving her hands in front of Ogden's face and giggling. Ogden looked anything but amused, and for the very first time Sully caught a glimpse of fear on his features. "Are you trying to tell me that there is a vampire in this room?"

Sully stopped smiling. "Her name is Marie."

"I don't care if she is Her Majesty, Victoria, the Queen of England. You are telling me that vampires could be all around me at any moment and I wouldn't even realize until they were touching me? Not only me, but also all my brothers and sisters in Manhattan? Wasn't it you who told me that the British deploy vampire soldiers against demons? What is to stop them from—"

He took a deep breath and calmed himself. "There are very few vampires left in the Americas. Nobody needs to know about this. I can rely on your . . . on Marie's discretion?"

Marie nodded solemnly, and Sully did her best not to laugh at the expression on her face. "She won't say a word to anybody."

Ogden brushed himself for imaginary lint and then settled back into his seat. "All is well then." He frowned. "How often has she been there when I was talking to you?"

"We just assumed that you were rude."

He turned slowly to look around the room, glancing at Sully for confirmation as he went. When she nodded, he said, a little too loudly, "I apologize for any offense that I gave, Miss Marie. I was not made aware of your presence."

Marie had drifted right around Ogden to come stand beside Sully behind his back. She let out a delighted giggle. "Oh, he's a charmer. You never told me he was a charmer."

Sully pursed her lips and Marie took it as an invitation. What should have been a chaste peck grew deeper as Marie leaned in against Sully's shoulder. Ogden coughed loudly and Marie pulled away giggling. "I just made you make fish-lips at your army-wizard work buddy."

Ogden was staring, a little perplexed, at Sully, but she discounted him for a moment. "What was that all about?" she asked Marie.

"Just saying goodbye properly, darlin'. He's here to drag you off to work again. I figured I would just stay here with my folks and try to smooth out some of the strangeness you made by tossing a dowry at Daddy."

Sully spluttered. "I was just being polite. You told me they were old fashioned. And besides, I'm not going anywhere."

Ogden coughed again, more forcefully, "Actually the Prime Minister sent me here to collect you—and I quote, 'by any means necessary'—for the strategy meeting this afternoon."

Marie quirked an eyebrow at her and Sully grumbled. "Fine."

After a hasty change into a new Hawaiian shirt and the battered leather jacket that Sully had won off of a were-snake in Laos, they went out into the courtyard and prepared their spells. With the lock on portals and teleportation that the Magi had leveled on the American continent to keep the British out, there were limited options for travel beyond the slow, mundane ones. Ogden had been using a flying spell for centuries, but despite the relative ease with which Sully had learned it, she still wasn't entirely comfortable flitting around the sky. It felt simultaneously alien and all too familiar. She conjured a parasol for Marie to see her safely back to the house now that the sun was rising and kissed her goodbye. Marie murmured into her mouth as she pulled away, "Don't be gone too long, darlin', I'll miss you."

Sully gave her a wink, then launched herself up into the red dawn sky.

It wasn't easy to talk with the wind whipping past his face, but Ogden still tried. Incessantly. "Did you really think that the Prime Minister would let you vanish in the middle of planning the first offensive action of the war?"

"I was due a holiday. I've been in every planning meeting for months. All that is left is for your people to finish the damn spell. Until that is done, I am as useful as a decorative fern."

"And what if I told you that the spell was complete?"

"Then I'd call you a liar."

Ogden laughed loudly into the bandana he had wrapped around his face. Sully wished she had borrowed a scarf from Clementine. She was genuinely concerned that she was going to swallow a fly while going fifty miles an hour.

He spun in to fly closer to her, lying on his back in the air. "You are correct in your assumption. The Magi still work diligently on your spell. Even so, you must have known that you would not be allowed—"

"Allowed what? A whole five minutes to myself without some tool in a suit talking to me like I'm there to make his coffee?" Sully poured a little extra power into the spell and shot off ahead of Ogden. The rush of frigid wind biting into her cheeks was less painful than listening to him prattling on. He caught up to her within a few minutes and she could tell at a glance that he was smirking under the salt-crusted cloth on his face. She pointedly ignored him and tried to keep herself pointed due north.

They had almost made it to the border of New England Province when the hair on the back of Sully's neck started to stand up and her arcane senses started to scream at her. She spun herself to glower at Ogden. "I suppose I'm meant to think this is just a coincidence?"

She could feel the wind of powerful wings beating against her skin. She could taste the blood of the battlefield. Ogden didn't even look ashamed. "I see no reason to hide my movements from one of my oldest friends and closest allies, Sullivan. I do not know why you are so afraid—"

She cut him off. "I'm not scared of shit. But you know I don't want to hang around with—"

Mol Kalath dropped out of the cloud bank above them, moisture turning to steam as it rolled off the oily black feathers of its wings. From a distance it could have been mistaken for a crow, albeit a crow of impossible proportions, but as it swung in close Sully could see the six burning green eyes arrayed around its head, and the way that its torso tapered so that it had a silhouette almost like a feather-coated snake's. The smell of brimstone still clung to Mol Kalath despite the time it had spent away from the hells and the stench rolled over Sully, even here in the open air. The demon closed the distance between them, only seeming to remember at the last moment that it was not swooping down to grab her. Its beak creaked open. "GREETINGS TO YOU, IONA SULLIVAN. GREETINGS TO YOU, MAGUS OGDEN."

Demons had no inside voices.

"Greetings to you, Mol Kalath, it is a beautiful day for a flight," Ogden bellowed back. Maybe neither of them had inside voices. Sully had certainly never heard Ogden whisper.

"YOUR SKIES ARE STRANGE. TOO SMOOTH AND TOO STILL. AT HOME THERE IS FLUX AND TURBULENCE. STORMS THAT LAST GENERATIONS. WINDS THAT WOULD STRIP YOUR MORTAL FLESH FROM YOUR BONES."

Sully shuddered, mentally blaming it on the cold rather than revulsion. It seemed to catch the demon's attention. "I HAVE COME TO SEEK AUDIENCE WITH YOU, IONA SULLIVAN. THERE ARE THINGS THAT YOU MUST KNOW. THINGS THAT ONLY I CAN TEACH YOU."

Mol Kalath had been pursuing her politely but relentlessly since Manhattan had returned from the far plane. The only benefit to the ridiculous work schedule that the new Prime Minister had been inflicting on her was that it gave her an excuse to avoid the demon. Right now, there was nothing but dead air between her, it, and New Amsterdam. She calculated the distance in her head.

"If I've survived this long without knowing, I'll manage a bit longer."

Sully put on another burst of acceleration, leaving the two gigantic pains in her ass spinning in her wake. For one glorious moment both Ogden and the demon shrank away to nothing but dark spots on the horizon, then they gave chase.

At first Sully tried to lose them by flitting through cloud banks, but both her pursuers were far more accustomed to flight than she and they closed on her easily. She couldn't beat them on skill and she couldn't beat the power of either a demon or a magus. She grinned, then she plummeted from the sky as though someone had cut her strings. She dropped a few layers of shielding ahead of her as she fell, and they wrapped around her like a cocoon, taking the friction from the air and dissipating it around her into a pleasant warmth. By the time she was about to hit the covered bridge beneath her, she was almost comfortable. She changed direction so hard that her neck snapped back and for one agonizing second she thought that she had done herself permanent harm, before the jarring pain started to fade. With the added momentum of the fall and another push of power, she opened up the gap between herself and the demon. She couldn't keep up this pace forever but she didn't need to, she just had to reach New Amsterdam before the demon could make itself heard.

New England Province was a darker shade of green than the farmlands that had made up most of their flight. The color felt rich to Sully as she rushed back to the only place that had ever felt like home. Forests that would have been stripped clear for farmland in other provinces were allowed to flourish here. The British might have mutilated their share of this continent for centuries, but they still liked to have somewhere nice to walk their dogs on the weekend. Sully swung low enough that the beating of her invisible wings ruffled the leaves on the treetops as she sped along. Mol Kalath was still trailing along up in the clouds. If it had been brave enough to come down and risk bumping its pinfeathers, Sully would have had to fly underneath the canopy, and would likely have crashed into a tree trunk for her troubles. She suspected that the demon knew that and was hanging back as a courtesy, which only irritated her more. She knew that her behavior was irrational and that demons were the allies of America—in the abstract she could accept that—but face to face with that creature she still felt the bone-deep terror that the nuns back in Catholic school had spent so long trying to instill in her. She hated feeling that fear, and she hated the big bird for making her feel that way, even if it didn't mean to. Especially if it didn't mean to.

Before too long, houses began to appear beneath her, the frayed fringes of suburbia stretching out into the beauty of the wilds. She slowed just a little, easing the drain on her reserves in case of a crisis. The city was as big, beautiful and lethal as it had ever been, climbing up over the horizon like a rampaging titan, surrounded by its own personal aura of smog and human suffering. Sully grinned as home came into sight. She didn't get to look in on the monster from the outside very often; usually she was in the belly of the beast. Even after all this time she still got choked up just looking at it. The strange spires of Manhattan had been an unwelcome addition to the skyline, but she had gotten used to them eventually. What she couldn't stand was the milky white expanse beyond the city where the barrier spells were layered against the British bombardment. You couldn't even hear the explosions. The Magi of Manhattan had done amazing work. She swept by the sentry stations posted around the city proper and felt the hairs on the back of her neck stand to attention as she was inspected by the multitudes of spells designed to spot intruders. She could have done without that, too.

The Brooklyn Municipal Building wasn't the tallest in the city, but the brassy quality of its fixtures made it stand out despite its lowly stature, that and the cloud of complex magical protections that had been layered over it. Sully drifted down to land on a balcony, staring down the barrels of a half-dozen rifles as usual.

"Gentlemen, if you don't point those somewhere else, I'm going to shove them up your asses."

She could hear one of the soldiers snigger but they still waited until their sergeant gave them the signal to lower their guns. Sully gave him a nod as she strode past, but it wasn't out of respect. Most of the soldiers that the part of America that used to be Nova Europa could field had been on the British payroll until this little coup got up and running. She trusted them as far as she could throw them. Which from this balcony was actually pretty far, so that was a bad metaphor.

She breezed past the swarming civil servants who were waving papers at her to sign and made meaningful eye contact with the one who had been offered up like a sacrificial lamb as her personal secretary this week. "I have a meeting with the Prime Minister in three minutes. I know that. Anything else I need to know?" The poor woman shook her head jerkily. The tangled bun of gray hair pinned to the back of her head started to unravel. She wasn't going to last long. None of them ever did.

In the cabinet room there were already various ministers and lords surrounded by their own buzzing hive of bureaucrats. Most of

Sully's retinue had dropped off at the door, but her secretary still hovered behind her like a mosquito suffering from stage fright.

Some of the men in this room probably believed in a new American Empire—in equality and fraternity and whatever other nonsense Pratt had had students spray-painting on college walls all those years—but Sully was willing to bet that the majority were opportunists who couldn't grab onto enough power back in Britain and were here now in America to take a little gamble. They might not have been the majority to start with, but that was the trouble with opportunists and career politicians, they were very good at gaining power and hanging onto it while lesser men got distracted by things like morality and fell to the wayside.

Sully hated everyone in the room on principle, but the burning loathing that bubbled up in her throat was reserved for Prime Minister Pratt. A man who treated every favor he did as a debt owed and who had blackmailed Sully into her current position with the threat of deporting Marie along with every other vampire on the continent. She tossed herself into a seat by his right hand and smiled at him beatifically when he glanced up from the mounds of paper in front of him. He smiled right back. They sat and smiled at one another while Sully fantasized about hacking him open from navel to neck. The last few stragglers made their way into the room and the meeting started right on schedule.

About five minutes later Sully started to tune it all out. Her opinion was not welcome on most of the subjects that they were discussing, as Pratt had politely explained after the third time Sully threatened to punch someone in the throat during a taxation debate. She was here to contribute on military and magical matters and to shut up the rest of the time. The conversation swung in her direction before long, as it tended to when the British were bombarding the city. Some lord, an overstuffed suit with a waxed mustache, was reporting on their allies' preparations. "The United Nations and the Republic of America have worked in conjunction on military matters in the past, so their lines of communication seem to be wide open. Our other allies, who do not share a border or look to benefit from our continued independence, seem a little more reluctant to commit troops. There is much to be said for—"

Sully spoke over him, "We don't need every ally to send us an army. The British Land forces are tiny. Their garrisons on mainland Britain are miniscule. They're spread too thin across their holdings. They have always relied on their navy and their Magi to maintain control. If you've got the Natives and the Republicans, we are good to go on an invasion."

Lord Wax-Stache blustered for a moment, then admitted. "Well, that is rather the problem. Neither group will commit. They have mustered their forces, but they won't bring them over until our rather wild promises regarding demonic allies from Europe have been confirmed with some evidence."

"So they aren't going to help until we prove we don't need any help. Great. Great allies. Just what we needed."

Ogden cleared his throat from where he was standing by the door. The demon Mol Kalath hadn't made it in past the magical protections laid against its kind, but the Magus was still nominally human enough to attend meetings. "Using the information that was provided to us, we have been making great strides toward bringing down the Veil of Tears and unleashing all the trapped demons of Europe onto the British Isles. We have only a few fine details still to iron out in the spell, then—"

Sully snapped. "So it still isn't ready and we can't do a damned thing until you, your Magi and your pet demons are done fiddling with it. This is the same story that we have been hearing for weeks."

A muscle in Ogden's jaw twitched, Sully could see it from across the room. "We are very close now. I would say less than a day of theoretical work remains before we can start the casting."

Sully slumped back into the soft leather of the seat with a grunt. After a long moment of silence while the politicians waited to see if she was going to launch into another tirade, they moved on to new business.

The meeting dragged on for so long that the sun actually set on them, but Sully didn't give one of the bastards the satisfaction of seeing her bored. She plastered on an attentive face and nodded along with whatever Pratt said like she was his little lapdog. The fact that his lapdog was silently plotting to tear out its owner's throat wasn't information that she needed to broadcast to the world. Pratt knew that he was going to get what was coming to him and Ogden probably had an inkling that there was some tension there, but the rest of them would just try to use the information as leverage.

Sully wasn't sure exactly when the meeting ground to a halt, but it must have been about dinner time, judging by the grumbling of the stomachs all around her. When the room came back into focus Ogden had vanished, *probably* not into thin air, and the rest of the scum were starting to drift away, with only a few still lingering to whisper into Pratt's ear. Sully started to slink out of her seat, only for Pratt to tut at her and shake his head. She sank back down and tried not to grind her teeth. Sully's secretary sensibly took that as a sign to make a break for it with her clipboard full of notes, although if the woman had any real sense she would quit before Sully's temper got the better of her.

One by one the parasites of the upper echelons of American government trickled out the door until finally only Sully and Pratt remained. He gave her an indulgent smile after he had finished signing papers. "Shall we order in some dinner? I hear that an absolutely marvelous little boutique Nipponese restaurant has just opened up in your old neighborhood. Raw fish served on little blocks of sticky rice. I could send a runner down and have us both satiated within half an hour."

"I've swallowed enough raw crap for one day, thanks."

"Perhaps some more traditional fare, then? I believe that there is a—"

Sully snarled. "I don't want to eat with you, Pratt. We aren't friends. I work for you. Can we just get to the point?"

"Ah, as tactful as ever. I am going to be relying on some of that famous tact of yours in the near future, as a matter of fact. You see,

I find myself in need of someone who is accustomed to the vagaries of the Imperial Bureau of Investigation. Someone who might be able to inveigle themselves into an active investigation and report any relevant findings back to me in a discreet manner. Someone who is respected within the IBI, but not beholden to its power structures or its chain of reporting."

Sully slumped down in her chair groaning. Pratt could turn a yes or no question into a twenty-minute soliloquy on the difficulty of making decisions. "What's the case and what do you think they aren't telling you?"

Pratt smiled again. "There have been a string of disappearances. No clear connections among the people who are vanishing. No signs of foul play. Just a steady stream of citizens of our new republic who are no longer there when someone comes to check upon them. The local constabularies have had no luck whatsoever in identifying the cause, or any methodology involved. There seem to be easily detectable traces of magic at every location. Indeed, there is an overabundance that renders the Schrödinger's magical detection devices altogether useless, but otherwise no clues are presenting themselves."

Sully leaned forward to rest her elbows on the table. She was interested, despite herself. You could take the girl out of the Bureau, but you couldn't take the Bureau out of the girl. "Yep. That all sounds like a case for the IBI. So why do you want me involved?"

Pratt glanced nervously at the door. "Beyond my obvious faith in your oft demonstrated investigative abilities, the high levels of magical contamination seem to indicate that it is possible our demonic allies may have been involved in these abductions."

Sully whistled. "Wow. I can see why you would want to keep that one under your hat."

"Yes, you can understand why this is something of a political hot potato at the moment. Without the demons we lose Manhattan, and without Manhattan we lose the war. On the other hand, we can't have them roaming around unchecked, feasting on our citizens as they please. This needs to be resolved discreetly, and I believe this may be better achieved through diplomatic channels rather than through the thorough and dogged police work of the IBI."

Sully nodded. "All right. What'll you give me for it?"

"I beg your pardon?"

"I told you before. We're not friends. You're a politician, asking someone else with power and influence to do you a favor. I might not like what you do, but I can grasp it, and if I need to use it, I will."

Pratt chuckled and settled back into his seat. "My dear Miss Sullivan, I have no idea what you could possibly want. You know that I cannot offer your dear Marie or her kind any further concessions without alienating some extremely important allies."

"I know all that. We've been over all that. I want justice. I want Ogden on trial the day that this war is over, and I want him to hang."

Pratt blinked. "My understanding was that the two of you had a rather convivial working relationship. Has he done something in particular to offend you?"

Sully drew in a deep breath and launched into the speech she had been practicing in her head for months. "He is a mass murderer. The stunt that pulled Manhattan back from the Far Realms killed about three hundred people, give or take? I'm not . . . I'm not jumping down your throat for welcoming Manhattan back with open arms. I understand that we need all the firepower we can get. This is wartime, and decisions need to be made based on necessity, but when the war is over, I want him tried. I'm not asking you to round up everyone who followed him blindly. They were desperate people stranded a long way from home, but he was their leader. He led them down that path and a price needs to be paid for it. Ogden should be the one to pay it."

Pratt stared at her, his eyes unreadable. "You know, I believe that may have been the most you have said to me since I made you a general."

"Have we got a deal, Pratt?"

He held out hand and they shook on it. "We have a deal, Sullivan. Make this problem go away and I will misplace Mr. Ogden's pardon."

She forced a smile onto her face and resisted the urge to wipe her hand on her trouser leg. "I will get back to you on the IBI investigation as soon as I have something useful."

"Thank you, Miss Sullivan. I look forward to hearing your insights."

Sully walked out of the building like she was on a tightrope, keeping any hint of emotion from reaching her face. Pratt hadn't argued about "political realities" or tried to make her feel like a petty idiot for asking for Ogden's head. He hadn't tried to explain that he was going to end up with an island full of enraged Magi that he had no real way of controlling without their anointed leader. Even if he had intended to give her what she wanted, he would have let her know how much it was costing him, so he could use it as leverage later. He was going to screw her over.

NOVEMBER 3, 2015

The Gobi Grill was a Mongolian joint on Staten Island. Of the different boroughs of New Amsterdam, Staten had always been the wealthiest and the most resistant to what the IBI used to call "foreign influences," but even here, the Gobi stood out. Amidst French cuisine, Italian pizzerias, Greek salad buffets and stolid British pub food, it was the only place with anything spicy on the menu. Sully had always hated it, which meant that every time it was her partner's turn to pick a take-out joint, the delivery came from there. On the late nights in the office, there was nothing that Ceejay had enjoyed more than watching Sully eat the spiciest thing he could find on the menu without flinching. Sully had always appreciated his sense of humor, even when she was the victim of it.

Right on cue at twenty minutes to nine, Ceejay swaggered in through the door in a sky blue Ophiran suit. He spotted Sully sitting by the bar and spun on his heel to walk back out again. He made it as far as the street before Sully's snort of laughter brought him back inside.

"General Sullivan! Haven't you won this war yet? I can't sleep at night with all the banging on the barrier. You are so negligent. It is amazing that I didn't steal your job years ago."

Sully got up to shake his hand but stiffened as he engulfed her in a hug. Softly he murmured, "It is good to see you." Then he stepped back and was instantly back to his full braying volume. "Two coffees, please, and four Nai Wong Bao."

They settled by the bar after Ceejay had made a big show of yawning and stretching so he could get a good look around the place. There was no breakfast crowd to speak of—a few people were grabbing take-out coffee orders and there was an old Oriental man snoozing over a bowl of fishy soup in a booth. As far as Sully could tell, the Gobi never closed.

The food was in front of them before Sully could get a word in. Ceejay asked, "You came alone? I thought you would have bodyguards and sycophants dribbling out behind you these days."

Sully scoffed, "Like I've keep telling you all these years, I can take care of myself."

He raised an imperious eyebrow. "I seem to recall your telling me that—just before I had to pull your ass out of the fire."

Sully prodded at the gelatinous white lumps on her plate. "What am I eating here?"

"Steamed buns. They have custard inside. Very British. You should like them."

She took a small bite. Swallowing took some effort. Ceejay waggled his eyebrows again. "No?"

"I didn't miss eating your weird food."

"I've missed watching you eat my weird food. Your face—"

She cut him off. "How's business? They haven't kicked you back down to the mailroom yet?"

Ceejay chuckled. "I think that if there was no war going on, all the polite white people would've had me taken out back and shot by now. But since you keep dragging your feet, I get to keep being top dog in the IBI."

"Well, I'll do my best to keep fucking up then. For your job security."

He gave a little mock bow of thanks, then tucked into his own buns as Sully tried to wash the texture out of her mouth with coffee. After a moment of comfortable silence she said, "I hear you've caught an interesting case."

"I catch all the interesting cases. I am like a net that hangs underneath a thousand useless constabularies, catching everything that isn't completely obvious." His voice was slightly muffled by the mouthful of food.

"I was thinking about a specific interesting case. One that is almost as interesting as the one that I had just before I left the IBI."

He sighed. "I don't know why I pretended this was a social call. You are here about work. You are always *all* about work."

Sully stared intently down into her coffee. "When things are settled and the war is over, there will be time to be friends again. Hell, I might even apply for my old job. You could be my boss."

That earned her a belly laugh. "I can just picture it—'Sully, I need you to investigate this terrible crime.' 'Ceejay, go to hell, I am hungover.'" His smile never faltered as he hissed, "Did you check that we are safe to talk here?"

Sully let her arcane senses sweep out of her body and through the restaurant. She could feel the fire runes in the kitchen like a crackling pressure at the edge of her consciousness, and the alarm charms woven into the doors and windows vibrated softly against her gentle intrusion. Laid over all of it was the sensation of her own magic, an almost imperceptible bubble blocking anyone from scrying on them. "We're good for now."

"No pattern," he started. "These people, they seem to vanish with no logic at all. They go to bed one night and the next morning, *poof.* Nothing. It is not isolated to Nova Europa. The Northern provinces of the Republic have been losing people too. I know that the United Nations have lost some, but they don't trust us enough to even give names or locations. They give me nothing but dates of the disappearances and then they expect everything that we have in return. Pricks."

"And the Schrödingers?"

"They go haywire. Spike off the chart. There is definitely magic at play, but if any of our guys have a clue what it is, they are keeping it to themselves." Ceejay knocked back the last of his coffee.

Sully sipped hers. "Any theories?"

"The smart money is on spies. Everyone knows that the British had them everywhere. Now that the hammer is about to fall, they are pulling them all out. The crazy power spikes may be some sort of pumped up portals to get past the blocks your friends cast."

Sully frowned. "That makes no sense .You don't withdraw your spies when you are about to fight someone, you keep them in place so they can feed you vital intel—troop movements, morale on the ground. I don't buy it."

Ceejay was scowling. "It doesn't matter what you buy. It isn't your job anymore. Remember? You quit."

A bitter laugh escaped Sully. "Yeah, lucky me."

It was only when he turned on her that she realized he wasn't joking. "Back off, Sully. You have your own business to be dealing with. Stay out of mine."

Sully's jaw clenched but she forced her temper down. She had a lifetime of practice at that. "I don't know what you think is going on, but I don't want my job back."

"What's going on is that just when I thought I was going to see my friend again for the first time in months, a spy walked in dressed in her clothes. Fuck you very much, Sully."

Sully did not blow up the Gobi Grill. She even paid the tab for the coffee and glutinous lumps. When she stepped out into the street, the gathering of three dozen crows perched on every flat surface was probably a complete coincidence and nothing to do with her mood. She shooed them away and waited to watch them circle up through the canyon between the skyscrapers to vanish into the chill blue sky. She blew out a warm cloud of breath after them. She didn't know what was worse: Ceejay's calling her a government stooge or his being completely right. Her phone started to vibrate in her pocket and with great reluctance she drew it out. She wasn't sure how Ogden had adapted to modern technology faster than she had, given that she had several centuries head-start, but there was his name flashing on the screen.

She grunted, "Sullivan."

He replied, "Ogden." She could almost hear the smug grin.

"What do you want, Ogden?"

"I just thought that it might be an auspicious time to invite you to visit with us in Manhattan."

Sully tried not to growl. "Why would anyone want to do that?"

"You could take a look at the unique architecture? Get to know your new friends and allies? Come and witness the ritual that we use to tear down the Veil of Tears?"

Sully huffed out another plume of steam. "You finished the spell."

"We have most assuredly finished the spell."

What Manhattan used to be could be seen in its foundations. As she soared over the water Sully caught a glimpse of wood and whitewash here and there. The ground gravel beneath her course still bore the shape of cobblestones in places and there was unmistakably dirt and dung beneath that. Once upon a time, this had been a human place. The moment that she looked higher than knee height the illusion that it still belonged to mankind vanished. Conjured stone twisted up into the skyline, jagged and impossibly symmetrical. The spires of Manhattan resembled nothing so much as gargantuan termite mounds and the fact that the doorways and thoroughfares of the city had been designed with residents many times the size of humans in mind just hammered home the idea that humans were visitors here. The outer wall stood at more than twenty feet tall and the smooth white expanse of it was oppressive, but it also hid the strangeness of everything within its circumference very well. There was no gate in or out of Manhattan; there was no need when every one of the residents could fly. Sully tried not to shudder as she saw the demons coiled along the ramparts beneath her, nesting in the belfries and lurking in the shadows between the towers. There were not as many of them as there were Magi, but the numbers were close. In all of the dull meetings since the war began, Sully had not voiced her suspicions that behind their impassable walls the Magi were summoning more demons to bolster their forces. It wasn't as though there was anything that could be done, even if they were; Manhattan was a law unto itself. That had been the problem since before it popped back into the world.

Sully took the scenic route down to the massive ritual circle in the center of the city where the mass of Magi were gathered. Intelligence about America's allies had been even harder to come by than information about the British in the past months, so she was making up for lost time. That was what she told herself to justify her slow descent. It wasn't because she was frightened to go down into a massive nest of demons that would eat her magic and tear her to shreds and it certainly wasn't because she was keeping an eye out for Mol Kalath. The bird could be here or not, it made no difference to her. Once she was sure that it was not, she dove to land gracelessly by Ogden's side. He was grinning. "A very pleasant afternoon to you, Miss Sullivan."

"Right. How long have we got until the fireworks start?"

He swept his arms out to encompass this little town square. "They have already begun the preliminary casting. Each component shall be bound within the circle and when all of the parts have been assembled—"

Sully grumbled. "I know how ritual magic works. I'm asking for a time."

When he laughed it tugged on the scars across his lips, making him flinch. "By this time tomorrow, the Veil of Tears shall be unpicked and all the hell of Europe will be unleashed upon the British. Even now we ready our envoys to meet with the trapped demons. We shall marshal our forces in France, then strike out before tomorrow ends. They will not stand against such an onslaught for long. I would expect surrender by the following dawn at the latest."

"Good job. Has Pratt been told?" Sully cracked her knuckles.

"The Prime Minister has been informed, yes."

Sully closed her eyes and felt the magic taking form, each caster stitching their spell onto the last, every spell simple and easy to replace if an error was made, but woven together into an immense, complex tapestry. She had punched through a few barrier spells in her day, but that was a momentary disruption of the stable patterns, not a permanent solution like this patchwork monstrosity of a spell. She could already see the shape that it was going to take from the gaps left in the framework that they had cast so far. Understanding the totality of it was probably beyond her, but she could appreciate the craft.

"So, did you invite me here to watch you all casting for twenty hours? Because I might need a seat or something."

Ogden shuffled his feet. "Knowing the little that I do of you, I had assumed that you would want to be at the front lines when the fighting begins."

"You assumed right." Sully flexed her hands. The dense magic that saturated the air was teasing little sparks of spellfire from her fingertips.

"Which is why our mutual friend has offered to carry you with the vanguard to Europe."

Sully grimaced at the tell-tale rustle of feathers behind her. "Hello again, Mol Kalath."

"GREETINGS, SHADOW-TWIN." The voice tore right through Sully every single time. Even the other demons roaming free around Manhattan chattering in their own tongue didn't make her head creak as much.

"I guess that you're my ride to Europe?"

"THE DISTANCE IS TOO GREAT FOR YOUR SPELLS OF FLIGHT. YOU SHALL RIDE UPON MY BACK AND AT LAST WE WILL HAVE TIME TO CONVERSE."

Sully ground her teeth together while Ogden clapped her on the back. "Just think, Miss Sullivan. In two days' time, the war will be over and we will have toppled the British Empire."

She unclenched her jaw. "All right. Let's do this."

Mounting the demon had been the biggest delay. The way that its feathers rustled with anticipation made Sully queasy, and when she finally got the courage together to touch them, they clung to her fingers like oil. She scrambled up onto the demon's back, straining to make as little physical contact as possible. With the first beat of Mol Kalath's wings, her apprehension was replaced by survival instinct and she pressed herself closely to the demon's back as it took flight. She tried to breathe through her mouth so that the brimstone reek didn't overwhelm her. Sully's eyes were crushed shut; if she could just pretend that she wasn't there then maybe the fear would stop. She didn't see her city fade into the distance, missed the last of the towers dipping beneath the water and the glow fading from the sky. They flew off to war and she didn't look back.

NoVEmBER 1, 2015

Sometime after midnight, Sully gave in and spoke to the demon. Despite herself, she was still pressed tight against its back for warmth as they flitted over the chill waves of the Atlantic and she wasn't even sure that it could hear her when she muttered, "I guess there is no getting rid of you, is there?"

"OUR FATES ARE BOUND TOGETHER, IONA." The demon's voice reverberated up through its back. Sully felt it as much as heard it.

"I don't get it. Why me?"

"IT IS NOT ONLY YOU. IT IS THE NATURE OF THE PLANES. EACH LAYER OF THE UNIVERSE IS THE SAME, DIFFERING ONLY IN ITS DISTANCE FROM THE SOURCE."

"Oh Christ. I didn't know that there was going to be an in-flight lecture."

"HERE THE LIGHT OF THE SOURCE SHINES WEAKLY. MAGIC IS THIN AND SPARSE. MANY CANNOT EVEN WIELD IT. THE WORLD IS BRITTLE. IN THE WORLD BELOW—IN OUR HOME HELLS—THE MAGIC FLOWS FREELY AND ALL IS IN FLUX."

"And beyond that there are the far planes where there is so much magic that you just might pop. I know this stuff."

"YOU DO NOT COMPREHEND. THESE ARE JUST THE PLANES THAT WE HAVE SEEN, THE CLOSEST AND EASIEST

TO TRAVERSE. YET IN EACH OF THEM WE EXIST. IN THIS WORLD, YOU ARE ME. IN MY WORLD, I AM YOU."

For a long time there was no sound but the beating of wings, then Sully said, "So if I had been born in the hells, I would've been a big black bird-thing."

"JUST AS I WOULD HAVE BEEN A SMALL PINKISH HUMAN THING."

Sully snorted. "But how do you know that I'm your shadow-twin?"

"WHEN WE SOUGHT ESCAPE FROM THE TORMENTORS OF THE FAR PLANE, WE FOUND THAT EACH OF US HAD BUT A SINGLE VESSEL THAT WE COULD POSSESS IN THE MORTAL WORLD ONCE THE ANIMATING FORCE HAD LEFT IT. YOU ARE MINE. IF YOU HAD CUT A DEAL WITH THE HELLS, YOUR FLESH WOULD HAVE BEEN MINE."

"Well, that's horrifying. Thanks for sharing, big bird."

"YOU ARE MOST WELCOME. AND I AM NOT A BIRD."

The silence of the night was sliced away with beats of the demon's wings, minute after minute, until Sully couldn't bear it. "So the things you guys are so scared of, the Far Realms versions of us. They were born right next to the source of all magic. That means they are more powerful than you?"

"THEY WERE POWERFUL ENOUGH TO PENETRATE THE WALL BETWEEN OUR WORLDS WITHOUT BEING SUM-MONED. THEY WERE POWERFUL ENOUGH TO PREY ON US FOR MILLENNIA BEYOND RECKONING."

"Then why haven't we seen them here?"

"PERHAPS YOU HAVE."

Sully sighed. "Well, we've got plenty of monsters and gods in the old books. They can't all have been your lot."

"IONA."

"What?"

"LOOK."

The spell flowed over Sully and the demon like a cascading rain-bow. Each Magus had added their own power to the mixture, their own unique signature blending into this masterwork of the craft. The shockwave hit the Veil of Tears on the horizon and threw the sea beneath Mol Kalath into a thirty-foot wave that batted the demon back as though it were a common crow. Sully grabbed a greasy handful of feathers to avoid being pitched into the roiling water.

Instead of opening herself up and experiencing the wonder of the Veil being torn apart, piece by piece, Sully clamped down so that it was only deafeningly loud and blindingly bright. Unbound magic rolled over them in waves as they struggled to stay in the air and, willingly or not, Sully and her demon absorbed it until they were so saturated with power that it started straining to get out. Sparks trailed from Mol Kalath's feathers. Sully's breath came out as puffs of smoke and flame. Still they drove on toward the center of the maelstrom.

Then, as swiftly as it had begun, it was over. The silence held for a dreadful moment before the cacophony of hooting, bellowing cries of the demons behind them filled it up. Even Mol Kalath brayed in triumph, and why wouldn't it? This was just what the demons had always wanted; free rein across the world. Dread was a dull ache in Sully's gut. As the odd pair drew closer to the spell-blighted cliffs of the French coastline, the great bird's cries were echoed back by its demon kin on the land. They swooped down to greet the first of their new allies.

The demons of Europe were a different breed from the thriving monstrosities that Manhattan had brought home with it. They were smaller, sleeker, and better shaped for life on the earth. They had a reasonable number of legs, fewer superfluous mouths, and the paucity of jagged teeth and raking claws on display was almost disappointing. They still started salivating when they laid eyes on Sully, though. They were still feral. When the first tentacle casually reached out to snatch her, Mol Kalath snapped it in half with a pinch of its beak and let out a hiss. "NO."

The other demons were twittering and gargling in supplication, begging Mol Kalath, "SHARE TREAT. SHARE MEAT. SHARE. SHARE."

"SILENCE."

The demons of Europe cowered. Mol Kalath rose up to its full height and bellowed. "THE WAR WITH MAN IS DONE. THEY ARE OUR ALLIES AGAINST THE ONES BELOW. THIS ONE LEADS THEM. THIS ONE WILL LEAD YOU IF YOU WILL LISTEN."

Sully had practiced this little speech a half-dozen times and had been privy to the eight thousand "little notes" that Pratt had provided to the withered old bastard of an ambassador who had been meant to make the proffer of alliance. "Here's the deal that we are offering. America will be your friends. We'll let you keep whatever land in Europe that you can hold without our help, and if it comes to war with a foreign power, we will do our best to help you out. In return, we need a little bit of help right now to deal with the people that trapped you in here to start with." She turned on the spot and pointed north. "Britain is that way. They are our enemy, and now that the barrier keeping you trapped in Europe is down, they're your enemy too. We are proposing that we fight them together and don't fight each other. Sound good?"

The crowd of demons had been growing denser with every passing moment as more and more arrived from the scattered nests they had burrowed into the corpse of Europe. Sully's words were being passed back in a chain of whispers. Mol Kalath spread its black wings and roared, "CRUSH THE HUMANS?"

Instinct took over and the demons began to bellow back. "CRUSH THE HUMANS."

Sully shuddered as the battle cries and shrieks rolled over her. When she spoke, it was mainly to herself. "I can work with this."

Given time, the message began to spread amongst the demons and most of them seemed relieved to have finally received permission to be in the world after however many decades they had been squatters. Some of the demons were set in their old ways and wanted to go on a rampage the moment that the Veil fell. It was taking considerable effort on the part of their friends to constrain them and explain the situation. There weren't a lot of them, but any number of rampaging demons was probably too many rampaging demons. After an hour of bellowed arguments in languages that Sully was pretty confident a mouth with only one tongue couldn't speak, she was fed up. She stalked off into the wilderness and tried her best to get her headache to recede.

France had been wiped off the maps before she was even born, so Sully couldn't work out where exactly they were, but the war-torn hell-scape that she had been expecting was strangely absent. In fact, it was idyllic compared to most of the modern world. Here and there you could spot the remains of old buildings overtaken by nature, but even they just seemed like a little flourish in a well-designed garden. Whatever war had been fought here had been over for so long that even the earth beneath her feet had forgotten it. She had been taught, and had believed, that the demons unleashed by the Great War were corrupting Europe somehow, that they were twisting it into a night-marish kingdom of horrors. The reality was disappointing—it was just abandoned land.

Mol Kalath ambled up to Sully. It was careful to keep its voice low; every word still grated across her soul, but she appreciated the effort. "WE HAVE COME TO A CONSENSUS. THEY WILL JOIN OUR CAUSE."

"Well, it wasn't like they had a lot of better options," Sully scoffed.

"THEY ARE FEW IN NUMBER: THE RIFTS THAT THEY USED TO TRAVEL HERE ARE LONG COLLAPSED AND THOSE THAT COULD FLEE BACK TO THE HELLS RATHER THAN FACE STARVATION DID SO SOON AFTER THE BARRIERS WERE RAISED. SOME THAT REMAINED LOST THEIR LIVES FIGHT-ING THE LOCAL FAUNA. THERE WILL BE ENOUGH, BUT YOU SHOULD KNOW THE MEASURE OF YOUR TROOPS."

Sully kicked a rusted-out helmet from amidst the undergrowth. "Uh. Thanks. For all your help."

"I WOULD DO ANYTHING FOR YOU, SHADOW-TWIN."

Sully shuddered. "There you go being creepy again. You can just say, 'You are welcome.' You don't have to make every conversation into some ominous doom-laden—"

"YOU ARE WELCOME."

"Thank you."

"YOU ARE WELCOME."

"Okay, that's enough of that."

From the north there came a deep resonating sound something like a trumpet, assuming you had made the trumpet out of a giant squid. Mol Kalath startled. "THEY ARE MUSTERING. WE MUST MAKE HASTE OR WE WILL BE LEFT BEHIND."

She leapt onto the demon's back and they took off at a sprint. It was only once they were in flight in the midst of the swarms of demons that Sully realized that mounting Mol Kalath hadn't felt strange at all, but then the tiny feathers on the demon's back seemed to twist and curl in her grip and the skin beneath shuddered appreciatively at her touch. At that, nausea bubbled up inside her and she swallowed it back down. "Eyes forward," she muttered to herself.

"EYES FORWARD," Mol Kalath echoed back.

Compared to the crossing from America, the English Channel was hardly worth noticing. At the pace at which the demons flew, there was just enough time to relay the battle plans, limited as they were, before land came into sight. Sully had never seen the White Cliffs of Dover before. Her time serving the Empire had always been out on the front lines and in the colonies. London overhung the cliffs, as unnatural looking as the demon-grown Manhattan could ever have aspired to. Here at the edge of the water, when whatever curse that kept it growing and spreading had found no more land, London had made a few feeble tries at bridges, and then had sprouted up into an ornate wall. Containing itself like a carcinoma. At the top of the wall, Sully could just barely make out the movement of redcoats scrambling around and over every inch of it. Frantically, they were raising defenses in a place where no defenses had been required for a lifetime.

There was a rumbling from within the demon beneath her, a regular, crackling sound that it took Sully a long moment to realize was laughter. Mol Kalath was not at the head of the pack, but it was charging on with the same blind abandon as all of the rest of them. A few spells were flung up from the walls of London but even the few that hit a demon just made the creature swell up larger and more powerful than before. The demon swarm dove for the redcoats manning the walls and—only an inch away from their targets—smashed against an invisible barrier.

Mol Kalath was one of the lucky ones; it had enough time to turn aside instead of plowing straight into the unseen, impassable wall. The demons' roars of triumph had turned into bitter shrieks. Sully had to scream to be heard over their wailing. "What is it, what happened?"

"A WISH. IT IS THE ONLY THING THAT COULD TURN US AWAY. THEY HAVE WISHED THAT DEMONS CANNOT ENTER."

"How could they make a wish when all of the demons are on our side?!"

Before Sully could get her answer, the British opened fire. Mortars had been emplaced all along the wall, and the exploding shells easily penetrated the swirling mass of demons. Creatures that had survived millennia died in an instant.

Sully was screaming at the demons to retreat. Slick ichor showered down on her amidst the sparks and buzzing metal. The explosions were so loud and so close that she couldn't even hear herself. Instinct had her throwing up shields but there was no end to the burning chaos. Mol Kalath was trilling at her in a language she didn't understand. A demon's head tumbled past her, looking halfway between an elephant and a man.

One lucky shard of superheated metal made it through, searing a line across her back and ruining her jacket. The next piece of shrapnel bit deep into her thigh and she burned her fingers digging it out. Her eyes watered from the smoke and her hands were sticky with her own blood. When she drew a breath to cast, her spell turned to a wheezing cough.

She fell. It could have been one second into the bombardment or an hour, she didn't know. All she remembered when she hit the water was that one moment the demon was beneath her and in the next all she held was a handful of bloody feathers.

The freezing sea washed away her confusion and she launched herself back into the air with Ogden's clumsy flying spell. Sucking in oxygen, she slipped past the firestorm, skirting close to the lapping waves, then rushed up the cliff face with spellfire boiling up out of her hands faster than she could shape it. She rose like a comet. For one awful moment the redcoats on the wall looked up at her and saw her fury before she rained death down on them.

Her concussion spells ruined the mortars' aim. Darts of white flame pulsed from her fingertips, shredding hastily erected defenses as they were cast. She landed on the wall without any interference from the barrier that had repelled the demons. Then the real work began.

All British eyes were still on the sky. Down on the ground, Sully danced through the assembled soldiers with a stolen saber in one hand and a whip of flames in the other. Her heart thundered in her chest and with every breath she cast another curse. It had been a long time since she had gone to war, but she had not forgotten the screams, the blood, the horror in her guts when she recognized that appetizing smell as roasted human flesh.

Arterial spray got caught in her defensive spells, swirling around her as she killed and ran and killed again without pause. There had been a hundred men stationed on the walls when she began at one end of the line of redcoats, soldiers, and artillery equipment techs. Now there were less than twenty still standing. Sully could not remember a single one of their faces. They had been only a blur of targets, only objects in motion. Not people. Not really. She couldn't stop to think that they were people or she wouldn't be able to throw the next spell that boiled away a young man's guts in a flash of putrid yellow smoke.

The deafening rhythm of the mortars had fallen to a stutter. When she had a moment to look up, the demons were fleeing to France. Her hands were shaking. Adrenaline or exhaustion or both. Blood thumped steadily from the wound in her leg. Marie was going to be furious—these trousers had been a gift and besides, that was her dinner going to waste.

Reinforcements were already boiling up the stairs onto the walls to take a last few pot-shots at the demonic stragglers. Sully staggered through the corpses to the edge of the wall, killing an officer in a pressed uniform with a sloppy backhand stroke before the snapped saber tumbled from her numb fingers. She caught a stray bullet from the far end of the wall in a hazy shield and let it drop to the ground with a little splash.

More and more soldiers rushed onto the wall, readying their Gatling rifles and bellowing out orders at her, as if she would ever have listened even when she was on their side. The dull ache in her chest told her that she did not have enough power to cast her flying spell again. In her frenzy, she had depleted not only her own resources, but had drained the oversaturation of magic from the air around her, too. All the excess power that the dissolution of the Veil of Tears had released had passed through Sully and come out as death.

There was no way in hell that she was letting the British take her alive. She turned to face them as they emerged from the stairwells and charged toward her. She raised her middle fingers to the whole country and jumped backward off the wall.

Mol Kalath caught her before she had fallen ten feet.

"YOU SHOULD HAVE LOOKED DOWN."

"And lose my nerve?"

The wheezing crackle started up in the demon's chest once again and this time Sully was laughing along with it. Mol Kalath spun in the air, dodging shells and bullets with a familiar grace. But now that the British gunners weren't spoiled for a choice of targets, every mortar on the wall was tracking their position.

"YOU MUST TAKE US AWAY FROM HERE. I CANNOT FLY AND CAST AT THE SAME TIME."

A bullet clipped off the top of Mol Kalath's beak, as if to prove the point. Sully buried her face in its feathers and groaned. "I've got nothing left. I'm empty."

"SHARE MY STRENGTH, IONA. TAP INTO THE WELL OF MY POWER."

A mortar shell shrieked by them and Sully had to cling tightly to avoid another bath.

She shouted, "Great plan. Except I have no idea how to do that."

"YOU HAVE DONE IT BEFORE. YOU HAVE DRAINED DEMONS DRY."

"That was... I don't want to hurt you. What the hell? I really don't."

"YOU WILL NOT HURT ME. BUT THE BRITISH WILL. CAST YOUR SPELL, IONA."

The barrier between Sully and the power that she needed was only as thick as her skin. The moment that she tried to draw magic from the beast beneath her it began flooding through like from a hole in a dam. In an instant her strength was restored, and an instant later spellfire started leaking from her fingers and her eyes. It was too much, too fast, and in the back of her mind she saw glimpses from the cases of magical overload that she had witnessed, bone fragments and puddles that were left behind. The power started to burn.

She cast her traveling spell without a full set of calculations, mostly from memory, while they dodged explosions and Gatling gun fire. With a thunderclap as the air rushed in behind them, Sully and her demon vanished.

NOVEMBER 5, 2015

Mol Kalath hit the barrier across the Black Bay like a fly hitting a windshield. It spun as it fell toward the battering waves below, shielding its precious cargo from the sight of the British Dreadnought along the coast. In the water Mol Kalath gathered power and reset its broken bones, then it launched itself back into the air, flying hard for land and passing through the spells blocking travel without even pausing to unravel and reset them. With one last effort it heaved itself and Sully onto a street by the bay-side. The demon collapsed in a sodden heap with one black wing stretched out over her and then it let exhaustion drag it down into sleep.

When it awoke, Mol Kalath was dry but alone. Their return had sounded no alarms and the docks had already been evacuated when the British bombardment began so there had been nobody to discover them sleeping through the early hours of the day. The demon did not see New Amsterdam as Sully did. Whatever romance she attached to the plumes of fog drifting between the blocky buildings, it did not ascribe to. To creatures of chaos, a city built on grids was a maze; it wasn't surprising that so many of them had chosen to grow wings rather than trying to navigate it from down here. With senses so arcane that humanity had no name for them, Mol Kalath started to hunt for Sully's trail.

There was a strange sense of familiarity as Mol Kalath passed through the streets by the Black Bay, not just from the oddments of architecture that reminded it of Manhattan, but a more profound sense of déjà vu, as if it had walked these streets in another life. It followed that déjà vu back to its source, an unremarkable apartment building that had its façade hidden behind a web of scaffolding. Mol Kalath shed as much of its size as it could and pressed through the front door into a hallway. There were traces of Sully everywhere; fragments of her spells, long since spent and discarded, littered the hall. One of the apartment doors had been kicked in—with Sully's temper in mind, Mol Kalath peered through the gap. The apartment had been stripped of all decoration and furniture, but even empty it looked hardly large enough for a person to live in. Still, to Mol Kalath's eyes, Sully's presence was ingrained in every surface. She herself was standing in the center of the room, staring into a corner, where once there had been a bed.

"IONA."

Sully spun to one knee, launching a barrage of spells at Mol Kalath before either of them realized what was happening. The magic hammered into the demon, making it swell larger and crackle with contained power. "IONA, STOP."

She didn't stop. When her first barrage failed to scratch the creature, she cast something on herself and charged with a guttural roar.

"IONA. IT IS ME."

Her fist caught Mol Kalath at the side of its beak and with her enhanced strength it was enough to snap the demon's head into the doorframe and shower them both with plaster dust. "IONA. I AM A FRIEND."

She cursed and hammered her forehead into the central cluster of Mol Kalath's eyes. The demon quailed and tried to pull its face back out of the room but Sully was as relentless as she was vicious. She hammered at Mol Kalath with both fists, slammed the door into its neck and roared defiance in the demon's face when it still would not fall. "SULLY."

She stopped dead. Ichor trickled from her knuckles to join the puddles on the floor. "I AM MOL KALATH. I AM YOUR FRIEND."

She spat. "I think I would remember making friends with a giant talking bird."

"THINK BACK. WHAT IS THE LAST THING THAT YOU REMEMBER?"

Sully's eyebrows drew down. With a whisper, she let her enhancement spells slip away. "I . . . I don't know what you have done to me, but . . ."

"SULLY. CONCENTRATE."

She stumbled back a step, then sat down heavily on the bare floorboards. "I asked Marie to marry me. She said that she would. She had a friend, who was a party planner. We were going to meet him after work."

The searing pain in Sully's brain started to ease and memories started to come back in a trickle. First a day at a time, then weeks and months. She turned pale. "Jesus. I burned out? I never burn out. What the hell did I cast?"

"A TRAVELING SPELL. YOU PULLED US BOTH FROM THE FIRE. YOU CARRIED US OVER THREE THOUSAND MILES."

Sully snorted. "Nobody can travel that far; you'd need a portal and Magi . . ."

"YOU CAN. YOU DID. REMEMBER."

She scrambled to her feet and darted into the only separate room in the apartment. Mol Kalath did not understand human digestion, but it did know that the process was meant to travel in only one direction and that the sounds coming from the bathroom were probably a sign of distress.

When Sully came back, wiping her mouth with her sleeve, she was shaking. She pointed at the demon and looked absolutely furious that her finger was waving around. "Stay away from me."

"IONA. YOU MUST TRY TO REMEMBER—"

"I remember everything. That's why I'm telling you to stay away. If you come near me again, I will end you. If you try to touch me again, you are getting an express ticket right back to the hells. Do you understand me?"

Mol Kalath backed out into the hallway, wincing as its feathers ruffled over the corner of the doorframe and tugged on its wounds. "YOU ARE INJURED. I CANNOT LEAVE YOU WHEN—"

"Get out of here. I've had much worse and I've dealt with it myself. Go find our army. I need some time to think."

Mol Kalath was not happy but it backed its way out of the building and took off in a shower of wilted feathers. Sully took one last look around the hollow shell of her old apartment and then limped inland to catch a taxi.

Breaking in to the IBI used to be a lot easier. Most of that was the confidence that had come with knowing she could wave a badge and make all the guns point somewhere else, but the current block on traveling spells was definitely a complicating factor. She probably still had friends in the Bureau, but she didn't want to put anyone at odds with Ceejay. Despite their disagreement earlier, Sully couldn't shake the idea that he was on her side and that she had to be screwing up a lot to make him this angry. The motor pool entrance gate had always been sticky coming back down, so she only had to wait half an hour behind a dumpster before she got her chance to duck in. The blind spots in the security down in the lower levels of the building were so gaping that she only had to use one spell to get through, a tiny concussion spell that was just enough to spin a camera to point the other way and yet it left her skull humming. She was going to have to be careful with magic for a day or two. She had no desire to feel ever again the void where a lifetime of memories was meant to be. Once she was in the guts of the building, she didn't have to think any more; she had trodden these halls so many times that her feet carried her to Raavi's lab without her input.

He had turned the place into a modern art exhibit while Sully was away. Huge hunks of white wood, crackling with magic and in varying stages of being carved into human likenesses, littered every flat surface. Raavi himself was shirtless in the midst of a heap of sawdust with flecks of it stuck in his oiled back hair, hacking away at another carving with a scalpel in each of his four hands and a manic glint in his eye. In other words, he looked more or less the same as usual. Sully made sure to slam the door as she came in so he didn't panic and drop the scalpels while she was in the danger zone. "Sully, my dear, what a delightful surprise! To what do I owe the pleasure of this—Oh. You're bleeding everywhere."

The pain had been manageable, but only until he pointed out her injury. Now she hobbled her way to one of the tables and hauled herself up with a grunt. "What do you say to a little surgery between friends? For old times' sake?"

"You know what. I'm not even going to complain. I am bored out of my mind. Get your trousers off and lets me get all this muck cleaned off me."

Sully flopped back onto the metal with a clatter and laughed. "No wonder you're single, with that bedside manner."

"I will have you know that I have been on two dates this week," he shouted over his shoulder from the sink at the far end of the room. Sully grinned as she fumbled with her belt.

"With the same person?"

"You do remember you're here for a favor, right? I am about to be sewing you up. Wouldn't want to stitch your elbow to your arse by accident."

She got the blood-soaked trousers as far down as her knees and gave up. "Come on, you miss the abuse when I'm not around."

His grinning face suddenly loomed into view above her. "I do actually. Most of the folks upstairs have no sense of humor whatsoever."

She hissed when he prodded at her leg and made a sound somewhere between a gasp and a yelp when he tugged on the edges of the wound to peer inside. "Half of this is cauterized. What on earth have you been up to?"

"Waging wars. Riding demons. You know, the usual."

The syringe was jammed into her leg before she had the chance to make her usual objections and in less than a minute, the cold metal beneath her started to feel much more comfortable. The pain was still there, but there was a handy layer of mental fluff between her and experiencing it. "So am I to assume from all of the bullet wounds that the war isn't going according to plan?"

"None of them ever do," she yawned, "I wouldn't worry about it though. Plenty more plans."

He was frowning when she caught a glimpse of his face. "Do plans B through Z also involve you getting pieces of yourself blasted off?"

"Wouldn't be a proper war if I didn't have some scars to show for it."

He tutted and set to work suturing her leg. For a few moments there was a companionable silence as he concentrated on the fine manual work, but that gave Sully long enough to pick out the soft voice on the radio. "What the hell are you listening to?"

"Oh, you haven't heard this? I half thought it was one of your ideas."

"Some girl reciting numbers?"

"Isn't it marvelous. Nobody has a clue what it is! There are theories though, so many theories. I personally subscribe to the idea that the British are using some pattern in the numbers to share intelligence with their spies across the Americas. Although if that was it, why wouldn't we be jamming the signal? Of course, it may be that we are the ones broadcasting it to communicate with our spies. So that would explain that. Whatever the code is, it must be terribly clever because nobody has been able to work out the pattern yet. They broadcast on the hour, every hour. It must be a recording, right?"

Sully lay still and listened. "Well, she sounds English, but so do you, so that doesn't prove shit. The numbers aren't random . . . there is definitely something linking them together, I can feel it in my teeth."

Raavi giggled. "Radio transmissions directly into your fillings, eh?"

"There *is* something there. Some connection."

"I have got so many message boards for you to visit." Raavi looked so giddy when he popped back into sight that Sully couldn't help but return his smile. "Maybe another time. What do they think about it upstairs?"

"They think that I need to stop bothering them with paranoid conspiracy theories when they are trying to do real police work, apparently. Right, leg is done, up you go and I'll clean up the rest."

With his help, Sully was hauled into a seated position. She blinked until the sparks at the edges of her vision faded away. "So what is up with the wood?"

"Ugh," Raavi cast a despairing eye at the state of his lab, "This is the new big case everyone is losing their mind over. People vanishing. Lumps of wood left behind. No logic. No pattern."

"I hadn't heard anything about the wood."

Raavi's eyebrow quirked up. "But you have heard about the case. Making some waves up there at the top of the food chain, is it?"

Sully hissed as he dabbed alcohol across one of her burns. "Pick a metaphor and stick with it, will you?"

Raavi smirked. "Well, upstairs think that there is no pattern . . ."

Sully caught his hand. "What have you found?"

"I've been documenting every lump of wood as it came in. Blew out two Schrödinger's before I realized the magic saturation was off the charts. Weighed them. Measured the depth of the carvings. The magic levels stay about the same, but the carving has been getting consistently better each time a new victim is taken."

"The weight?"

His grin threatened to take the top off his head. "The weight was all over the place, no logical progression. Until you compared it to the weight of the missing people. Then you discovered that it was a perfect match each time. If one hundred and sixty pounds of Jeff Milquetoast went missing, then one hundred and sixty pounds of weird white wood was left in his place. And before you ask, no, nobody is being turned into wood. The Magi have searched for any trace of transmogrification and found nothing. Somebody is taking people and leaving their weight in wood."

Sully laughed despite herself. "That is really bizarre."

"Does it help?"

She caught the sly grin on his face. "Everything helps. And no, I am not investigating this. So keep your insinuations to yourself."

The next half hour went by quickly. Raavi caught her up on the latest office gossip—which she hadn't cared about even when she worked there—and on the progress of their bowling team, which she still vaguely resented having to give up despite being one of the worst players. He was just starting in on his appalling love life when he realized that he had run out of injuries to attend to. Whatever narcotics he had jammed into her leg were starting to wear off, leaving Sully listless and queasy. "You need to sleep that off now. A good twelve hours of sleep and you will be right as rain."

She blinked at him. "Chance would be a fine thing."

He took her by the arm and helped her back onto her feet. A few staggering steps later, she felt sure that the stitches were going to hold and clapped him on the back. "Thanks, Raavi. You're one of the good ones."

"Pfft. I am the best one, thank you very much."

She paused at that and glanced up at him with an enigmatic smile. "You are, actually. You are the best man I know."

He had the good sense to look nervous. "Sorry?"

"I've got a party coming up. Just me, Marie, and some of our nearest and dearest. I was wondering if you fancied coming along, maybe holding a ring for a while."

"Sully, you dark horse! You're finally settling down? Of course, I'll be your best man! Oh my goodness, I just realized I have to organize a stag party for the biggest lecher on the East Coast. I'm going to have to hire every stripper from here to the Northern Territories."

Sully held a finger up to his face and a flicker of spellfire leapt up to singe the tip of his nose. "No strippers."

"No strippers."

With a little bit of help from Raavi, Sully made it out to a taxi and headed for home. It was only when the evacuation notices came into sight that she realized she had sent the driver to her old address. She corrected herself and when they finally arrived at the right apartment, she paid him double the fare to make up for messing with him. Still, though, it left a cold weight of dread in her stomach that she had—at least for a moment—forgotten where she lived. Normally Sully took doctor's orders as mere suggestions but after the day she had just suffered through, she was more than happy to slip into the big empty bed and breathe in the faint perfume that Marie had left behind on the sheets.

MARCH 3 1986

The first week after the British had surrendered, Iona drank. She didn't mean to, but the state dinners dragged on for so long, and if a little whiskey made the time pass quicker then a lot of whiskey could reliably turn the whole thing into a blur.

On the second week, her long overdue honeymoon started. Ayomide took her through a portal to Ophir to finally meet her parents, but the conversation had been so stilted and awkward that Sully started to miss the state dinners. They'd lasted only one night in the sleek white stone buildings of Kinshasa, trapped in separate rooms, before they moved on to the next leg of their journey. Maybe in the years to come Iona could make friends with her in-laws, but for now the hurt was still too raw. She'd taken their precious daughter away from them and there was no turning back the clock on that.

They took a cross-country bullet train to the Egyptian Congo, basking in the lush green of one of the last true jungles on earth, listening to the chiming birdsong from the sweat-soaked sheets of their sleeper car. It was as close to heaven as Iona was ever liable to get.

On arrival, their cabin with a view turned out to be more of a treehouse, but neither one of them gave a half a damn about a ladder. They had magic, they had each other, and they had all the time in the world.

Iona was bored within three days, though she wouldn't admit it. After a lifetime of dedication to a singular cause, having that focus taken away from her was troubling. She should have been ecstatic, but nobody had informed her emotions of that fact. She still snapped awake at the break of dawn, ready to pull on her boots and head into the field. She still lay awake at night, listening for Redcoats that were never coming. If Ayomide had expected her to open up and relax now that the war was done, she gave no indication of disappointment. From the moment that they met, she had known Iona better than Iona knew herself. If Ayomide wasn't worried, Iona wouldn't be either. She'd heard that time healed all wounds, she had enough scars across her body to prove the truth of it too, so the waiting game began.

On the third week, Iona and Ayomide came home. Their honeymoon had been short and sweet, still feeling languorous and indulgent for a relationship forged in the heat of battle, but by the end, Iona felt like she was hiding out, so they caught the next portal back to Ireland.

She had expected a heap of demands to be waiting in her office, but what she found was polite invitations. Weddings mostly. A few remembrance vigils for the veterans of the war that never made it across the finish line. She took Ayomide to as many of the weddings as they could manage: Iona in her best pressed uniform and Ayomide in dresses so bright and beautiful they put the brides to shame. She went to the vigils alone, incognito. The other players in the war were parlaying their success into political positions and fame. Neither held much appeal for Iona.

It was now rolling into the fourth week of Irish Independence. Ayomide was interviewing for a post-graduate position at Cork University, finally bringing her carefully constructed technomancy out to be torn apart by the world of academia. The day seemed to stretch on and on without company.

There was no wedding invitation waiting in her office this time, only Leonard Pratt, reading a book in the corner and waiting patiently. "My dear Mrs. Sullivan, what a pleasure to see you again."

"Pratt. How are you?" She had long since stopped being surprised by his appearances.

"Quite well, thank you, and your dear lady wife?"

Iona couldn't conceal a smile. "Perfect."

"Ah, grand. I am so glad to learn that even in troubled times, love finds a way. I only regret that I could not be here for the ceremony"

Iona perched on the edge of her desk. "Hard to get an RSVP when you're in a warzone."

"Yes, quite. Quite."

The pause only stretched out for a moment before Iona filled it. "I don't have any soldiers for you Pratt. I already told you we aren't getting dragged into America's war."

"My dear Mrs. Sullivan, nothing could have been further from my mind." He pressed a hand to his chest in mock dismay. "Rather, I was hoping that you might help me with a work related matter rather than assisting me in my extra-curricular activities."

That piqued her interest. "You're here curse-breaking?"

"Yes indeed. It seems that one of the British billets was discovered to have been furnished in a rather abnormal manner, and a request was made for me to lend my talents in deciphering the particular curse that was used."

"The human furniture in Tulsk?"

"Ah, the matter has already attracted your attention?"

Iona cracked her knuckles. "I'm the one who found them like that, after I'd killed the piece of shit who did it to them."

"While I am sure you were thoroughly morally justified, I must admit that the caster's demise has made my job rather more difficult."

"Well the prick was trying to make me into a chair at the time."

"Morally and aesthetically justified. Whatever your virtues, I do not believe that anyone could be convinced that you would make for good decor."

"The hair, right? Clashes with everything."

She caught the flash of Pratt's smile before his good manners could stifle it. "Would you countenance a field trip to examine the afflicted with me?"

"If you think I'll be useful."

He rose from his seat with a minor tectonic shift of gut providing his momentum. "My dear Mrs. Sullivan, you always have been in the past and I see no reason you cannot continue to be in the future."

Traveling spells were only meant for one person, but Iona's work-around had been adopted world-wide after it was seen in use on the battlefield. Sure, technically Pratt was dead for about a second while they traveled but there was no denying that it was more efficient than portals.

While Pratt got his breath back and his palpitations slowed, Iona found the constable in charge of the warehouse. He was in the area where the younger and more attractive folk of the town had been stacked under dust-sheets. There had been some notes and books about how this had been done in the Redcoat's little laboratory, but what hadn't been destroyed, had been lost in the fight. Pratt had nothing but his own expansive mental library to draw upon.

He whistled while he worked. Cataloging in a little moleskin notebook the different transformations and the likelihood that certain spells were involved. Boredom took hold of Iona once more, and she dithered between the rows, only startling out of her reverie when one of the nesting tables blinked at her.

By the time she returned, Pratt was standing beside a human being who still had a paper tag with his name and address dangling from his wrist. The boy seemed to be struggling to talk, but too much time as an ottoman probably did that to you. He embraced Pratt, then ran for the door. Iona moved to stop him, but Pratt halted her interception with a barely perceptible shake of the head. "Let him go. He has a family to go home to."

"You've cracked it?"

Pratt moved to sit on a loveseat then thought better of it at the last moment. "It is all rather uninspired really. Fairytale ideology. True love's kiss."

"I didn't know you and the ottoman felt that way about each other."

Pratt chuckled. "Picture your darling wife. Imagine that you are pressing your lips to hers, then plant them on that cupboard and we shall see if it works."

The cupboard in question became a pretty young blonde with admittedly broad shoulders. She managed to mumble out some thanks before shuffling awkwardly to the door, swinging her hips with each step.

"Nicely done." Iona put an arm around Pratt's shoulders and then, because she couldn't help herself, said, "You'd better not have been thinking about Ayomide too."

"There was a young street wizard, once upon a time—several years back, during the brown-outs in New Amsterdam. We worked together to break a curse that was destroying so many young lovers that it seemed almost like a plague. In the end, he expired in the spell-work. But I shall not forget him anytime soon."

Something in his voice brought Iona up cold. Pratt had always kept to himself. The world that he lived in, full of backstabbing politicians and conniving academics, took anything he said and twisted it into a knife. He'd trusted Sully with something that could sink his career. Sully tightened her grip on his shoulder. "I'm . . . sorry you lost him."

"It would never have worked out in the long run, but it is sufficient for our purpose today." He gave the loveseat a peck on the cushion and it immediately started bucking back into human shape. "Come along Mrs. Sullivan, do not leave all the work to me or I shall have chapped lips by the end of the day."

They must have spent hours kissing their way through all the furniture in the warehouse, but when they were finished, neither one could complain about the results. Word had spread, and the town had gone from silent on their arrival to an overjoyed carnival atmosphere by the time they emerged. When Pratt tried to beg off, claiming exhaustion and indisposition, Iona dragged him into the street party. Music filled the air, a bonfire burned bright against the night sky, and there was a drink being pressed into the heroes hands every time they turned around.

At some point after midnight, Iona and Pratt found themselves sitting on the grass, probably ruining Pratt's suit in the process, and staring up at the stars. "You did good today Pratt. You made things better."

"Your company was much . . . appreciated Mrs. Sullivan."

The screams were so distant through the whiskey haze that Iona didn't even realize what she was hearing. In the sky above them, the stars blinked out in a wave.

"What?"

The same dark void was rushing toward them across the town. Already the warehouse, bonfire and revelers had been swallowed whole. Iona stumbled to her feet, fumbling through a protection spell, but it was already too late. The darkness swept over them, and they no longer existed.

NoVember 6, 201C

The hammering in Sully's head matched the sound from her front door and was a subtle hint that she had not slept as long as she needed to. She was halfway across the living room before she thought to check that she had clothes on and she was relieved to find that she still wore her bloody and tattered rags from the night before. Ogden was rocking on his heels outside and he looked furious. "What in the hells happened?"

Sully yawned and beckoned him in and he stomped right across the rug with his muddy boots. "One minute you are flying off to war, the next we have messengers screaming that you were killed, that the British can repel demons, that they have their own demons. What is going on?!"

Sully pointed at the couch, and with all the grace of a child in a tantrum, Ogden threw himself down on it.

"The British knew that we were coming. They had been preparing for it. There was artillery set up along the southern border. They've made a wish that demons can't come onto British territory. Somehow."

Ogden cursed. "Well, General, what do you plan to do about it?"

Sully licked her cracked lips. "I plan to have a coffee. Take a shower. Put on clothes that are still clothes, then go get screamed at by Pratt for an hour before I lose my temper and blow him into the Atlantic."

With the bandana stretched across his face, it was hard to tell when Ogden was smiling. You had to watch the corners of his eyes for wrinkles. "And in the long term?"

Sully stalked off toward the bathroom. "Maybe breakfast? See if you can make the coffee machine work. It's too new for me to work out, but I'm no super genius Magus from another world."

He had managed to brew two cups of coffee by the time that she was dressed, but it was so atrociously bad that Sully poured it down the sink and bought some on the street corner for both of them. That was bad, too, but Sully judged coffee on a sliding scale and at least this cup tasted recognizably of coffee. Before Ogden had the chance to take flight, Sully flagged down a taxi and bullied him inside.

"I do not understand why you insist on traveling like this."

"Because I'm still tired as hell. If I nod off here, it is embarrassing. If I nod off in the sky, they have to pick bits of me off the street. Besides, we need to talk."

Ogden peered at her imperiously. "Is that a fact?"

Sully cast a quick glance at the back of the taxi driver's head. Loud African rock was thumping out of the car's speaker and he was bobbing along to it, oblivious. "Has Pratt asked you to kill me yet?"

Ogden's eyes bulged. "What?"

Sully cast a barrier behind the driver and the music fell silent. "He hasn't asked *me* to kill *you* yet, but he needs you gone. Manhattan is a great ally during the war, but the minute the war is over, you become a liability. All those Magi? All that power outside of his control? Pratt might hate the British, but he's just as pragmatic as any of those blue-blooded bastards."

Ogden scooted closer, but his eyes never left Sully's hands. "How would killing me help him?"

"That's how Pratt thinks. You're their king. If you're gone, then there's a chance for him to either seize control himself or install a puppet."

"What is your evidence?"

Sully scoffed. "He offered to put you on trial after the war. There is no way that your people would stand for that. He'd have a civil war on his hands, and Manhattan would wipe the floor with him."

Ogden's hands were flexing in his lap, ready to cast the moment Sully made her move. "In exchange for our alliance, he made assurances that—"

"He makes a lot of promises. Never pays up. Funny how that works out."

She pulled a cigar out of her jacket and leaned over so that Ogden could grudgingly light it with a whisper and a twist of his fingers. He leaned back and sighed. "If all of this is true then why would you warn me? Why give me the advantage?"

Sully grinned. "Because Pratt hasn't got a lot of choices when it comes to killing me. He's with you every day, so he can work on you in steps. Try to convince you that putting me down is the smart option. But here's the thing—you're an old-school kind of guy. You believe in honor and duels and all that. Now you're going to feel obliged to give me the same warning I just gave you when the time comes."

Ogden leaned back in his seat and let out a ragged breath. Eventually he nodded. "That is only fair."

"That's what I thought." Sully settled back to stare out at her city rolling by. The taxi moved on in silence for a moment before Sully's temporary barrier fell and the screaming Yoruba lyrics washed over them in a crashing wave of noise.

Pratt was holding court in the Brooklyn Municipal Building again. Sully suspected it was because of the close proximity of the city's best restaurants. The day to day running of the Empire had been left to the underlings while the rich old men with no tactical skills beyond their boundless sense of superiority settled in to argue about the course of the war. Ogden drifted up into the sky to meet with his underlings and a pair of soldiers fell in at either side of Sully as she got out of the taxi. Pratt may have been trying to intimidate or shame her but it was hard to march someone in like a prisoner when they strode ahead of their minders with such confidence. Sully led her bemused honor guard into the conference room.

Pratt glowered from the far end of the table with such fury that she was surprised it didn't set the heaps of paper in front of him alight, but he did nothing to interrupt the arguments all around him. He was going to make the only person with anything useful to contribute to the conversation wait to speak. She remained at attention, staring out the far window at the sky between the buildings, but internally she scoffed. Like this was the first time she'd had to wait for a dressing down from a superior officer. Eventually, the stuffed suits that lined the table noticed her and fell silent, and with no more excuses, Pratt rose up and barked, "Would you be so kind as to furnish us with your long overdue report, General Sullivan."

"We removed the Veil of Tears. We contacted the demonic presence in Europe and formed an alliance. On our first expedition, we encountered resistance. The British had forewarning of our attack."

Pratt's eyes narrowed to slits. "Pray tell, how did you overcome this resistance?"

"We didn't. The demons suffered heavy bombardment and were forced to retreat."

One of the waistcoats and elevenses crowd opened his mouth. "Poppycock, the gentlemen downstairs driven off by a little gunfire?"

Sully clenched her fists and smiled. "The British wished that demons couldn't enter their territory. I have the Magi contacting their counterparts in the world below to find out precisely how that wish was made when we had assurances that no more deals were being offered."

There was another outbreak of grumbling and muttering from around the table as the politicians all raced to have their baseless opinions heard. Pratt was grimly silent until the hubbub died down again. "Regardless of the details, it seems quite apparent that your plan has failed, General Sullivan. We cannot rely on the demons to provide us with any sort of victory in the British Isles, so it may be time to start pursuing diplomatic solutions."

Sully's knuckles were turning white. "With all due respect, Sir, a fight isn't over just because the first punch doesn't connect. We have an army of our own and many allies that could contribute troops and materiel. We have an excellent beachhead established in Europe that will be unassailable to any and all counterattacks. We are still in a very strong position."

"You promised us victory and you have delivered us little more than scraps."

Sully growled. "I promised you nothing. This isn't a game and it isn't one of your little political squabbles. This is war."

She wasn't great at illusions, but this one had been on the school curriculum. A routine chore for the only witch in the class. Shimmering coils of spellfire drifted up from her hands and spun until a sphere hung over the table, until with a grunt of effort it became a map of the world. Sully didn't give them a chance to talk over her. "Hong Kong has barely manned defenses. If we took down the barrier around the fortress city like we did with the Veil then it would fall to the Khanate in days. The Black Hole of Kolikata has always been unstable—with just a few Magi we could completely destabilize it and drive the Empire out of India permanently."

Each imperial base lit up on the globe as Sully mentioned its name. "There is a substantial redcoat presence in Botany Bay, but with assistance from the Dreamers we could create enough chaos to force the British either to reinforce there, weakening their home-front defenses, or to abandon their hold on Oceania completely. The base at Anguilla is in easy striking distance. The Virgin Islands. The Faroe Islands. The Spire of Ascension. All of these isolated targets are within our grasp. The British Empire is overextended to its breaking point. All that we need to do is apply pressure at any one of their overseas holdings and we can regain momentum."

Pratt sneered, "And what price shall we pay for you to wage your little campaign of vengeance? How many of the lives of our citizenry would have to be tossed into the meat grinder to satisfy your bloodlust, when the British would likely listen to our terms even now?"

Sully's globe blinked out. "If you think that they're going to let us go without a fight, then you are a fucking idiot."

He almost smiled. "Please, conduct yourself with some decorum, General Sullivan."

A deathly silence filled the room as Sully's jaw clamped shut. Her next words came out in a soft hiss. "We can all see you hedging your bets, Pratt. We're not stupid. You're too much of a coward to be a hero in war, so you're going to paint the people who do have the balls to fight as warmongers. No matter which way the fighting goes, you stay safe in your cushioned palace. If we win, you kept us monsters in check. If you lose, then you were the voice of reason when the British come around looking for ringleaders to execute. I see you, Pratt. I know you. You're a spineless piece of shit."

In the awkward silence that followed, it was finally quiet enough to hear screaming coming from outside.

A half-dozen soldiers burst into the room, barking, "Evacuate! Evacuate the building! Everyone out!"

The politicians had barely started to rise from their seats when an impact rocked the room. That got them moving. Sully stripped off her jacket and tossed it aside as she ran to the window, spellfire starting to seep from her fingers. She had made it as far as where Pratt was gathering up his folders when the wall tore away. The masonry cracked like a gunshot and the metalwork screamed. A dark shape passed through Sully's vision, dragging the far end of the room away to shatter on the streets below. It was too fast and too huge for her to comprehend. She lashed it with a bolt of fire purely on instinct. Black scales, each as big as Sully's hand, showered into the room as the mass vanished out of sight. She forced herself forward to the breach and hung out the side of the crumbling building to get a look at the enemy. She still couldn't make sense of what she was seeing.

The body was impossibly large, scraping against the tallest buildings on either side of the street, and it was vaguely turtle-like. She could grasp that, but it was when she looked up at the mess emerging from the massive shell that her mind started to rebel. When she concentrated her gaze, narrowing her attention, it was easier. She could make out a snake-like neck supporting a head with a conger eel underbite and milky eyes. But there were dozens of heads on dozens of necks, all coiling and tangling around each other. Each one moved independently. One was hammering the thick bone of its brow ridge against the side of a building. Another was swooping low to scoop up a whole squad of infantry in its jaws. The head that had so casually ripped a side off the municipal building was lashing upward to snap at Ogden and his Magi in the air. Behind her she heard Pratt screeching over the roar of the wind outside. "What in the nine hells is that thing?"

Sully was still gawking in wonder. "That's a Hydra. But I'm pretty sure they're extinct."

"Well, what is it doing here?"

A head passed by the building, so close that the rush of air almost knocked Sully off her feet, and then there was a muted scream from above them as the jaws snapped shut on whatever Magus it had been pursuing. The Hydra uttered no sound, no roars or hisses. It moved methodically, eliminating one threat after another with startling precision. Though its eyes were blank, the intelligence behind them was calculating.

Sully flashed Pratt a grin. "I'll go ask it."

Her flying spell caught her just as she hit the ground and she rebounded up to where she could see Ogden readying some huge complex working. His spell came together just as she arrived beside him and a torrent of lightning leapt from his outstretched hands, enough to have powered the city for a month. When it hit the Hydra, the beast jerked convulsively and every one of its necks fell suddenly limp. Heads rained down into the streets below and for a moment Sully thought that the fight might be over. She was only fooled for a moment.

Three heads reanimated themselves and lunged up at Ogden and Sully like striking cobras. Nothing that big should have moved that fast. Ogden was half exhausted from his last attack. He barely had enough time to toss up a shield before the Hydra's jagged teeth were scraping over it, tossing him a block away with the force of the impact.

Sully had more time to think and with a surge of power she spiraled up out of reach of the snapping teeth.

As she rose, she peppered the top of the Hydra's heads with fire. It didn't stop their attack, but she took satisfaction from watching the monster flinch. As it strained upward, more necks unfurled from inside its shell, but they were headless and ended in cauterized stumps. *Someone had hurt this thing before. It could be done.* She burst up out of the fog hanging over New Amsterdam and the whole world fell away beneath her. She and the pursuing heads were alone in the void between the fog below and the clouds above.

Away from the chaos on the streets, Sully found her focus. With the same methodical pace that the Hydra had used in demolishing the defenses around the municipal building, Sully ran through her repertoire of spells, testing each one against the Hydra's hide and finding each one wanting. She conjured blades to cut it, flames to scorch it, ice to freeze it and razor-sharp crescents of pure arcane force that inflicted only superficial damage. Each time that she moved on to the next spell, the wounds from the last had already started to close. The Hydra just would not die. For a moment she sensed hesitation in its attacks and that was the only warning she had before three more revived heads burst out of the clouds around her.

"Shit." Abandoning her experiments, Sully fled for the questionable safety of the earth. The Hydra's heads lunged for her, moving in concert now, perfectly synchronized like a flock of birds. She drove straight down into the roiling fog and immediately crashed into another head that was on its way up.

She bounced off its snout and tumbled up between the monster's blind eyes. She hit the brow ridge traveling at full speed, knocking the air out of her lungs. The spells she'd been forming died on her lips and she lay limp on the calloused hide, trying desperately to take a breath. If she just had one second to think. One moment to cast. The Hydra flicked her up into the sky with a jerk of its neck. She tumbled helplessly through the air into another waiting mouth and the jaws snapped shut around her.

The stench of rotten fish enveloped Sully in the total darkness. Every surface was slick with a thick slime that was soaking through her clothes, stinging when it reached her skin. Her hair was plastered with it and her scalp was burning. There was nothing to grab onto once she was past the jagged teeth. Beneath the spongy mucosa of the mouth were hard ridges of bone that battered her with every movement of the Hydra's head. Gravity had started to do its work and Sully was slipping toward the Hydra's throat.

She finally got enough of the fetid air into her lungs to cast but she couldn't tell up from down. She cast the flying spell hoping that it would stop her from being swallowed. She collided with the roof of the Hydra's mouth, where the pulsing vents still dripped venom. That was enough to put the world back into perspective. She cast again and though the first lance of flame ricocheted harmlessly off of the Hydra's teeth, the next cratered its gums. The monstrous head whipped from side to side, knocking Sully from one jawbone to the other. Her head rang like a tolling bell. That was enough of that.

Her concussion spell had started out as a little industrial cantrip used for blowing glass and making lightbulbs. She had amped it up to smash windows and flip cars. It didn't take much more power or terribly complicated math to turn it up again. It doubled the casting time, but she could work out that kink with a whiteboard and an hour when she wasn't in the process of being swallowed. Adding a delay at the end so she had time to stick her fingers in her ears and cast a shield so that she didn't go deaf or die was a nice touch, too.

Even though she was braced for it, the concussion hit Sully like a sledgehammer and knocked her down the back of the Hydra's throat again. For one awful moment she was falling, then she pulsed more energy into the flying spell and launched herself back up into its mouth. Until she saw daylight, she thought that the she had missed her chance, that the Hydra had snapped its jaws shut again before she could escape. But the mouth was still gaping open, much wider than it should have been. The concussion had dislocated it, and while the Hydra's impossibly fast healing was at work again, it wasn't fast enough. Sully burst out into the open air with a whoop of triumph.

Every single one of the Hydra's heads snapped around to track the parabola of her flight. All those dead eyes were suddenly far too attentive. The Hydra surged forward—its speed again belying its size—and Sully had to concentrate all her energies on just keeping ahead of it. They were almost to the water before she realized how far she had traveled while she was inside the monster's mouth. It had gulped her down and then headed straight back to the sea, crossing a dozen blocks of Brooklyn in the time it took her to remember the difference between up and down. The Magi were still trailing after it, but since it was retreating, they seemed to have stopped their assault.

Sully dove down into the water to clear off the worst of the venom that was stinging her skin. By the time that she broke the surface she was certain that the Hydra had lost all interest in everyone else. It was here for her. That made just about as much sense as an extinct reptile the size of a small island showing up in New Amsterdam—and it played nicely into her healthy sense of paranoia—but Sully accepted it as fact. If the Hydra wanted her, though, it was going to have to work for it.

She stayed low, dancing along the top of the river, and teasing the monster out onto the water where it was less likely to roll over a civilian. That turned out to be a mistake. Once it was in the water, its massive flippers were able to fulfill their purpose. Any intention that Sully had of getting clever vanished as she burned down the coast as fast as her spells could carry her. Red Hook was passed in a minute and the Magus tower in Owl's Head Park loomed large on the horizon. Sully didn't dare to stop and look back, but she could hear the Hydra in close pursuit. Its flippers were churning up the Black Bay and its bow wave was huge beneath her. Once or twice she heard the snap of jaws close at her heels. She put on another surge of speed even though she could feel her power dwindling by the minute.

The pain in her head had graduated from the expected tension headache into something new and terrible. If she closed her eyes, she was fairly certain that she was going to see colors. It didn't matter. If the Magi hadn't been able to scratch this thing, she didn't stand a chance. Admitting that, even to herself, stung. Sully truly hated to retreat but she might be able to use its fixation on her to get it away from innocent people. The low broad blocks of Fort Hamilton came into view. Just a little bit further and she would have a clear shot out across the ocean. If she didn't have to keep putting on more speed, she might make it as far as Bermuda before she was completely burned out, although she probably wouldn't remember who she was by the time New Amsterdam was out of sight. That was worse than dying, somehow. Running and running until there was nothing left but fear and incomprehension.

Thinking of that possibility, Sully's resolve faltered and the spells keeping her in the air weakened and came apart, dumping her onto Brighton Beach. She turned to face the Hydra. If she had hoped for one last glimpse of New Amsterdam, that hope was going to go unful-filled—the writhing mass of the Hydra dominated the skyline. The heads reared up as its shell hit the sand. For one long moment her death hung there, before every one of the jagged maws came plunging down.

The impact knocked the air out of her again. There was no pain. Or at least, there wasn't any more pain than there had been before. Sully forced her eyes open and her vision was filled with feathers. "I CANNOT LET YOU OUT OF MY SIGHT FOR A MOMENT."

Sully was laughing despite herself. "Didn't I tell you to piss off back to Europe?"

"I DID. THEN I RETURNED."

Whatever membranous barrier there had been between Sully and Mol Kalath's raw power in the past had been stripped away when they last connected. Her reserves refilled in a heady rush. "It is after me. We need to lead it away from people."

"WE NEED TO FIGHT."

Sully climbed Mol Kalath, scrambling and yanking at feathers as she tried to get up onto its back. The Hydra loomed into sight the moment she passed the demon's wings, so big that looking up at it triggered her vertigo. She shook her head. "How do you fight something like that?"

"THE SAME WAY THAT WE FIGHT EVERYTHING ELSE."

Spellfire was coiling out from Sully's fists, her shadow-twin's power flowing through her as easily as she would draw a breath. Fear and confusion were forgotten as the raw power coursed through her. The demon flew in an ever-widening spiral around the Hydra. The mass of heads tracked their movement as they ascended, coiling and weaving around one another. "It's just a big turtle, right? So, let's flip it."

Laughter rumbled beneath her and they dove for the Hydra's flippers.

Sully cast as they fell, the complex formulae for increasing the power of her concussion spell unneeded as she poured more and more raw power into the working. She had been using the spell for decades. Tinkering with it for even longer. This latest change wasn't even difficult—it was what the spell had been fighting to be all along.

She tumbled from Mol Kalath's back when they hit the sand bar, but she rolled to her feet without missing a single syllable of the spell. The spellforms that she had traced in the air rained down all around her, and with only a moment of hesitation Mol Kalath was a reassuring weight braced against her back. The instant that the Hydra had seen them land it had lunged for her once more, but it was too late. Sully raised a hand and snapped her fingers.

The impact of the concussion tore her from her feet despite Mol Kalath's support. The demon, too, was flipped end over end. Both of them went skipping over the tops of the waves until they hit the beach. The shockwave rolled over them, deafening and huge. The windows of the warehouses along the waterfront imploded. The lampposts rocked back and forth like ears of corn in a windy field. Sully scrambled over the downed demon to see what her spell had wrought, just in time to catch the wave that it had thrown up directly to the face. She spat out the mouthful of saltwater and scrubbed at her stinging eyes. The

Hydra was nowhere to be seen. She cackled, then kicked Mol Kalath playfully. "Did you see that?!"

"THE HYDRA HAS BEEN LAUNCHED FAR FROM THE LAND. WE HAVE TIME TO PREPARE OUR DEFENSES."

"At this point, I'll take whatever I can get."

Ogden dropped from the sky to land between Sully and the demon, looking even more windswept than usual. The experience of being hit by the shockwave had done nothing to temper his good manners. "What the hell did you do?" he bellowed.

November 7, 2015 AM

A little after three in the morning, Sully's head lolled over to bash against the train window and she snapped back to attention. A cigar had turned to ash where it was dangling from her lips and it had sprinkled into the little plastic cup of gin that the bar had let her take back to her compartment. She stared down into the swirl of gray and after a moment of deliberation, grudgingly decided it was undrinkable. Arrayed around her on the table of the cabin were a scrying mirror, two cellphones, and a pad of paper where she was working through the calculations and formulae of all her usual spells, to see just how easy it would be to amp them up with a little demonic backing. One of the phones was buzzing incessantly because Sully couldn't work out how to turn it off; it was the one that Pratt had the number for. The other one had been given to her to call friends and family. She had reluctantly called Marie's parents and left the number of the new phone on their answering machine, but there had been no reply yet.

The surface of the scrying mirror rippled and Mol Kalath's croaking whispers came through unbidden. "IT LURKED DEEP WITHIN THE CASPIAN SEA. THE ANIMALS AND HUMANS TRAPPED WITHIN THE BARRIERS AROUND EUROPE WERE HUNTED TO EXTINCTION BY MY KIN IN THEIR FURY. THIS CREATURE STILL PERSISTED. IT WOULD NOT DIE NO MATTER HOW THE DEMONS WAGED WAR UPON IT. THERE WERE OTHER

CREATURES, LESS FEARSOME BUT EQUALLY ETERNAL. FOUR OF THEM IN ALL."

Sully dropped the butt of her cigar into the plastic cup. "In the classical myths there were gods and monsters that couldn't die. Immortals. We assumed that they were just stories. If they were real, then why weren't they still running around?"

"ON THE RARE OCCASIONS DURING ITS HUNTING SEASON WHEN THE HYDRA WAS INJURED BADLY ENOUGH BY OUR ALLIES IT RETREATED INTO HIBERNATION. PERHAPS THE REST WERE SLEEPING WHEN YOUR KIND RULED EUROPE."

She drummed her fingers on the table beside the mirror, watching the surface ripple with the vibrations. "I don't buy it. Everything can be killed."

"MY KIND DO NOT DIE NATURALLY. AND THE MAGI OF MANHATTAN HAVE CEASED TO AGE."

"But if I cut you, you bleed. If I blast Ogden with a fireball—like I frequently want to—he isn't going to get over it and come back after me once he has had a nap. Everything dies. That's a pretty firm rule."

"IF THEY CAN BE KILLED, OUR ALLIES DID NOT HAVE THE WHEREWITHAL TO DO IT."

Sully plucked a fresh cigar from the dented silver case that she had rescued from yet another destroyed jacket. "Do the demons have any idea why this thing is after me?"

"ALAS, NO."

She lit the cigar and rolled her eyes. "Well, thanks anyway. Keep in touch."

"BE SAFE, SHADOW-TWIN."

The mirror's surface flattened out once more and Sully let out a huff. She kept catching herself being polite to the demon, and she wasn't sure why she was so annoyed about it.

Everyone knew that Europe had gone to hell during the Great War. The Romans didn't give a damn what they were calling up by the end of it and the Entente hadn't been much better. When the decision had been made to open the barriers, there had been a lot of trepidation about what they were going to be unleashing on the world. With the promises from Manhattan that the demons could be controlled, it hadn't crossed Sully's mind that there might be anything else lurking in the ruins of the continent. Of course, the fact that there was some unusual fauna in Europe didn't explain why a giant primordial turtle had swum around the world to murder her specifically. The phone finally stopped buzzing, so Sully picked it up to listen to the voicemails. The first eight were secretaries asking her to return various politician's calls. The next three were Pratt's secretary, sounding increasingly nervous about the fact that Sully wasn't answering his calls either.

The last one was actually helpful, a report from one of her subordinates about the Hydra's movements. It had made landfall again in Carolina Province, ignoring the local population entirely as it worked its way inland, pausing only briefly when it "came into contact" with a herd of cows that promptly became fast food. The plan to keep Sully moving inland, away from population centers, was working, but the hope that the Hydra was going to slow down once it was away from its natural aquatic environment had been in vain, and they still had no idea how it was tracking her position.

Sully picked up the personal phone and called Ceejay. She wasn't sure why, but it was probably the same impulse that made her pick at wounds that weren't healing fast enough for her liking. Despite the late hour and the way that they had last parted, he answered on the third ring, and she could hear the smirk in his voice. "What do you want, despicable traitor?"

Sully was smiling back before she meant to, startled by the reflection of her own teeth in the black glass of the window beside her. "Burning the midnight oil again, Ceejay? Working on your big case? Anything you want to share with the government's evil spies?"

He tried to muffle his belly laugh, but he had never been very good at keeping them in check. "I wish that my life was that simple. Instead I am sitting in an office that is bigger than my apartment in the middle of the night trying to find the appropriate forms to file when some idiot brings a big pissed-off turtle into the middle of my city and lets it flop around."

"To be fair, I also kicked it out of your city."

"And I thank you for that. But now I need to find the appropriate forms to send to every constabulary across the whole colony telling them not to go and shoot the giant turtle rolling through their back gardens because it will just eat them." He rustled something beside the phone for emphasis.

"Come on, you remember our arrangement. I kill the monsters, you do the paperwork."

He grumbled. "That wasn't an arrangement. You just wouldn't sit on your ass at a desk long enough to do anything constructive."

Sully cackled. "You can't prove that."

"I have got literally eighteen memos on file about your inability to sit on your ass. I only wrote ten of them myself. It is well documented."

"I never knew the Empire took such a keen interest in my backside."

He muttered a spell down the line and the connection crackled with static. When he spoke again there was an echoing metallic quality to his usually buttery voice. Anyone scrying on them would have one hell of a migraine if they went on listening. "You would be surprised just how thorough the Empire's records on you really are. The IBI has had you under surveillance for a very long time, since your navy days. I know much more about your personal life than I want to. Some of those women were very ugly, Sully."

Sully scowled. "I'm Irish. The IBI probably thought I was one bad day away from sedition."

Another laugh, bizarre through the distortion of the spell. "Who knew that eventually they would be right?"

With a fizzle as he lost concentration on his masking spell, his voice returned to normal. "So you want to hear more about my big case, do you? Well you can tell your masters that I was right. It was just spies abandoning their positions."

Sully snorted. "You got anything to back that up?"

"If it was anything else, then why would it have stopped?"

"It stopped?"

"No new missing people. None. Not in the last two days. Not since you came poking around in my basement with your four-armed freak friend. And don't you think that I don't know what is going on under my own roof ever again, thank you very much."

Sully's scowl had started to ease, but now it was back. "Why would it just stop?"

"Why would it just start? Mark my words, it was spies. British spies."

"All right. I will tell His Majesty it was just spies. You know your job."

Ceejay let out a whoop of triumph. "You are actually admitting that I was right for once? I take it all back, Sully. The bloodsucker you are shacked up with is doing wonders for your temperament. She must be sucking out all of the bile instead of the blood. I like this new, amicable version of you far better than the old crabby one."

Sully lit a cigar off the stub of the last one and stared out at the fields flowing by, bleached to stark whiteness by the moonlight. It jogged her memory. "Yeah, I'm a delight now." She waited for his laughter to die down before asking, "Could you check up on something for me? It isn't about work. Just curiosity."

"Whatever you need, amicable Irish princess."

She sniggered. "Could you look up any reports of crop circles for me? I was at a farm down in Georgia and they have some. Apparently, they've had a few around about there."

She could hear that damn smirk again. "Consider the reports collated, stapled and emailed to you."

She took another pull on the cigar. "Right. Thanks."

"I had better return to this quagmire of bureaucracy that you have left for me. Try to get some sleep, yes?"

"I will put it on my to-do list."

He was still laughing when he hung up.

Sully realized that she needed a drink, a meal, and a solid twelve hours of sleep to recharge her reserves. She would settle for the drink. She didn't know if the bar would still be open at whatever hellish time of night this was, but she forced herself out of the compartment and into the corridor. Gin would help her sleep—it was medicinal—and every bar sold those little packs of nuts. They were practically a balanced meal by Sully's reckoning, containing all three of the important food groups; crunchy, salty and greasy. She doubted that twelve hours of peace were on the horizon, but even a couple of hours would be better than nothing. She bumped into the door at the end of the car and stared at it blankly for a moment before reaching for the handle. Apparently, she really needed that sleep.

The next car wasn't the bar. Neither was the next. She had a vague memory of the train being relatively short when she was being hustled onto it amidst a barrage of questions from all quarters, so the treacherous thought that it might not even have a bar was starting to prey on her. The next car rocked from side as she stepped in and she had to grab onto one of the empty seatbacks to stay upright. The lights flickered out. Sully didn't panic—it wasn't in her nature—but she took a moment to reassure herself that the Hydra was still halfway across the country and that she was in no danger.

Something skittered over the metalwork above her head and she quickly reassessed her assumptions. She was also starting to revise her opinion of trains. Being trapped in a metal tube, hurtling across the landscape with everything completely out of your control, was seeming less and less like a good idea with every consecutive journey.

The scrabbling sound stopped almost as soon as it started, but Sully was certain that something was on the roof of the car. She let a tiny trickle of spellfire slip out and pool in her hand, illuminating the cabin. Her full strength wasn't close to returning yet, but it wouldn't take much to catch a would-be assassin unaware. She stayed perfectly still, straining to hear where the roof-rider was. The train turned a bend and just at the edge of the roof Sully heard a tiny squeak of pressure being applied to the metal. A lance of raw conjured force leapt from her hand and tore through the pale faux leather that upholstered the cabin roof.

Blood dropped into the train in a congealed dollop before splattering across the seats. A gargling avian cry made Sully clap her hands over her ears. Even as she recovered from that it was replaced with the deafening screech of tortured metal as the thing above peeled back the roof like a sardine tin. Sully hated being the fish in any analogy. She wasn't idle as the looming shadow tore its way into the train. Her first lance was followed by a blast of fire and a non-lethal ray of moonlight meant to freeze everything it touched. Each slowed the progress of her attacker, but none of them stopped it. The whole situation was starting to feel a little bit too familiar, like a recurring nightmare.

In the gap in the roof, illuminated by the distant stars and the barrage of her spells, an image of the creature started to take shape. Here was a patch of white feathers, singed by her fireball. There was a golden flank, encrusted with fast growing scabs where another of the spells had left its mark. There were claws of too many different types digging through the metalwork, bird and cat in quick succession. The creature decided that the hole was big enough and started forcing its way in. The hole was not big enough. It tore itself on the ragged metal and blood ran down the walls all around Sully.

Sully stopped her steady assault and backed toward the door, casting quick protections over herself and infusing her eyes with the dull red glow that let her see in the dark. The mangled thing passed the point of no return and dropped into the train. It had the face of an eagle, but its neck was snapped and the once-noble head hung limp and useless. Atrophy and rot had set in. The eyes were dry and shriveled amidst now filthy feathers. Its wings could barely fit into the cabin, and they spasmodically twitched and twisted, battering off the walls and cracking the windows with each flex. Behind the flurry of falling feathers Sully could make out the rear half of the beast, a lion's body grown to twice the size of the shoddy specimens she had seen in the Ophiran touring zoo.

"A gryphon. Holy shit. They are *definitely* extinct."

It tried to cock its head, which flopped over and hit the chairs on the other side of the aisle. Sully stared at it. "You can hear me, can't you? Do you understand me?" The head flopped back, bones grinding and popping noisily within the gryphon's neck. "I don't want to fight you. I don't know what you and your Hydra friend want from me, but—"

The gryphon charged.

Concussion spells knocked it back before it could build momentum and Sully retreated into the previous car, tossing up barriers as she went. Spells would normally bounce off a conjured barrier, a demon, and anyone else who could use magic. The gryphon brute-forced its way through them as though they were cobwebs. Sully made a tactical retreat as fast as her legs could carry her.

She made it to the back of the train in under a minute, with the sounds of the gryphon's progress through the furnishings and walls behind her serving as constant motivation in her efforts. Looking behind her down the corridor, she had enough space to breathe now. Enough space to come up with some big ingenious solution to her problem. With a tiny pilot light of spellfire on her fingertip, she started scribbling calculations on the wallpaper. The situation was different, but she had a spell that might work. It was just a shame that old notebook from the IBI was currently moldering somewhere in the ocean. She had just seared a circle to work in on the floor when the gryphon arrived. Frantically she dumped power into the magic circle, weaving it into spellforms after the fact and hoping like hell that she wasn't about to accidentally blow off her own elbows. It was hard to close her eyes when the gryphon was bearing down the corridor toward her, but she managed to blink for long enough to extend her awareness out of her body, to feel the forces being exerted just beyond the protection of the walls around her and to capture all of that raw kinetic power.

Claws extended, the gryphon pounced, and Sully slapped it back with the full force of the speeding train. The train suddenly slowed, losing all of the momentum that Sully had borrowed from it. She was flung from her feet, tumbling along the corridor after the gryphon.

She caught onto a cabin door. It stopped her, but it also jerked her shoulder clean out of its socket with a wet pop. She hit the carpet and tumbled to a halt, blessing her protection spells with one breath and cursing them with the next.

The pain didn't come right away. In Sully's considerable experience of bodily injuries, that was a bad sign. That meant she was either in shock or had done damage so permanent that her body was refusing to acknowledge it. She dragged herself up with her other arm, sitting, waiting for the world to stop spinning. Then she tried to get her dead arm to move. She had almost managed to clench a fist when pain finally joined the party and brought nausea along as its plus one.

With bile burning her throat and tears burning her eyes, Sully wrestled her way up the wall of the train until she was standing. The swaying could be blamed on the movement of the train—she was fine. The daggers of pain that were dancing all around her neck and back meant nothing. On her third attempt, Sully managed to take a deep breath. A compartment stood open and empty in front of her. She took a staggering step to one side, lining herself up carefully, then she charged forward. Her injured shoulder hit the doorframe. The ball relocated itself in the socket with another, quieter pop and Sully spun around to land in one of the bench seats. It would have looked like a pretty smooth and deliberate operation if she hadn't immediately thrown up everywhere. She didn't know how long she sat there trying to force the encroaching darkness from the edges of her vision, but the gargling screech of the gryphon drew her back out of her trance.

She trudged along the length of the train until she reached the bar, just behind the locomotive itself. She had nearly made it the first time, before she was so rudely interrupted in her hunt for a drink. The gryphon had completely trashed the place when it landed. Sully couldn't see a single intact bottle anywhere but the mirror behind the bar had somehow survived. She looked at herself, bruises blossoming all over her face amidst the cuts and scars from her earlier fights. Despite the hiss of pain it dragged out of her, she grinned. "You should see the other guy."

The gryphon had lost a wing somewhere in its journey along the length of the train. There were feathers scattered everywhere and Sully was so punch-drunk that she hadn't noticed the feathered lump wedged in the door of a bathroom as she passed. The other wing looked like it had been snapped neatly in two. Each of the creature's legs seemed to be broken, twisted at odd angles. The neck still hung limp, and now it was turned right around to look back at the open wound where the missing wing used to be. Ribs poked out through one side. Blood coated the floor in a thick, sticky slop. Still its great chest heaved up and down, even as more blood misted out of its mouth with each exhalation.

Sully kicked it, but there wasn't much feeling behind the violence. The grunt that came out of it confirmed her suspicion that it was still conscious. The only sounds in the bar were the distant rattle of the train along the tracks, the wheezing of the beast, and the quiet creaking of its bones as they tried to bend back into shape. Even as she watched, the nub of bone jutting out from its back seemed to have gained more meat. It was healing. Just as the demons had warned her.

Sully squatted down beside the gryphon's head. "I guess you can't speak but you can listen. I don't know why you are after me. I don't know what you want. But I can tell you that what I did to you just now is only the beginning. If you come back, I will flay you down to your bones and I will smile as I do it. Do you understand me?"

With agony in every trembling movement, the gryphon lifted its head and swung it forward at her like a blunt instrument. There was little strength behind the blow, but there was enough weight to send Sully back across the sodden carpet. When her shoulder hit one of the surviving stools the whole world went dark for a moment. Sully snapped back to attention and scrambled to her feet just in time to see the gryphon's front legs straighten out. That was faster than she had expected. She started shaping another spell, something huge and fiery to fulfill her gruesome threats, but she didn't cast it. Not yet. This was probably the last gryphon in the world, and she wasn't quite ready to wipe them out. Not when there was a chance it might listen to reason. "You can't win this. Give it up."

The gryphon didn't lunge for her, it didn't even move closer, it just reared up onto its hind legs and slammed its claws down through the flimsy sheet metal of the floor. Sully opened her mouth to cast but it was already too late. The gryphon's claws hooked into the tracks and the wheels beneath them. It was dragged down into the ragged hole, wedged partially in and out of the train. Sully turned to run but there was no time. The irresistible force of the train in motion and the immovable object of the gryphon strained against each other for an instant, then the carriage jerked sideways. The train derailed. The deafening roar of the train's brutalized engine, the shrieking metal as the solid structure twisted apart and the agonized cries of the gryphon all blended into a nightmare cacophony, and then blissful silence fell as Sully's head cracked off the side of the train.

Sully could taste blood. All the pains of the last week reared up out of the comfortable oblivion that surrounded her, dragging her back to consciousness despite her best efforts to cling to the numb dark. She spat and one of her teeth pinged off a bit of hot metal near her face. Only one of her eyes would open when she finally gathered the courage to see how bad the damage was. The shoulder might have been dislocated again, or the pain might just have been the swelling from the first time around. There were pieces of the train everywhere, recognizable only from tiny details. A decal on a chunk of glass by her cheek. A flutter of cream colored leather, singed at the edges and draped over the twisted hulk of what might once have been a chair. Sully's protective spells had done their job, but now she was hollowed out from the loss of the raw energy that it had cost to keep her alive. Assuming that she wasn't actually in seven bloody pieces right now without realizing it.

Her left hand was still good, so she brought that up to probe at her face, ignoring the blood and the pain to confirm that underneath the mass of swelling her eye was still intact. That was lucky. She was pretty attached to depth perception. She took her time, hauling herself upright. The shoulder screamed at her, but it was part of a chorus of cries from all over her body now, and the arm was moving so she had avoided the worst of it. The wound in her leg had opened up again, but there was no terrifying flood of red, just a damp patch on her trousers. She didn't love the pain, or that her face was more than a little mashed, but the fact that she was about to walk away from a train crash silenced any complaints that she might have thought of voicing. Waves of dizziness and nausea took their turns washing over her as she clambered to her feet, but she paid them no mind. The sun was hanging high in the sky and the woodlands around Sully seemed hostile, with no shadows stretching out to hide her. She had lost half a day. How close would the Hydra be now?

She staggered to the tracks. The locomotive was a smoldering wreck, lying on its side in a ditch belching black smoke. She held out no hope of pulling anything but the charred skeleton of the engineer from it. A few of the rearmost carriages had been flicked off into the trees almost whole but the ones around her were scrap. The plinking sounds of the cooling metal might have been almost musical, but Sully could smell something under the ozone reek of the overheated steel. Roasted meat.

It didn't take long to find the gryphon. She followed outlying pieces as they inched their way across the gravel toward the central mass of it. The head and torso were mostly together, although a big chunk of the beak had snapped off. Fresh feathers were just starting to sprout along that side of its face, which probably meant that side of its face had only just grown back. Sully spat on it and wished that most of the saliva wasn't red. "You stupid bastard. I gave you an out. What the hell did you go and do that for?"

Sully had thought she was spent, but looking down at the mangled monster she found a deeper reservoir. Spellfire leapt unbidden to her hands and she started to trace out some of the most dangerous spells from her artillery days. The fury that usually nested in Sully's gut like a coiled viper wanted control. On a normal day it would writhe and simmer and she would spit abuse at whoever was closest, but when the fighting started, she let it take over. There was no fight to win now—there was no chance that the gryphon was going to defend itself in its current condition. Sully knew that she was never going to get a better chance to finish it for good, but it was hard for her to kill in cold blood. She had been beaten, shot, and flung across the ocean. She had been hunted and haunted by creatures that weren't meant to exist. She had faced down a monster so gargantuan that she couldn't wrap her head around it. Sully had done enough running and now she was angry.

The first torrent of flames leapt from her hands, enveloping the gryphon and drawing a fresh round of shrieks from its broken body. The backwash made Sully flinch and she could smell the popcorn aroma of her own hair burning. A blast of flame, blue hot, was next, over so fast that Sully almost couldn't remember casting it. That spell had cut through steel hulls to sink ships, but though the gryphon was red and raw, when the fires died down it was still moving. Still stitching itself back together. Old military spells weren't going to be enough—she needed more heat. She needed more power.

Dante's Inferno was simple enough in the beginning, similar to a thousand other spells to evoke fire, but while the others had limitations written into them to keep the caster from draining their reserves completely—and dying—the Inferno did not. Sully had been tinkering with it since college, an intellectual exercise that was the closest thing she had to a hobby, outside of drinking and womanizing. Now Sully began layering her own modified version of the spell together in stages, tracing each spellform with painstaking care. She had never actually cast it—not when the risks of failure were so steep—but in this moment she didn't care about the risks. The burned hunk of meat on the tracks had been given a chance to back down and it had chosen death.

Reserves of power that had seen Sully through the worst battles of her life ran dry as she poured more and more spellfire into the Inferno and she had to strain to drag more magic into her body from the air, using the same channels that let her tear strength from Mol Kalath. It was like trying to draw breath through a wet cloth, but she eventually got enough to finish. The gryphon opened one baleful golden eye in the charred, sticky remains of its face, that one tiny part of it briefly rejuvenated by its destruction and rebirth. The final words were on Sully's lips, begging to be spoken, when she heard the ringing.

Sully stood frozen in that moment, hearing the electronic chiming of the bell and seeing the mass of runes and sigils hanging in the air all around her, intercut with the connecting lines and sacred geometry of the universe that it would take the uninitiated a lifetime to decipher. She took a deep breath, wresting control back from her anger. She reached out for the spellfire and felt warmth returning to her exhausted body as she pulled it back inside.

It took only a few moments of digging through the coiled innards of her seat to find her personal phone beside the shattered remains of the official one. She flipped it open on the last ring. "Hello?"

"Darlin'? Are you all right?"

Tears pricked the corners of Sully's eyes when she heard Marie's voice, stinging like hell on one side. It had been a hectic few days; it wasn't surprising that she was getting a bit emotional. She was probably still in shock.

"About the same as usual. How are you doing?"

Marie's voice was so tight you could have strung a banjo with it. "I need you back here, darlin'. As quick as you can."

"Are you safe?"

There was a long pause on the other end of the line, then Marie huffed, "I ain't sure."

"Find somewhere safe and hole up. I will be there in . . ."—she did some frantic calculations—"about four hours. Is there anyone local you can trust? Anyone that can help?"

". . . I—I don't know. Just hurry, darlin'."

The line went dead.

With a jerk of her hand, Sully drew all the scraps of spellfire back inside her, then cast the flying spell without a second thought for the golden eye that was still following her every movement. She had more important things to worry about.

November 7, 2015 PM

Georgia looked completely unchanged from her last flight over it, although Sully could only see half of the view at any given moment thanks to the swelling of her black eye. The crop circles in the fields around the Culpepper plantation were easy to see from above, strangely intricate from this distance. Not just one circle but many, forming patterns that set Sully's memory alight. She knew these patterns and the geometry they conveyed, but she did not have the time to think on how she knew. Not now when Marie was so close she could almost smell her.

Sully dropped into the courtyard and stumbled into the fountain as her leg gave out. Raavi was going to be pissed that she had torn out all his careful stitches. The farmhouse and the guest house looked as pristine as when she had left them. There was a gentle breeze carrying the last warmth of the day through the orchards. Whatever had scared the hell out of Marie was damned subtle. Sully scooped up a handful of water and scrubbed the worst of the blood from her face. In her distorted reflection, it looked like the swelling on the eye might have been going down, but it was hard to tell between the bruises and the rippling of the water. She had been prettier. If Marie hadn't already been terrified, there wasn't a chance that Sully would have let her see her in this state. She mumbled to herself, "Eyes forward."

Sully crept around to the patio doors with a freezing spell readied.

There was no telling what the situation was going to be inside the house. Marie's family could be hostages. Sully couldn't risk rushing in, spells blazing. There was a record playing in the kitchen, some old country tune about a truck with a busted spark-rune. Clementine was singing along softly as she coated chicken legs in flour, her voice cracking at the highs in the chorus. Marie was sitting at the table, staring at her mother with an intensity that she usually reserved for blood and musical theater. As Sully crept into view, Marie's eyes flicked over and widened briefly, but she didn't say anything, just returned her gaze to her mother. Sully let her magical senses roll out over the house. There was no sign of anyone else using magic, beyond the usual household enchantments. She slid the door open carefully and stepped inside. Clementine cast her a glance as she came in; maybe she was too polite to mention her bedraggled state. "Iona, welcome back, child. I wish Marie had told me you were heading this way, I would have got more chicken."

Sully looked at Marie and got nothing. "That's very kind, but I don't think that I can stay for long anyway." She sidled over to Marie and leaned down to place a kiss on her cheek, murmuring, "What the hell is going on?"

Marie popped up out her seat. "I'm just going to show Sully where the bathroom is, Momma."

"All right, darlin'. Don't be too long. Your father will be back soon, and those potatoes need peeling."

Out in the hallway, panic flooded Marie's face. "What the hell happened to you? You look like you were in a train crash."

"Uh . . . my train crashed."

"Jesus. Are you all right?"

Sully shrugged with the shoulder that wasn't screaming at her. "I've had worse days."

Marie stared at her for a long moment and there was a sadness in her eyes that Sully wasn't used to. "You really have, haven't you?"

The sympathy was getting too uncomfortable for Sully's tastes. "Why am I here? What's going on?"

Marie looked nervously toward the kitchen door. "That ain't my Momma."

Sully blinked. "What?"

"She sounds like my momma, she looks like her. She even has my daddy fooled. But that ain't her."

"Why do you think that isn't her?"

"She don't smell right, Sully. She's wearing Momma's honeysuckle perfume and she has all the right kitchen smells, but underneath it she don't smell like blood."

"Your mother usually smells like blood?" Sully was trying to keep her voice calm and neutral like she was still a detective.

"Y'all smell like blood, Sully. Everybody. You're full of it."

Sully wet her lips. "Have you tried questioning her? Asking her questions that only your mother would know the answer to?"

"I've just been playing along. I figured that if she realized I knew, then . . . I dunno. This ain't *my* day job, Sully. This stuff freaks me out, you know that."

Sully took her hand. "It's going to be okay. I'm here now. We can work this out."

Marie let out a shaky breath. "Okay."

Sully had half turned to go back into the kitchen when Marie caught her by the chin and kissed her. It was soft and unexpected, and for a moment Sully froze. Marie kissed her way up Sully's cheek and whispered, "This is gonna hurt a little."

Marie bit into the swollen lump over Sully's eye with a single needle-sharp fang and then latched onto it like a suckling baby. There was an initial sting, but the easing of the pressure was such a relief that she clung to Marie gratefully while the vampire drank her fill. When Marie was feeding from her, the world was a much quieter place for Sully, without magic or rage buzzing away just below the surface of her skin. It was almost like Sully had found her true purpose in those few precious moments each month when Marie was draining her life away. When it was over and the crackle of magic had returned, she opened both of her eyes and caught a brief glimpse of Marie, blood-drunk and lustful, before dread reasserted itself on that perfect face.

In the kitchen Clementine was still tinkering away at the counter, doing something to sweet corn that Sully couldn't understand. "Jeremiah said that you were having some problems with the fire runes, so I'm just going to cast a few diagnostics, if that's all right, Clementine?"

"Oh please, you're our guest. Shame on that man for trying to put you to work."

Sully smiled. "I like to keep busy."

"Well, if you insist."

Sully started running through her repertoire of half-remembered forensic spells. A glamour as complex as a full-body disguise should have lit up her senses like she was on fire, but there wasn't even a hint of magic hanging around Clementine. Frowning, Sully tried another spell.

"Momma, can you remember my first school play?"

Clementine chuckled, "The nativity? Oh darlin', how could I forget? You were so darn angry that you had to be the angel. I still remember you hanging from those wires, face red as a cherry and ready to pop. When we got home you made us act out the whole thing with you again, but with you as Mary."

Marie was smiling, but it didn't reach her eyes. "Which doll did we use for the baby?"

Clementine cast her a confused glance. "Now don't tell me you've forgotten. That was the year that your daddy won that piglet at the Province Fair and you both insisted on keeping it in the house like a puppy. Curly! That was your baby Jesus, and our Christmas roast the next year."

Sully snorted, earning her a scowl from Marie, but she kept on casting, wandering closer to the oven that she was meant to be studying. Marie didn't miss a beat.

"Who was that cousin who always said they were coming to Christmas but never showed up?"

"Ulysses? He was on your father's side of the family, of course.

Every year we'd get word he was coming. Every year we'd set him a place at the table, and every single year we'd get a card three days later to say he was sorry. I am not entirely convinced that he exists, you know. I've never met him. After all these years I am starting to suspect that Ulysses Culpepper is some sort of practical joke that your father is playing on me. Or a plot to make sure there's plenty of leftovers."

Marie had the next question ready but Clementine cut her off. "Iona dear, since you are tinkering with the fire runes, could I trouble you to light up the back-right ring?"

With a flicker of attention, Sully lit the fire beneath a pan of oil, then returned to probing Clementine. As did Marie, in her own way. "Is that your famous fried chicken you're making there?"

"I most certainly am, darlin'. I know that you can't have any but . . . well, old habits die hard, I guess. Your Grandma always had to have something cooking when she had guests, even when they were stuffed to bursting. Tell me, will you be joining us for Christmas this year, Iona?"

Sully's latest spell sputtered and died in her hands. "What?"

The oil had started to hiss.

"Well, the way that I hear it, you're planning on making our Marie into an honest woman. And with your family being all the way across the sea, it only seems right to have you here."

Sully looked at Marie. Frustration and confusion competed for real estate on Marie's face as she said, "You ain't got no right inviting people here."

Clementine staggered against the sink. "I beg your pardon, darlin'?"

Marie lurched up out of the chair, abandoning all pretense. "Where's my momma?!"

"Darlin', I'm right here?"

"You ain't my momma. I know my momma like the back of my hand and you ain't her. Now you tell me where she is or so help me—"

Her last diagnostic spell had returned nothing and Sully was out of options. Something wasn't right. Between Clementine's nonchalance about Sully's injuries and the way that she was hiding at the far side of the kitchen, the little niggling part of Sully's brain that had made her a good investigator was screaming that something didn't add up. Sully stalked over to Clementine's side of the room to see what the response would be, but the old woman just gawked at her. There was no fear at all. "Iona, is something the matter with Marie?"

Sully smiled. "I'll calm her down. You just cook that chicken and let me worry about her."

Clementine's eyes flicked from Sully to Marie and then across to the stove. "Could you put the chicken in the pan? My hands are shaking something dreadful."

Sully's smile twisted into a smirk. She conjured a flame into the palm of her hand and Clementine's panicked expression was all the confirmation she needed. "Marie, get down!"

Everything happened in the same moment. The faux-Clementine made a break for the patio doors. Sully launched a dart of flame at her back. Jeremiah stepped into the room and dropped the paper bag of groceries. Marie leapt for her father.

When the fire hit Clementine, it was like she had been doused in gasoline. She exploded into a tower of flames, scorching the counters, charring the roof black, knocking Sully off her unstable feet and flooding the room with thick black smoke. Clementine didn't scream. Sully expected some sound, but instead the flaming mass just stumbled outside. Without exchanging a word, the remaining Culpeppers and Sully gave chase. Clementine darted around the house and threw herself bodily into the fountain to douse the flames, but it was too late.

The water turned black and little hunks of sodden charcoal drifted up to the surface. Sully reached into the water and dragged what was left of her future mother-in-law out. The shape was still mostly intact, but there was no mistaking it for flesh now that the human veneer had burned away. Most of it was blackened with soot, and cracks ran along the grain all over it, but it was unmistakably the same white wood that had filled Raavi's laboratory. Sully turned to Jeremiah and Marie with the burned husk in her arms and said, "It wasn't her."

OCTOBER 31, 2005

The gold leaf script on the door was a nice touch. Sully wasn't sure how Marie had managed to afford it, not with a waitress's salary and an actress's credit card bills. It wasn't much, she supposed. Just the words *Private Investigator*, but it felt like a lot. Sully had bought the furniture herself. She didn't get a pension from the Imperial British Navy any more, for fairly obvious reasons, but the Nova Europa Provisional Government seemed content to pay her a general's pension even though she had only technically served for seven months—instead of the seven years you were meant to, according to Pratt's never-ending guidelines and laws. She suspected she was going to be the exception to a lot of Pratt's rules. He'd always been willing to lose his puffed-up airs and graces with her, and what had started as mutual admiration had gradually developed into the kind of friendship she'd never suspected that she could find in her life. An intellectual equal, Pratt saw her for what she was.

It was easy to be friends with somebody when you'd made all their wishes come true. Nobody had hated the Empire the way that Pratt did. He'd been the backbone of the revolution once it started, but he had needed one last push to get the ball rolling. Sully still couldn't believe that push had been her. Her name, her face, they were going down in history books right now. When the redcoats had surrounded the protesters in Victoria Park, she had had no idea what the consequences of her actions would be. When she threw up that barrier and the spells had deflected back out at them, she had had no idea that she was starting a war. All that she knew was that Marie was in that park with all her idiot arty friends, waving badly spelled placards with mottos half of them didn't understand blazoned across the front. "No Taxation Without Representation," might have sounded catchy, but if a single one of the actors, dancers, singers, choreographers, costume designers or musicians out there had ever paid taxes in their life Sully would have been stunned into silence.

Her pension had to stretch to a bigger apartment up in Red Hook—closer to Marie's new job in the cabaret bar—food, clothes, whatever new taxes Pratt invented next, and miscellaneous expenses, so Sully had bought the furniture second-hand. She preferred it that way if she was being honest. The smell of old leather, the scored surface of the wood, gave her office a patina of authenticity. Like she was a real private investigator and not just playing pretend so that she would have something to fill up the hours of the day. She didn't have any cases yet, but technically she'd only been open twenty minutes, so she wasn't too upset about it. By the end of the day, the local constabulary would have a half-dozen different crimes that they couldn't understand, and they'd be looking for a witch to hire. Sully was going to be that witch, because the IBI was in tatters and crime didn't stop just because a war swept through.

There was a knock on the glass and a dame with tanned legs for days sidled in wearing a floral print sundress and a pair of shades that hid half her face. Sully suppressed a smile. "Can I help you, Ma'am?"

"Ain't you the private investigator?"—low and breathy. She tossed her head and her golden curls cascaded around a face that had been made for the silver screen. When Sully gave her an amused nod, Marie sauntered forward and sat in the scuffed leather chair. "You've got to help me. You see, my wife's gone missing and I don't know where to find her."

"A missing person. Where was the last place that you saw her?"

"Well last night before I passed out I'm pretty sure that I saw her somewhere around here." Marie tugged at the hem of her dress and slowly parted her legs.

Sully cast a pair of quick spells at the door. One to seal it shut. The other to soundproof it. "Well then, I suppose that I'd better start my investigation there."

She rose up from her chair. Marie's eyes were sparkling in the sunlight pouring through the window. Sully couldn't believe that she deserved to be this happy. It made her chest ache, just looking at the beautiful woman that she got to call her wife.

The sparkle faded suddenly. The whole room dipped into shadow and the tantalizing smile on Marie's face evaporated in fear. "Sully? What the hell is that?"

When Sully turned it was just in time to watch the row of buildings opposite them vanish beneath a wave of pure darkness. It rushed at the window and Sully threw every barrier that she knew in a shell around Marie and herself. When the darkness hit it, the shell cracked, but the moment that it held gave Sully enough time to wrap her arms around Marie and whisper, "I love you." The void closed over them and they sank away into nothing.

NOVEMBER 8, 2015

The hysterics hadn't been pretty, but at least Sully had an out. She had her job. She had lives to save and monsters to catch. Marie had nothing but a missing mother and a broken father who had never dreamed that one of the hidden horrors of the world might end up on his doorstep. Sully sequestered herself in the guest house and started making phone calls as soon as could be considered polite after incinerating your host.

Her first and most begrudging call was to Pratt's office to update him on the many situations that were in play. Luckily, he was too petulant to take the call so Sully was able to relay things through a secretary. The next call was to her own offices. She reported the gryphon attack and the destruction of the train to a horrified aide, then got a report back from another one. The Hydra had stopped tracking her, it had waddled back toward the sea at about the moment when her train crashed, proving beyond any doubt that all these creatures were in cahoots, there was no update from Europe, and Mol Kalath and the much-diminished horde of demons were holding their position and waiting.

With those calls out of the way, Sully was able to get on with her damned job. She called Ceejay. "Hello, despicable traitor, do you care to tell me how you knew about the crop circles or do I have to torture it out of you?"

Sully didn't have the energy to act surprised. "What?"

"The crop circles. Everywhere that they were reported we had had missing people. I don't know how you knew, but now that the crop circles are on the map too, we have a pattern. A bigger circle. Drawn around the whole of America. Outside the circle, nothing. Inside the circle, missing people."

Sully let out a breath. "Okay. You're going to have places with crop circles and no missing people. That's where we need to focus our efforts. The abductions didn't stop, they just got more sophisticated. They are replacing the victims with simulacra. Some sort of golem carved out of that weird white wood. The disguise is perfect. The replacements have the same memories as the victims. The only way to detect them is that they're extremely flammable."

Ceejay let out a woof of laughter. "You want me to order the constables to go around burning everyone? I'm sure that's going to be a popular decision."

"Tell them you are just following my orders. Pratt is already trying to paint me as a psychopath, so I doubt this will make much difference to my reputation. I don't know what these things are doing, or what they're capable of, and frankly I could die happy never finding out, as long as we get rid of them."

"Do you have any idea how these abductions are happening, when traveling spells and portals are blocked?"

Sully had run out of cigars and she was getting twitchy. "It's a circle, right? A summoning circle?"

"You think that someone is calling up demons?"

"The demons are all on our side, remember? But the British have got something else. They've been making wishes without demons. They've found some new patrons."

She had expected a groan or a quip, but Ceejay didn't make a sound. She was almost startled when he spoke again. "We really have no idea what's being called up?"

"Not a clue. But at least we know who's doing the calling."

There was some rustling on the other end of the line. "What I do not understand is how they could have drawn a circle around us without anyone noticing. A man cannot walk his dog without a constable getting a report, but somehow the British have built something the size of a continent under our noses? I've sent agents out to find the nearest edge of the circle, to break it if they can. But how could the British have laid down a solid circle without everyone being able to see it. How could they have closed the circle without everyone who uses magic feeling it? None of these things make any sense to me, Sully."

She drummed her fingers on the breakfast bar. "We just need to work the parts of the case that we've got. We know that there are wood-people out there pretending to be citizens. We need to deal with them before they move on to whatever they're meant to be doing next."

"I know that I joke, but you must tell me; how did you find out about all of this?"

"They took Marie's mother. I burned the fake."

Ceejay whistled. "I'm betting that you're not the most popular person right now."

Quietly, Marie let herself into the guest house. Sully coughed. "I've had better days."

She hung up on him so Marie wouldn't hear the rumble of his laughter. It didn't seem appropriate right now.

"Hey, darlin'."

Marie slumped onto the stool beside her and rested her head on Sully's shoulder. She murmured, "I thought I was going crazy, but you didn't even have to think twice. You believed me. You trusted me."

Sully kissed Marie on the top of her head and was enveloped by the faint scent of apple-blossom in her hair. "What else was I going to do?"

Sully's arms wrapped around Marie automatically as she leaned in closer. "I kinda wish I had been going crazy. That would've been easier. Daddy is . . . he ain't all right. Don't know that he ever will be again."

"What about you?"

Marie's voice broke. "I could have had her. All these years I was ashamed and hiding and I could have had her and now—now I'll never see her again."

"We don't know anything yet. We don't know where they're being taken. She could be fine for all we know. On a beach somewhere, sipping cocktails."

Marie laughed through her tears. "She'd hate that. Sitting around with nothing to fuss over? She'd lose her mind."

"If she's still out there, you know I'm going to bring her back for you. Don't you?"

Marie turned and caught Sully's lips in a salty kiss. "You ain't God, Sully. You can't fix everything yourself."

Sully kissed her back. "I can try."

There was a gentle knock outside and the women let their heads drop so that their foreheads were touching. It was just a coincidence that they both whispered "I love you" at the same time. Sully got up and walked over to the door. Marie had spent all evening with her father, Sully could at least take this hit for her. She pulled the door open gently because she didn't want to startle Jeremiah after his already traumatic day. When she looked out, the courtyard was full of monsters.

The gryphon was still looking rough after the train wreck and the fire. It had a few new feathers sprouting out of its bald front half but it still looked distinctly like a roasted turkey. Its head was back to hanging limp and it seemed to be struggling to dunk it into the fountain for a drink. The other two monsters were new additions, but Sully assumed they made up the rest of the eternal pains in the ass that the demons of Europe had reported. One of them loitered by the front door to the main house. He was shaped like a man, coated in shaggy hair and standing so tall that his head was brushing the upstairs windowsills. Once upon a time he probably had an eye and a nose under the thick brow on his face, but now there was just a blackened hole above the slack jaw. He was clearly the muscle, and Sully had never been intimidated by the muscle in her entire life. Not since the first time a nun snapped a ruler on her ass.

The other one was a lot more interesting. She was standing coyly a few steps away from the door, looking for all the world like a naked woman with long black hair. Sully's eyes automatically completed their tactical assessment of the monster by running up and down her body. Definitely naked. She was also smiling and holding a pair of handcuffs. All of these elements were usually good omens for Sully but judging by the jagged teeth in that otherwise pretty mouth and the dull way that the moonlight was reflecting back from a pair of manacles that were clearly made from cold iron, she suspected that fun probably wasn't in the cards.

One of them, Sully's bravado insisted, she could have handled. If there had been only two of them, she still would have taken a swing. But three of them, with civilians so close. With Marie so close. It wasn't a gamble she was willing to make. The woman bowed gracefully at the waist with the faint sound of rustling feathers and then introduced herself. "Iona Sullivan, I greet you. I have had many names, but those gathered here call me Alecto. Behind me are Tartalo and the last gryphon. I believe you have already met."

Sully stayed very still so that nobody got the wrong idea. "Don't suppose you care to tell me why the four of you have been trying to murder me all week?"

"We had very strict instructions not to murder you, in fact. But with the pain comes a loss of focus and purpose. I apologize for any confusion we have caused you." Alecto's smile was not reassuring.

"So who is giving you these instructions?"

"Lord Blackwood of the British Empire made his requests, and his offer."

Of course it was the British, who else would it have been.

Sully wondered aloud, "What could those pompous pricks offer you to make all this worthwhile?"

Alecto's polite smile faded and her pupils dilated until they filled her almond eyes. "An end to our curse. Oblivion is our reward. Imagine an eternity of pain, Iona. Wounds that will not heal but cannot kill you. Do you wonder that we can be bought with the promise of release?"

Sully tried to imagine living with the pain she was feeling right now for a year. She remembered the bottle of gin that had kept her company after Marie left her, and the next bottle of gin, and the next. She could understand wanting oblivion all too well. "The British aren't your only option, you know?"

"It will take a wish to undo what a wish has wrought." Alecto stepped a little bit closer to Sully. Danger radiated from every inch of her gaunt frame.

Sully kept her eyes locked onto the creature and wet her lips. "I've got a whole hell full of demons on speed-dial."

"We have had an eternity vexed by this curse. Do you honestly think that we did not try the children of chaos? They could not help us. The British have new allies—strong allies—that can"

Just as she had suspected. Not that being right helped much if you were dead. "Can you at least tell me how you found me?"

"My kind have a gift for tracking. We can sense an oath-breaker wherever they may be. You broke your compact with the British when you turned against them. It was a small oath that you put little of yourself into, but it was enough. The one lurking behind you would be so much easier to hunt. Breaking an engagement has left a stain on her that my sisters and I could taste from a world away."

Marie cursed softly under her breath, then stepped forward carefully to rest her hand on Sully's back.

"Are you going to introduce me to your friends, darlin?" There was barely a quaver in her voice when she spoke. Sully felt suffocated by her pride in her lover.

"Alecto and her friends are working for the British. I think that I am going to go away with them now. But first they are going to give me a minute or two to say goodbye?"

Alecto nodded indulgently, so Sully stepped back into the guest house, closing the door just as carefully as she had opened it.

Marie started shaking the moment the door was shut, and pink-tears started to roll down her cheeks a moment after. "You're just giving up? You?"

Sully smiled. "I can't beat all three of them. Not like this. If I go with them . . . The British want me alive. I'll escape. I'll come back to you."

"Darlin', if you can't get away from them now, how are you going to do it in chains?"

Sully's smile slipped. "If I fight them, you're going to die. I can't—that can't happen. That can't ever happen."

"If I bite the leader and she loses her magic, you can take the fried chicken and the grass man. Right?"

"They aren't Magi. They're monsters. They don't need magic to do the things they do, they're just different."

"So you can just—"

Sully caught Marie around the waist and dragged her in for a kiss. At first Marie slapped helplessly at Sully's arms, but gradually they melted together. When they parted, her tears had already started to dry in red streaks down her cheeks. "I need to go now. And you need to stay inside until I'm gone."

Marie opened her mouth to object, but Sully stopped her with a finger across her kiss-swollen lips. "I love you Marie, and I am going to come back to you."

Marie pushed her away and forced bravery back into her smile. "You'd better."

Outside, Alecto was arrayed in all her glory. Six wings were spread out behind her back, huge and black feathered. Sully hadn't seen the injury on her before, but now it was obvious. The wings hung heavy with pus and rot and for every feather there seemed to be another broken arrow shaft lodged among them. Marie gasped in awe in the corridor behind Sully. "An angel."

Alecto's grin spread until it threatened to take over her whole face, jagged and terrible. "A Fury."

She tossed the manacles to Sully. "We must depart. Put them on."

At the first touch of the metal Sully shuddered. Her magic blinked out. The well of power that had burned within her since her first memory was just gone. This wasn't like the gentle respite that Marie's bite brought her. She felt like someone had taken an apple-corer to her insides and left her hollow. She dutifully strapped the manacles onto her wrists until they made a clicking sound and then turned to take one last look at Marie. "Goodbye, darlin'."

"See you soon."

Alecto pressed against Sully's back, draping her arms around her with obvious relish. "No, she won't."

Then the wings started to beat around them, the arrow shafts rattling together with each stroke and thick black ichor trickling down to patter on the ground beneath them as her wounds were tugged open. They took off, and without her magic, Sully was a dead weight. She watched the immortals scatter away from the plantation. Then she stared down at Marie, standing proud and safe in the courtyard as they rose up into the sky, until the clouds took even that away.

NoVeMBeR 9, 201C

The flight to England had been pretty unpleasant the first time that Sully had flown there, what with the cold and the demon beneath her. This time the company was more aesthetically pleasing, but the conversation was worse, not to mention the putrid smell. She had tried asking Alecto a few questions as they traveled but the answers had been abrupt at best. She had been around for as long as there had been humans. She had been cursed after a little misunderstanding regarding an evisceration. She had kept to herself for a while after that, hiding from the sight of mankind, whom she considered to be inferior to herself. She had met the other immortal creatures during the long silence following the war, when the demons had started to cause trouble. Sully got all of these answers in quick succession, but very little more. Maybe the long periods of isolation had made the Fury socially inept. Besides, Sully didn't feel like she had anything more to say to the monster that was dragging her off to execution or worse. Somehow the boredom, combined with the intensity of the last few days, lulled Sully off to sleep somewhere above the Atlantic. Sully had seen it many times at the IBI—when she finally caught the bad guy and they knew that they were going to be executed, all of the stress that had been haunting them faded away and they slept like babies.

The tightening of Alecto's grip when London came into sight stirred Sully from her dreams.

The gothic spires rose up ahead of them, as tall as any great skyscraper that New Amsterdam could boast, but grown rather than built, born from the curse that kept the city spreading ever outward, consuming all in its path. Someday, unless the curse was undone, all of mainland Britain would be London and it would stretch tenuous bridges out to all of the islands nearby and consume them too. Nobody was certain which of Britain's enemies had cast the curse. The more poetically inclined said that it was the Romans who flung it out as a final vengeance as their cities burned and the Veil was erected. The prosaic strategists placed the blame on the Mongolians, whose spies had reported back that the Empire was close to overspending its resources, even without the strain of an ever-expanding city. Sully didn't care for either of the political theories. To her it felt personal. Somebody had fallen in love with London once upon a time, just like Sully had fallen for New Amsterdam, and when the relationship finally went sour, they lashed out in the way that people do. There were rumors of a second curse, one that made all the people who lived within the city forget about the very existence of a world outside, but that just sounded like living in a city to Sully.

Having spent a lifetime in New Amsterdam, the spread of London beneath her shouldn't have felt so impressive. She felt almost treacherous, looking at another city that way, but it was just so damned big. She was lost almost immediately and that was looking down on it from above. She couldn't even imagine how the people in the streets made sense of it all. New Amsterdam was a grid laid over the land, but London coiled and tangled in ways that made no sense at all. Side streets and stairs led to nowhere. Main streets came to abrupt ends at monuments and fountains commemorating battles and generals that nobody could name anymore. To go north you had to walk east. To go south you had to walk north. The only constant seemed to be the clouds of pigeons that the Fury snapped at as they passed, and the coating of shit the birds left on everything.

Alecto swooped down into the streets of London and dropped Sully neatly between a pair of redcoat guards outside an unremarkable building made from white marble. They seized her immediately and gave Alecto such a brief glance that Sully wondered how heavily the Fury was doused in illusions. Sully hadn't expected anything further from her, but the creature swooped down for one moment and placed a sharp-edged kiss on Sully's cheek. "I thank you for your sacrifice. I will think of you as I receive my reward."

Standing there in enemy territory, in enemy hands and in chains, Sully did what she always did when the odds felt insurmountable. She grinned. "Just make sure you get paid fast. I don't plan on hanging around all day."

Alecto launched herself back up into the sky, lost to sight in the smog and shooting straight through the wide circle of pigeons that hung over Sully.

The guards jostled her into the building and into an elevator, and she didn't resist. Not yet anyway. She wasn't going to get away until she found a key to her shackles, and she doubted that these meatheads were at that pay grade. Sully's smile was robust. "Lovely city you have here. Shame I never got to visit as a tourist. I hear you've got the best libraries, and more pubs per head than anywhere else in the world."

The redcoats didn't engage with her, which was probably sensible, but it made for a very boring journey down into the bowels of the city. Without knowing how fast the rickety elevator was traveling, she couldn't work out just how far down they had gone but the journey seemed to go on for much longer than it should have. Sully half expected to step out into the earth's molten core when the doors finally opened.

Instead, she was greeted with a beige corridor and a fresh duo of redcoats with slightly more pips on their lapels who took her deeper into the catacombs of bureaucracy. She was handed off twice more and she started to suspect that this was all an elaborate farce and that they were walking in circles. Eventually they stopped in front of a walnut door with a tiny brass plate on it that read *The Archive*. They knocked three times, then stepped back to let the door open. Inside of what could easily have been a broom-closet there was an archway carved out of a single solid piece of ivory and completely encrusted with pictograms and runes. Sully couldn't feel the magic radiating from the archway, but even crippled as she was by the cold iron, she could see the pool of radiant light that was bound inside. The redcoats dragged her, reluctant, into the light.

Pratt had theorized about a place like this. Somewhere that you could keep records of every wish ever made without their being obliterated when the universe was changed again. A little cul-de-sac off the regular planes of existence where you could keep your paperwork in order. Sully couldn't conceive of anything that more fundamentally explained the British than this. An infinite cosmos of planes to explore and they set up camp on their own front lawn and started filling out the appropriate forms.

In practice, it didn't look vastly different than the building that they had just come from, although here the walls were blazing white constructs of pure force rather than plaster. Every breath felt stale and everywhere that Sully looked there were shelves. Row after row of shelves stretching off toward every horizon. Beyond the portal and its far newer twin there were enough card catalogs to make a librarian orgasmic. In the midst of the endless files there was a neatly appointed desk and behind that desk sat the smuggest man Sully had ever seen. Most of the British politicians that had crossed her path enjoyed their working lunches a little too much, putting considerable strain on their waistcoats as a result. This one was almost skeletally thin, and his expensive clothes hung off of him like he was a coat rack. He had thinning hair slicked over to one side, a pencil mustache, and bugging eyes that would have made him look perpetually surprised if they hadn't been so sunken. When he glanced up from the papers he was working on, he let out a sigh.

"How many times do I have to kill you before you stop coming back to trouble me, Iona O'Sullivan?"

Sully stared straight ahead and said nothing. She had done enough interrogating in her day to know that offering up information just got you to the hangman faster.

"I apologize for my terrible rudeness. I may have met you many times before, but for you this is our first encounter. I am Lord Blackwood, and as far as you are concerned, I am the British Empire. His Majesty may sit on the throne and the great and powerful may gather in Westminster to debate details of policy, but I am the one who turns their proclamations into reality. In short, they may know that a killing has been ordered, but I am the man who knows where the bodies are buried."

Sully suppressed a groan. He was like a skinny, white version of Pratt. She wondered if maybe the Fury had killed her and this was her own personal hell. Blackwood rambled on. "Have you ever wondered how it is that such a tiny island as Britain came to dominate every part of the world? We had no special advantages. We are not particularly numerous or strong—indeed in the early days of our great nation our magic could not even compare to the Celtic savages or the invading Romans—yet we noble few have mastered this entire globe at one time or another. Did it never strike you as strange?"

Now that he mentioned it, Sully wondered why it had never occurred to her before, but she wasn't going to give him the satisfaction of knowing that.

"It is quite simple really. The truth is that history is a terribly malleable thing if you have the correct tools and the correct environment to work from. The Romans discovered this in their conflict with the Greeks. The ancient Greeks had their own pocket dimension where they could track the comings and goings of the "gods" that they made sacrifices to and how their prayers were fulfilled. After the Roman conquest, the dimension became theirs and they laid claim to half of the known world. As each great empire rose, it found a place like this or it was wiped from the page of history by those of us who had the wherewithal. This is the great game of empires. Not shuffling troops and brokering deals. Rewriting history and carefully observing the ways that others have rewritten it so that we may benefit from their poor planning."

"Why wouldn't you just wish them away?" Sully's face snapped back to neutral after she realized her mistake, and she mentally kicked herself.

"Ah, Iona, I am so pleased that you have decided to join the conversation. There are two glaringly obvious reasons that we do not simply wish our foes away, the first being that each of our real competitors has a bunker rather like this one, from which they could remake their empire, in some form, with a wish. The second, and rather less expected, is that the gentlemen downstairs are creatures of honor. They will not undertake a wish if it runs contrary to one that has already been granted; therefore, wishing away the possibility of our annihilation in the service of an enemy's wish is the rather standard line of defense. Indeed, the abject impossibility of undoing a wish is the entire reason that we are having this conversation."

He paused to see if she would slip up again, but Sully remained silent.

"As I am sure you can imagine, the remaining empires have been at something of a stand-off for many decades now as a result of that inability to countermand a previous wish. The demons' usefulness was depleted more and more with each wish that was granted until we came to the current sorry state of affairs. Or rather, the sorry state of affairs before you turned the entirety of the hells against us in one fell swoop. Things proceeded without interruption for millennia, played out painstakingly by my predecessors and me, until you took our trading partners among the gentlemen downstairs out of operation. It would have given me great pleasure to toast such an excellent move in the great game, and to admire your mastery, were it not for the tragic fact that you performed it entirely by accident, without any grasp of what you have done."

Sully smirked. "I get it. I broke your toys and now you're pissed off."

Blackwood's perfect composure did not flutter. "I do not believe that you do 'get it,' Iona. You have always had trouble grasping these concepts in the abstract. So allow me to make them more personal for you. Please, take a seat."

With barely a word, he conjured an ornately carved chair out of the air in front of his desk. Sully couldn't feel the magic that he had used, through the crushing presence of cold iron, but for it to have been so simple, the whole room must have been saturated with magic. There was more magic in the hells, and the Far Realms had so much that it had permanently mutated the residents of Manhattan into Magi. She wondered just where on that spectrum of planes this little enclosure was placed. She slumped into the seat with a bored yawn and then went back to staring past Blackwood.

"There are two abiding theories among historians about the way that events unfold. One is that there are social trends which gradually blossom into inevitable results. I can understand the appeal of this particular theory, especially for academics—after all, it entirely absolves the individual of any responsibility. The world has gone awry because of an amorphous trend rather than the work of any one person. I imagine that this is rather how you Catholics view religion. Anyway, the other theory—the one that I must profess to subscribe to after my many years of practical work in this field—is that there are great men, individuals who, despite being born in many different circumstances, have such a strength of will that they can reshape reality to match their vision. Alexander the Great. Julius Caesar. Queen Victoria. These individuals are the pivot points on which history can be swung down a new course." He frowned slightly as Sully went on ignoring him.

"The first time that I killed you was in the late 80s, I believe. You had fulfilled your mother's wishes and rallied the free people of Ireland to your cause, leading an uprising against the British occupation and successfully driving our forces out. You looked terribly young in the ragtag uniform that your little militia had stitched for you. Terribly young and terribly proud. I believe that you had a wife at the time, a young lady about three years your junior. She was part of the Ophiran International Brigade that had rallied to your cause. Black as night yet cute as a button. The two of you were quite the charming couple." He smiled faintly, lost in his memories.

"It wasn't the first time that we had to resort to extreme measures to counter an Irish uprising. You are a very resilient people. It is commendable, if a little wearing. I met you on neutral territory, The Isle of Man, I believe, and we discussed your terms of secession from the Empire. Or rather, you believed that we were discussing terms, while I gathered all of the necessary information to complete the wish that would rid the world of your little insurrection. You can imagine my surprise when we discovered that you couldn't simply be wished out of existence. Your mother is a very enterprising woman, she sold herself quite highly. Not only were you impossible to remove, your magic could not be snuffed out either and the same seems to have been true of your rebellious streak. I may have some contempt for the way that you have interfered in the great game, but given the correct resources, I believe that your mother would have been a grand contender. It is unfortunate that she was born in a swamp rather than in a seat of power. I can only imagine the damage that she could have done if she had been given stewardship of a place like this. But I digress . . ."

He registered Sully's bored expression and sighed. "Alas, we find that this personalization of the grand work remains too abstract to concern you. This Iona is too distant from you to excite any sense of kinship?"

Sully continued to stare ahead blankly. He pressed on as if she were listening. "The rebellion was undone and you were directed away from your mother's tutelage at a younger age. Combined with your natural inclination against authority figures, you can imagine our surprise when you joined the navy. We had hoped that this indicated a natural improvement in your disposition and a possibility that you would become a contributing member of society. Of course, it also provided us with ample opportunities to redirect your anger. We placed you on the front lines of our conflict with the Mongols, on the assumption that your hatred might be diverted toward the Orientals, or that you might have an unfortunate accident in the line of duty, allowing us to stop tracking your every movement. Imagine our dismay when you relocated your rebellion to our colonies in the Americas."

He tipped his head to one side until he caught Sully's eye, then offered up another thin-lipped smile. "That would have been the second time that I killed you. 2005, I believe? The quagmire that you had created was considerably more complex but thankfully we found that you were once more at the epicenter of it. We did not try to remove you or your power on that occasion, nor did we make any grand sweeping changes to the world. Such things are not necessary when there is only a single course to be corrected. The woman that I killed then would have been in her late thirties, I suppose. Almost the you of today. That Iona had shed the Irish from her name, cut off her curls and married some American woman. A blonde in the mold of what I believe you colonials call "cowgirls." This would be the Marie that you are still pursuing in our current iteration? Well, not quite the same Marie, of course, some adjustments had to be made to ensure that you remained unstable. And that you would not renew your convivial relationship with the United Nations."

Sully leapt over the desk and had his stupid bloody cravat in her hands before he could let out a yelp. She hammered her forehead into his face, but instead of the satisfying crunch that she had expected there was just pain. Pain and the sound of a thunderclap. The spell flung her back across the Archive to land in a heap next to the portals and the redcoats. They hoisted her boneless body back into the seat as she tried to blink the blinding lights from in front of her eyes.

Blackwood was resting his elbows on the desk and his chin on his hands when he finally came into focus. "I am glad to see that we have finally made an emotional connection, but I would strongly advise you to keep your hands to yourself in the future. In the current scenario I have magic and you do not. Perhaps this will be a learning experience for you. A glimpse at how the other half lives, scared and powerless while people like you burn the world down on a whim."

"Fuck you," she slurred.

That damned smile again. "I don't believe either of us has the appropriate inclination for that."

"Why are you telling me all of this shit? What do you want?"

He leaned a little closer. "I simply need you to guide me through the chain of events that led us to this moment. I need you to tell me how the island of Manhattan was returned from the far planes where my predecessors deposited it. I also need you to tell me how you defeated my useful acquaintance Adolphous DiNapoli, although I will readily admit that is more out of a personal interest than any true necessity."

After a long silence Sully cackled. "You don't know? I thought you're meant to have spies everywhere? I thought a mouse couldn't fart in the colonies without His Majesty hearing about its inferior aroma. Some spymaster you are."

"If you would be so kind as to walk me through the events, I will be happy to ensure that your next iteration has a more comfortable life. We can restore your wife to her previous state of vitality, find you an isolated ranch in the old United Nations perhaps? I understand that you have some inherent urge to hunt, and the game there will be a good match for your abilities. Wouldn't you like a comfortable life with the one you love, Iona? Wouldn't you like peace?" He peered at her with a querulous eyebrow raised.

"Sounds like peace is going to cost me too much, if you're trying this hard to sell it."

"Ah, but you would not even know that you had paid," he chuckled, "To you it would seem that your life was going on as normal."

Sully smiled. "It doesn't matter anyway. Even if I told you everything. Which I won't, because it's the only reason I'm still alive. You don't have any demons to make a deal with."

He sat back and crossed his arms. "You and your Manhattanite friends actually furnished us with a rather neat solution to both of my current annoyances—your recalcitrance and the matter of wishes. We may not know precisely how you drew that island back from the Far Realms, but the channel that you opened between the planes remains quite permeable. We have been in contact with the residents of the Far Realms since the moment that the Americas descended into chaos. The beings that dwell there are more powerful than you would believe. As the demons are to human men, so are they unto the demons. Our experimentation with them has been limited but successful so far. Most importantly, we have discovered that they can and will quite readily overwrite demonic wishes. You thought to sever us from the source of our power, and instead you have handed us the keys to the kingdom. The whole world is ours for the taking now. Your demonic allies quail before the Fair Folk and they will not dare to return to our world. In one blow we can create a perfect Empire and rid ourselves of any hint of demonic influence once and for all. Best of all, the Fair Folk do not possess the demons' chaotic and emotional nature. They are beings of pure reason, much more fitting allies for the greatest of all empires."

Sully grinned. "None of which is going to matter, because I'm not going to talk."

Blackwood smiled back at her. "I must apologize once again, Iona, for I haven't been entirely forthright with you. The purpose of this exercise was not to share information with you, although it was nice to have someone to talk to. I am sure that you can imagine that this is a lonely life, and there are so few people that I come across that could grasp the magnitude of my work. No, the reason that I am telling you all of this is to prime you for interrogation. It is necessary for you to be thinking about the details of the time preceding your retrieval of Manhattan, and for you to be sufficiently emotionally compromised that you will be unsuccessful in hiding those details. You see, I rather suspected that you wouldn't talk to me, but I am nothing if not a fair man." He smiled. "I wanted to give you the opportunity to choose the right path. Before you spoke to him."

Sully's magic was bound deep down within her and her senses extended no further than the limits of her skin. She had not felt the second portal opening. She had not even sensed the thing approaching. She leapt out of her seat when she caught a glimpse of it in the periphery of her vision, then she scrambled back over the desk. Unthinking. Desperate to escape.

In the brain of every human being there is some small part that still lives in the forests where mankind first came to be. The part that forces them to freeze, if only for a moment, when they hear the howl of a wolf, or to jump when they see the scuttling of a spider. That primal fear took hold of Sully when she saw the creature looming over her chair. It bypassed her brain, moving her body as the fear screamed that the thing she was looking at should not exist.

She was relieved to realize that she herself hadn't screamed, but she had to clamp her hand over her mouth when she saw the Fair One move for the first time. She wanted desperately to look away, but she was petrified by the thought of what it could do when it was out of her sight.

It loomed over her even now, almost double her height but so thin and spindly that it looked like it should sway with each movement. There was no color anywhere upon its bare rubbery skin—things that lived their whole lives in darkness deep beneath the earth might not be so pallid and dead looking. Corpses didn't look as dead as it did. Its arms stretched down past the sexless joining of its legs to reach its knees. Too many fingers on each hand were spread and swaying like the tentacles of some deep-sea squid. Sully forced herself to look up into its face, even as tremors and nausea vied to distract her. She had never backed down from a fight, and it would take more than her own brain screaming in terror to make her back down now.

Two huge black almond-shaped eyes dominated the creature's swollen head and though it had no mouth, she could hear its voice hissing into her head uninvited. *"I shall extract all that is needed from you directly. Then on to the experiments. Your master has given you to us freely in exchange for this service. Do not give in to fear, your suffering will last only a moment at a time."*

NOVEMBER 10, 2015

Blackwood had gone back to his paperwork, and the white thing had driven Sully through the chamber with the threat of its proximity until they reached a space that was clear of furniture and files. It drew walls up from the floor around the two of them and then sealed Sully inside an enclosed space so that her screams could not distract Blackwood from his work. The Fae did not have names, as those were a by-product of emotion; and besides, Fae rarely gathered in one place in sufficient numbers for it to be necessary to designate beyond pronouns. Sully knew all of this, because the creature was still hissing into her head. Every thought that crossed its mind forced its way into hers. It explained that this was how the Fae communicated and that soon that communication would be a constant exchange of ideas flowing both ways, once she was acclimated and primed to share. It was obviously some kind of magic, but Sully was cut off from her own and had no way to defend herself. The creature advanced on her when there was a lapse in communication, driving her back into the corner of her perfect white cell.

Sully refused to scream, even when it reached for her with those dead-spider fingers. It didn't hurt when it brushed them over her face; in fact, the pain that had been her constant companion for days started to fade almost immediately. Huge black eyes still filled her vision. *The damage here is deeper. I must touch it to heal your wounds.* Sully nodded wordlessly, still trying to keep her shaking in check. This time, when the fingers brushed over her shoulder there was discomfort, then a dull ache. When she couldn't bear it anymore, she looked down and she could see those awful fingers inside her, burrowing into her through the tattered remains of a Hawaiian shirt. It whispered as it worked. *"I must heal your wounds so that you understand that you are utterly powerless. Even your body is not your own. Even your pain can be taken from you. I can heal or harm you as I see fit and there is nothing that you can do to change this fact. You are nothing."*

Sully tried to wrench away but the fingers were still lodged inside her shoulder, flesh merging into flesh as if they were one creature. She lost control and vomited, but there was nearly nothing in her stomach. A tiny splatter of bile decorated the plain white walls and Sully couldn't help but feel that that was a tiny victory. The Fae turned to look at the stain, then turned back to Sully. If there were expressions on its face, Sully couldn't see them. *"Your wounds are healed and now I will leave you here to become afraid. You will contemplate the things that I will do to you when the waiting time has elapsed. This fear will lead you to speak sooner. As it has with our previous subjects. You will not know where I am, or if I can hear your thoughts. I will be close, and I will return later than you would expect but sooner than you would hope. Very few subjects manage to sleep, but if you do, I will enter your dreams."*

It conjured a door into the wall with a simple gesture, then ducked almost double to pass through. It didn't need to look back at Sully. The door made an ominous clunk as it closed, but Sully ran over to try it anyway. It was locked.

In the center of the room, Sully slumped down and sat cross-legged to take stock of her situation. She was no longer injured, which was the good news. The Fae could toy with human bodies like a child with modeling clay, which was the bad news. She was still shaking but now that the Faerie was out of sight her fear was starting to recede. She clambered up onto her knees to check her pockets. She had two pounds in loose change, which probably wasn't enough to bribe anyone with. She had the clothes on her back which had seen better days and a half-decent pair of boots. She had nothing that she could use as a lock-pick to get the damned shackles off and her magic back and then blast her way out of this cell. The cold iron felt heavier than a normal metal should, but Sully supposed that might just be emotional weight. The honesty of the Fae was pretty refreshing after listening to Blackwood talk himself around in circles. It was leaving her here so that she could get scared. That was where it had made its fundamental mistake, because outside of that initial awful gut reaction, Sully didn't get scared. She got angry. The longer that she sat there thinking about everything that Blackwood had said, and the Faerie had threatened, the angrier she got. Sully's magic and her anger had always felt inexorably connected. When she was enraged, she could feel her magic crackling beneath her skin. Now that she was separated from her magic, she was surprised to find that less of it had been about power, and more of it had been about purpose. She didn't sit and plan her escape. She didn't let her thoughts drift to any ideas that she might have had about ways out of the current predicament. Instead she just experienced the slowly simmering rage until she drifted into a shallow stiff sleep for a few minutes at a time, resurfacing for just long enough to stoke the flames of fury before drifting off again.

Sully heard the door to her cell opening, but she kept her eyes closed. She could not afford to flinch. She could not afford to be afraid. Fear was not going to carry her through to the other side of this.

"You do not quake. Are you going to try to escape? Without magic, you are harmless. You are nothing. Shall we take it from you permanently? I have not completed that operation so far. You could be my first success. Your body is mine. Your mind is mine. Shall I make your magic mine also?"

She could feel the Fairie's presence. Not like she did with magic, rather just the sensation of air displacement as it leaned in close to her face. She opened her eyes, saw the oily black orbs of the Faerie filling her vision and she swung her fists.

The cold iron chain wrapped around her knuckles took the brunt of the impact. The Faerie staggered back and hit the wall. Sully felt the ache of the punch on her own face. The Fae was still in her head. She leapt after it, letting the chain fall from her grip. She looped it around the creature's wrist as it tried to flick her away and whatever magic it had been trying to call up died. Without waves of glamour rolling off of it, this "Fair Folk" didn't look nearly as imposing. Sully drove her forehead into its midsection and it doubled over. There was something spongy and moist about the texture of the creature, like it wasn't flesh but fungus. Sully grinned and looped her chains around the creature's neck. She rode it to the ground, catching tiny glimmers of its thoughts when the chain broke contact. She could feel herself being suffocated for a moment, but it was only that moment before the chain bit in and she got some good leverage. The Faerie clawed at her hands with those horrid fingers, but they had no strength. The Fae had nothing without their magic. Sully still had herself.

It stopped flailing after a few minutes, and after a few more Sully was pretty certain that it was dead, but she wasn't taking any chances. She looped the chain around its neck properly, then sawed the cold iron back and forth until it had cut all the way through. The Fae had no blood or bones. They were the same pasty material all the way through. If Sully ever saw tofu again, she would probably throw up, but that wasn't a huge departure from her usual response to tofu.

She kept low as she ran through the maze of bookshelves and filing cabinets. Her memory of her arrival was a little hazy thanks to the Faerie's mind-altering interference, but it didn't take long for her to orient herself and head for the portals. Blackwood wasn't at his desk but the portal back to London was still open, so he hadn't been gone for long. He would be back to debrief the Faerie soon. The first interrogation was always a short, sharp shock to see if your perp would talk without a greater effort. Sully dithered for a moment, then started digging through the desk drawers, hunting for the key to her shackles. She found more files than she knew what to do with.

The original file about "The Manhattan Insurrection" was written on what felt like animal skin instead of paper; newer files had clearly been typed on a computer and then printed off. Her own file came in several parts, each one chronicling another of the lives she had lived before the British took it away from her. If they thought that she was their enemy before, they had no idea what they were in for now. Sully had never had much time in her life for revenge. Most of the people that wronged her were either so protected by layers of society that she couldn't touch them, or they were dead. Now she had the loss of two happy marriages and two decades of freedom to even the scales for. She had never known why she was so angry before, but this seemed like a pretty good explanation. Even if she had forgotten.

She abandoned the search for the key after dumping out the contents of every drawer and carefully mixing up the pages of every file. She would have to find another way out of the cuffs and she was painfully aware that every second that ticked by was another moment when she could be recaptured. With one last backward glance at the Archive, she drew in a deep breath and stepped through the portal back to earth.

NoVember 12, 2015

Sully walked directly into Lord Blackwood as he tried to come into the room. He opened his mouth to cast and found that it was suddenly full of chain links. His head was in a vice-like grip and Sully's face was rushing toward him with an expression of unreserved glee plastered across it. This time when she head-butted the secret ruler of the British Empire in the face, it felt right. His nose collapsed, he made a squawking noise that was going to keep her warm through the cold winters' nights, and the best part was that she was holding onto him by his ears, so she could do it all over again. "Hello, Blackwood, fancy meeting you here. I hope you've got the keys to these cuffs because otherwise this is going to get embarrassing and painful for you quickly."

There were redcoats on the other side of the door but Blackwood's skinny frame was blocking them from getting a clear shot at her, which was just delightful. His hands were flapping at his sides as she reared back with his blood running down her face. "Keys. Now."

He let out a muffled scream into the chain and the redcoats pointed their guns around the doorframe.

"Keys, or they shoot us both."

He scrambled in his pockets until he produced the tiny key to her manacles. "Good boy. Put it in my hand."

He reached up slowly and did as he was told. Sully caught him by the wrist and with more practiced movements than she would care to admit, Sully undid the cuffs and then snapped them onto Blackwood, never stepping out of the cover he provided for a moment. As soon as she let go of the metal, her magic was there again as if it had never left. Relief flooded through her. Sure she was in a secret underground bunker in the middle of London with about a million soldiers between her and freedom, but at least now she could throw a fireball at them.

She called to the redcoats, "All right, boys, we're coming out."

Then she cast her traveling spell.

She didn't have Mol Kalath's power to fuel her this time, and she hadn't adjusted her usual calculations by much more than aiming upward and hoping for the best, so it came as a small surprise when both she and Blackwood landed on a hillside with a clap like thunder rather than plowing into a solid object and dying like she had half expected. Blackwood fell to his knees and it was only pure determination that kept Sully from toppling right down with him. She dragged in a breath and tried her damnedest to remember her own name. The long dreadful moment stretched out, an echoing silence in her head as she desperately tried to retrieve anything except her knowledge that she hated the man on the moss beside her, then her memory snapped back and despite the migraine it had brought with it, she heaved a sigh of relief. She really had to be more careful. Blackwood was talking again. "You know that there is no way you will get away with this. Every soldier in the British army will be searching for me, every Magus and redcoat in the entire Empire will be scrying to find us."

Sully grinned. "I'd better kill you quick then."

"You wouldn't dare!"

She squatted down beside him and let him get a good look in her eyes. "You read all those files about me. Do you really think I wouldn't dare?"

He had started to go red as he got into his rant but now all the color drained from his face. "It—it doesn't matter. I am not the only keeper of the keys. I am not the only custodian of the Empire. Another will take my place and Britannia will prevail as she always has."

"I wonder about that, actually. How many times your beloved

Empire actually won and how many times it was just you liars chang-ing the story after the fact. I bet even you don't know anymore."

He opened and closed his mouth. "All that matters is victory."

Sully cackled. "Oh, she is going to love you."

"Who is?"

"My mother. I've just worked out where we are."

She gave him a kick in the ass that knocked him off his knees and into the dirt, "Come on, it isn't far to walk. Even for a city boy like you."

He bristled, but he got back on his feet and was led down the hills toward the thickets and swamps that Sully had spent the first years of her life calling home. She tried to muster up a little bit of nostalgia, but all that she managed was contempt bred of familiarity. It didn't take long before the trees started to remind her which way to go. That copse had been struck by lightning once. The stream that Blackwood had just splashed through in his fancy leather-topped wingtips used to run on the other side of a big rock that looked like a rabbit if you squinted. The air felt so different here that Sully had to stop and just breathe for a moment. There was that undercurrent of decay and rich earth in the air, the peaty aromas of the cycle of rebirth. All the poisons of the city were missing. She had spent her whole life trying to get away from this purity. She still loathed it from the bottom of her heart, but now she wondered how much of that hatred had been planted there by scum like Blackwood and his cadre of liars.

The sky started to darken as they moved down amidst the leaf-less trees and boot-sucking mud. Sully sincerely doubted that it had much to do with the setting of the sun. She couldn't remember a sin-gle moment of sunshine in her mother's house, just the chill misting rain and the rich darkness of perpetual midnight. There was a certain point in the swamp where the old standing stones that might have drawn a casual explorer that far all sank out of sight and marsh-lights danced over the waters. From there she kept a tight grip on the back of Blackwood's collar to keep him walking only where she wanted. There were more bodies in that hungry water than she could guess at, and there would be more before all was said and done. Even when they left the land behind and waded out into the stagnant water, Sully's feet never left the path of slippery stones just beneath the water's surface. After all this time her body remembered the way, even if her mind didn't. Something shifted under the surface of the water up ahead, sending ripples dancing toward them, and Blackwood almost fell over in fright.

"What in the blazes was that?"

"Nothing to worry about, just a snake."

"There are no snakes in Ireland. Everyone knows that."

"Everyone knows that?" she smirked, "Because some Saint came stomping around, driving out all the witches and wyrms? Look around you. We're still here."

He fell back into sullen silence for the rest of the hike.

The cottage was easy enough to find. There was a ring of time-worn standing stones on a hillock in the middle of the swamp, still pulsing faintly with magic even after millennia of disuse. From there Sully just followed the trail of scrawny trees until they came upon the next patch of solid ground. Nothing had changed about the cottage since Sully had left. There was still a dip in the middle of the thatched roof and the slimy mold creeping up the walls showed no signs of clearing up without some serious intervention. Oily black peat smoke was rising from the chimney stack, although there was no other sign of life inside. Sully pushed Blackwood ahead of her like a shield as she ducked inside and the sense memory of her childhood in this dark enclosure came rushing back. The fire was the only light, and it set all the shadows around the house flickering. There were animal bones mounted on the walls and scattered all over the place. Books too, if you were willing to dig around a little. Far more books than you would expect to find in a battered old hovel in the middle of a swamp, anyway. Winter was coming on, so Sully wasn't surprised to see a bedroll and a heap of furs down by the fireside, although she was dismayed to see that there were sparks and embers on the hearthstone right beside them. With a grumble she started over to pull the guard around the fire when the heap of furs moved. Sully froze. "Mother?"

Gormlaith O'Sullivan didn't look her age. Nobody with magic ever did. Sully herself looked like she was barely pushing thirty despite having been around for half a decade. Her mother's face was a mass of wrinkles stretched over a far-too-prominent skull, topped off with the surviving wisps of a once full head of bountiful red curls. She looked at least a century old, but that didn't reach halfway to the truth. There were ridiculous rumors that Gormlaith had been there to see the first ships of the British occupation arriving on Irish shores. Sully knew for a fact that she had seen and supported every uprising against the invaders over the last two centuries, at least. The old woman slithered out of her bed and rose to her full height, in a tattered patchwork dress and weighed down with strings of bones. She stood chin to chin with Sully. Her voice had lost none of its power since Sully left. She still sounded like she gargled with gravel and whiskey every morning, although only half of that was true. "Never asked you back."

Sully didn't snap at her. Just met her milky stare. "You didn't need to ask me back."

Gormlaith stabbed a finger at Sully's chest. "I'll not be forgiving you. Not for abandoning me. Not for abandoning our people when they needed you."

Sully sighed. She had hoped that she might get a whole minute before all of this kicked off. "Forget about that for now. I brought you a present."

Gormlaith sniffed at the air. "Papers and ink. Leather and wool. Cold iron and silver."

"Lord Blackwood, I'd like to introduce you to Gormlaith O'Sullivan. I hear that you are a fan?" Sully smirked. "Mother, this is the English twit who handled all of the Empire's deals with the hells."

Despite the circumstances, Blackwood tried gamely to be polite. "It is a pleasure to finally meet you, madam. I am a great admirer of your work."

"Why did you bring that bull's pizzle into my house, Little I? Are you trying to impress me with the lofty cocksuckers you're rubbing shoulders with?"

Sully let out a bark of laughter. "He's my hostage, actually. Have you stopped paying attention? The Americas have seceded. We're at war with the British. Same as you."

"Is that meant to make up for it then? Is this meant to pay back all those long years I didn't know if you were breathing or not? You're finally fighting the British? You were meant to be fighting them thirty years ago when you were in your prime. You were meant to set us free and instead you ran. You've your father's cowardly blood in you, no doubt. I see none of me. I tell you that for nothing."

Sully took a deep breath. "Mother. Can you stop? We're on the same side. We want the same things."

Gormlaith spat in the fire and it roared to life. "You're a coward, and you'll run the moment the road gets rough. I've no use for you."

"You're my mother." Sully hissed through clenched teeth.

"Blood? You want to talk about blood? My piss runs thicker than blood these days. I'm the only one still fighting this war," She crept around the room as she spoke, as if Sully weren't there, snatching up bits and pieces from the shelves and out of baskets amidst the chaos. "You ran away, signed on with the enemy, lived it up in some big city with your fancy girls and now you want to come back here like you matter a damn to anyone? You don't matter. Not to me. Not to Ireland."

She came over to Blackwood with a pair of rusty scissors in her hand and snipped a lock of hair from his nape while he stood frozen in fear. She bound the hair to a little sack-cloth doll with some black thread as she strolled back to the fire. Sully kept her anger at a low simmer and asked, "What do you want, Mother?"

"Want? What have I ever wanted? You were meant to be a general, and you settled for being nothing. You were given all the power you could need; you were given protections you couldn't even understand. You were kissed by the fire like every Irish witch of my line stretching all the way back to the Queen of Ravens herself and you left us. You coward. You weakling. You had everything you would ever need and you ran from the fight without throwing a punch. You're no daughter of mine, Little I. My daughter would have stood in her place at my side and she would have burned the British off the face of this land. She would have made this country ours again. Made us masters of our own destiny instead of slaves to the Empire. I want what I've always wanted. I want a free Ireland."

Sully expected a rush of anger. She expected to scream and possibly to throw some spells around. This was exactly what she had always expected if she returned home. It was the nightmare that had kept her away. Now that she was living it, there was no half-remembered bogeyman of a swamp witch screaming hatred at her. There was a sad old woman who had lost her daughter and her dreams on one bad day. Sully looked into Gormlaith's blind eyes and she couldn't muster any rage at all. She sighed, "Don't tell me. Tell him."

Gormlaith opened her mouth to spit some more poison, but Sully cut her off. "I mean it. Give him a list of your demands. He is a hostage, but he's the man in charge, too. He can negotiate for his own safe return."

Blackwood had been edging toward the door, but he froze in place when the witches looked at him. "I mean . . . I am not certain that I . . ."

Sully grinned. "He gave me a big speech earlier about how he makes all the decisions. He is the British Empire all packaged up in one poorly fitted suit, and he wants to make it out of this alive. Right?"

Both Gormlaith and Blackwood nodded. "He thinks that he is going to go back to the Fae and wish this all away anyway, so it doesn't matter to him what he has to give you as long as he gets to go home. He'll give you anything."

The mounting glee vanished from Gormlaith's twisted knot of a face in an instant. "The Fae? The Fair Folk?!"

Sully rolled her eyes. Of course, her mother knew more about everything than anyone. "The British needed to replace the demons after I took them away. They put in a call to the Far Realms."

Gormlaith covered the distance to Blackwood in the blink of an eye and the back of her hand caught him across the face. The personification of the British Empire fell on his ass. Sully winced in sympathy. He might have been the enemy, and a real prick, but that old woman had hands like mahogany.

Gormlaith crouched over him and screeched, spittle flying from her mouth and blind eyes bulging. "You worthless pox-bottle. Do you even know what you've done? You can't make deals with the Folk. You can't reason with them any more than you could reason with a storm. You can't trade with them because there's nothing they won't take without a thought. They'll take whatever they want. They'd skin a babe alive just to hear it wailing and you geebags invited them in?!"

"Madam! The Fae have been true to their word."

"Their word?! What word?! They don't have words! If you think you've got a deal, that is just because you haven't said no to them yet. You've fucked us all."

Blackwood crab-walked backward, wailing. "The situation is under our control!"

Gormlaith's face had gone hard and cold. Sully recognized that expression. She was already throwing up a shield between them before the spellfire came flooding out of Gormlaith's hands to wreath her. "Mother!"

The old woman drew her magic back inside and swallowed enough of her fury that it started to show on her face again. She snarled at Sully. "This is your fault as much as his. If you'd stayed like you were meant to. If you'd learned our history like you were meant to then you'd have known what it meant. You'd have known better."

The opaque shield collapsed unused, and Blackwood was almost to the door before a whip of flame leapt from Sully's hand to snare him around the ankle.

"Mother, can we please focus?"

"You think those rocks out there were for nothing? Summoning circles grew like mushrooms? You think the magic got called into the world by chatting with the hopeless gobshites in the hells?" The old woman hunched down by the fire, stirring the embers with a wave of her hand. "The Folk have been before and every one of the langers that were calling them thought that they had it under control. That the circles would hold them forever. Even the weakest of the Folk knows magic the way a fish knows swimming."

Blackwood had stopped squirming. He was curled up on himself on the bare floorboards, scrubbing at the smoldering wool around his ankle and listening to every word intently. Gormlaith breathed life into the fire again, stoking it up until the whole room felt like a furnace. As if the warmth could ward off the chill her words were spreading through every one of them. "Every night they'd come around. Them that could afford it wore a bit of cold iron round their neck to ward the Folk off. Those were the days witches commanded respect. When we were all that stood between man and the hunt."

Sully could still feel the touch of the thing in the Archive in her shoulder. With a touch they could kill. With a thought they could conjure like a Magus. How did you fight something like that? How did you even face it? "It took us all together to stop them. Wishes and spells to patch up the walls and block the way. It were a thousand years before they stopped coming. Before we could start over and build again."

The lines cut into Gormlaith's face were deepened by the shadows and for a moment she almost looked her age. "If you had a child, you never took your eyes off it. The Folk loved them the best. But they'd take anyone and keep them forevermore. If luck was with you, they'd kill you quick, but few enough were lucky."

Sully could only muster a whisper. "When they took people . . . They left something behind?"

Gormlaith turned to her slowly. "A stock. That's what we called them. Carved wood."

Sully's expression was all the confirmation her mother needed. "Started already, has it?"

They both turned to look at Blackwood. He was still curled up on the floor. Staring into the fire. Sully walked over to him calmly and when he looked up at her she kicked him in the face.

He went down hard and Sully dropped on top of him, fists moving of their own volition. She watched it happen as though somebody else were doing it. So fast she couldn't even keep track of her own movements. She hit him and hit him as if all the evil he had done could be broken as easily as his cheekbones.

Gormlaith dragged her off before the old man died, but it would be a long time before the mess on the front of his head was recognizable as a face again. Sully's hands were aching. Blood was dripping onto the floor. Some of it his, some of it hers where the bone had bitten into her knuckles. He was sobbing and wailing through the mangled mass of swelling and bruises. Still alive, still conscious. That was fine. That was all Sully needed from him. She went to the mantelpiece and plucked out one of Gormlaith's tarry black cigars. They were foul smelling things that used to turn her stomach when she stole a puff, but now she found she needed one. At the door she paused and looked back at her mother where she was lingering over the beaten man. "Prop him up and settle your terms—Ireland secedes from the Empire today, we'll keep him safe and return him when the fighting is over—the usual kind of deal."

She lit the cigar in her hand with a flick of her fingers. "Give me a shout and pull out the mirror when you're done. I've got an army of demons hanging around France, just waiting to chew the redcoats out of Ireland and make us a beachhead."

She turned, then paused for a moment. "I never got a chance to say, I don't forgive you either. You never loved me. You never wanted *me*, just what I could do for you, and you asked for more than any girl could give." Gormlaith didn't have the decency to deny it. She just hoisted Blackwood toward a chair and let Sully walk away.

NOVEMBER 13, 2015

Mol Kalath and Ogden were together in Manhattan when Sully's mirror-call reached them, her voice echoing up out of a puddle near the town square where they were arguing, until they finally found a mirror that was more or less intact in an old tavern house. They had a few questions that Sully tried to get through as quickly as possible, but after the first rush of relief, they put Pratt on speakerphone and completely ruined her good mood. "I've established a beachhead near Cork in Ireland. And Ireland is no longer a part of the British Empire, so the wish that was keeping the demons out won't affect us here," she said.

"Kindly explain to us this extraplanar Archive that you have visited, Sullivan."

Sully sighed. "It is exactly what you thought it was, Prime Minister. A pocket plane where they could track any reality alterations."

There was some crackly chuckling. "Oh, the pompous hypocrisy of the British. Condemning everyone and anyone for working with the demons while secretly using them to orchestrate the mechanics of the entire Empire."

Ogden interrupted, as he so often did, "Tell us more about these fairies everyone is so frightened about?"

"They are ten-foot-tall monsters that are more powerful and dangerous than demons. They don't care about deals, they use humans like guinea pigs in their experiments, they are native to the Far Realms and they are probably what harassed and murdered you the entire time that Manhattan was trapped there."

Mol Kalath's voice was strangely comforting. "SHADOW-TWIN. I THOUGHT THAT YOU HAD DIED. I COULD NOT FEEL YOU WHEN YOU WERE IN THIS ARCHIVE."

Sully smiled softly and watched her own distorted grimace rippling across the surface of the silvered glass. "I'm all right. I'm probably better off than when I went in, to be honest. I need to know what I've missed, though."

Ogden spoke over the others. "The Hydra has returned to the sea. There is no trace of the other monsters that your fiancée described. The British have maintained their desultory bombardment and now we know why they were in no rush to push. The demons of Europe and the majority of the Magi who are not involved in our home defenses are in France at the moment. We can have them with you by the end of the day, although Mol Kalath and I will probably be a little later. We will have to establish portals to get our troops in motion. The natives have been restless since you vanished. The Republicans, too. It is almost as though they trust in your skill as a general and were disheartened by your loss."

Gormlaith was smirking by the fireplace. "Surely not."

Sully shot her a warning look. "Get here as quickly as you can. We need to start laying plans if we are going to take the Archive."

Pratt spoke over the others. "Arrangements are already being made, Sullivan. Secure your position and wait for reinforcements."

There was some commotion on the other side of the mirror and then Ogden sighed. "It seems that Mol Kalath was not content to wait. It will probably be with you before everyone else."

Sully smiled. "What is happening with the stocks? The wooden people?"

"We are conducting door to door testing under the guise of a health crisis and on average it has turned up a population loss of around one percent across the colonies, the United Nations and the impacted areas of the Republic, in the regions that our constabularies have canvassed so far."

Sully blinked. "Wait. One percent would be almost two million people?"

The mirror smoothed out in the painful silence that followed until Ogden murmured, "Two and a half million."

Sully felt numb. Everywhere that the Fae had touched her, that numbness spread like ice over her skin. "You understand that they are being tortured to death right now? Those two and a half million people."

Pratt chimed in. "We have no way of knowing precisely what is happening to them, Sullivan. It is just as possible that they are being held hostage in comfortable environs so that they could be of use in negotiating a later peace on favorable terms."

Gormlaith shook her head sadly but kept quiet.

Sully dragged her eyes back to the mirror. "Have we been able to work out how the Fae are being called in without summoning circles? The crop circles couldn't work. They aren't solid enough. Summoning needs permanence."

Ogden fielded that one. "We are still seeking more information."

Sully laid her hands on the rough wood of the mirror's frame and sighed. "Let me know if you work it out. And try to get here soon. The longer we wait, the more people we lose."

Pratt butted in again. "Hold your position and await reinforcement, General."

"Yes sir." Sully raised both of her middle fingers to the rippling glass.

The spell broke while she was still standing there like that. The surface smoothed out until she could see herself clearly; manic grin and all. She frowned and lowered her hands to her sides. She had forgotten how quiet it was out here after sundown, when all of the swamp bugs finally shut the hell up for the night. The thatch still rustled, and the cottage groaned as it settled, but beyond the walls there was nobody else. There was no world outside of this hut. Blackwood spoiled the illusion slightly by letting out a nasal whine from where he was lying in the far corner. A tincture of whiskey and herbs had put him under, once the agreement had been signed, then Gormlaith had set about coating his whole face with the bog mud to help it heal quicker, though Sully wasn't sure why she bothered.

The old woman spat into the roaring fire. "Sad days when demons is the only ones you can trust, Little I."

"You've got a problem with demons now? From what I hear, you dealt with them plenty before I was around."

The old woman slumped down onto her makeshift bed and grumbled. "If you'd stayed, you'd know."

Sully stalked over to the fire, drew in a deep breath and then settled herself cross-legged beside her mother. "Well, I'm here now."

"Pah. You'd rather have your book learning. Rather run around the world than listen to me." Gormlaith rolled over so her back was to the fire. Her spine was pronounced under the thin covering of her dress.

"I'm not fighting with you. If you want to tell me something, then tell me, but I've had enough bickering."

Gormlaith grumbled some more, then rolled back over. "The demons, they understand magic. How the worlds all slot together. They understand that there is rules to it. We just guess at them rules but the rules are why we haven't been up to our tits in Fae since the beginning. They need invited, same as a demon does. That's the only way to come up. Your demons, they understood you can make rules to the invitations, too. That's how their deals work."

"Conditional invitations?" Sully nodded along gamely, as if she hadn't heard all of this in a dozen lectures over the years.

Gormlaith let out a wet cough. "They don't bother with the fancy laws your college made up. Physics and the like. They've got contracts. That's their laws. They can't break their word, you see. Can't lie. Not any more than a rock can be a bird just by saying so. Where they're from, it is all changing. If you aren't true, you'll get swept up in the change, too."

Sully snorted. "So you're saying to trust the demon I already trust?"

"I'm saying there's consequences to everything and you'd do well to remember that."

Sully shrugged. "Cause and effect. Feel like we've covered that before."

She ducked under the little dart of green fire that her mother flicked at her. Smiling while somebody tried to kill you probably wasn't a healthy response, but she blamed her mother for that weird response. Just like she had blamed the old woman for so much more. She nodded at Blackwood where he lay paralyzed in the dark. "You know he had a lot to say about you and me when I first met him. He told me about the deals you'd cut to make me into a weapon."

Gormlaith growled. "Not saying sorry, if that's what you're after. I made you what Ireland needed. Never going to be sorry for that."

Sully rolled her eyes. "That is all manner of fucked up. But it isn't what I'm trying to talk about." She pointed to Blackwood. "He had met me before—twice—and he'd tried to wish me away and failed. You know why he had to do that?"

"No doubt you'll tell me," Gormlaith grumbled.

"Because I didn't run off to college. I didn't go find my own life. I stayed here. I fought your war for you. And I won. They had to remake the whole damned world to undo what you had made me into. So, you don't need to go on feeling bitter. You got your way."

Gormlaith drummed her fingers on the hearthstone. "You didn't betray the cause? You didn't leave in the middle of the night without a word? You didn't leave your mother to rot?"

"I did. And I'm not sorry. I'm nobody's tool. Not theirs. Not yours."

"Too much of me in you," the old woman scoffed, "Never liked being told what to do neither."

"I'm just saying that before they interfered, I was the daughter you wanted me to be. Maybe you can find some comfort in that."

For a long time Gormlaith said nothing. Then she mumbled,

"You'll freeze in them rags. Your old clothes won't fit you. Have a look through mine for something."

This was the most maternal Sully could ever remember her mother being, so she made the most of it. For half an hour she dug through heaps of old clothes until she found a woolen dress that she didn't hate. Her jeans weren't in too terrible a state beyond the bloodstains, and the dress covered that nicely. When she settled beside the fire again, Gormlaith gave her a nod of approval. Which instantly made her doubt her choice. They sat peacefully for a while, then the smoke and the dark started to get to Sully. She hadn't expected to sleep again for the rest of her life after seeing the Faerie, and she'd felt fairly certain that the idea that her whole life had been scrubbed and rewritten over and over every time she became a nuisance would have given her some sleepless nights. As it turned out in the end, exhaustion beat existential dread.

The sound of beating wings woke Sully with a start from her nightmare. She didn't like to dream—she'd seen enough of war to know how easily it could follow you into your head—but it seemed like the old house was bringing back old habits. One of Gormlaith's eyes snapped open when Sully stirred. She patted the old woman on the leg as she rose. "That'll be my army."

Gormlaith looked like she was about to say something, but then she thought better of it and rolled back over. Sully borrowed another cigar without asking and walked outside feeling strangely light. She had spent the night in her mother's house and had a conversation that hadn't ended in anyone screaming. The world really was changing.

The gryphon hit her as she was coming out of the door. Talons bit into her back and she only had the time to let out a strangled yelp before it dragged her into the air. Sully opened her mouth to cast and suddenly found herself free-falling back toward the swamp. It had learned its lesson from last time, it wasn't giving her a moment to think. Tartalo the blind giant was waiting beneath her, his head cocked to one side so that he could hear her coming. He'd uprooted one of the few solid-looking trees in the swamp to use as a club. Sully got a shield half formed before the wood smashed into her. She didn't die from the force of the blow, but it was enough to knock the wind out of her as she flew toward Alecto the Fury hanging in the air ahead, glorious in her full aspect of vengeance. Her pus-dripping wings were spread wide in the moonlight and a razor grin split her face. The hands that had embraced Sully so gently in flight had twisted and elongated into chitinous claws. Sully managed a dart of white flame, but with a slash of those claws it dispersed in a puff of light.

Just as Sully was sure that she was going to hit the Fury, Alecto turned aside with a giggle. Sully soared right past. Straight into the waiting gryphon. There was no attempt to catch her. It raked down the length of her body with its claws and she dropped in a shower of her own blood. That was when the pain caught up to her. The punctures in her back. The cracked ribs. The fine ribbons of skin and flesh that had been torn from her chest and her stomach. Her lungs, straining for air. They burned. It all burned.

She dove into the shallow water and for one wonderful moment the chill calmed her wounds, then she sank into the grasping mud, realizing that she couldn't get free. She struggled down there in the dark. Squirming and jerking. Trying to reach clear water. Trying to reach air. She couldn't remember which way was up, but she still strained for it with all her strength. The mud held on and for a moment Sully had clarity. She was going to die in a muddy puddle, within a stone's throw of the hovel where she was born, and a whole lifetime of running hadn't saved her.

Spellfire boiled the water around her hands away and lit the bottom of the swamp. She couldn't breathe to cast but this was low magic. The sort of thing kids did by accident and gave themselves headaches. She pointed her hands down and pushed.

She burst out of the water and Tartalo caught her in one massive hand, rumbling with laughter. The gryphon and the Fury circled above them. Sully hadn't seen the Hydra yet, but she had no doubt that it was on its way. She spat out a mouthful of water, dragged in an agonizing breath and then went to work. She cast her concussion spell by the giant's ear and he roared in agony and let her drop. The flying spell caught her before she returned to the swamp. She whipped herself back up and launched herself at the gryphon like a cannonball.

There was no way that she could outrun them and no point in escaping even if she could. They had forever to hunt her and nothing to lose. She cast a torrent of spells as she rose, one after the other. She hit its wings with a bolt of moonlight, freezing them solid. She hit its dangling head with a fireball that stripped it of feathers all over again.

Darts of force and flame. Coils of lightning. Anything and everything that she could conjure she flung at the falling beast as gravity and velocity brought them closer and closer together. Sully couldn't see Alecto in the night sky, didn't know how she would fight a Fury even if she did spot her. From what she could remember, the Erinyes were closer to gods than animals, but the gryphon was just a monster. She knew exactly what to do with monsters.

Her last spells before she collided with the gryphon infused her with strength and surrounded her with layers of protection. She punched her fist into the blackened hole that she had already cursed into its side and dug around inside for its heart. The gryphon was screeching and Sully screamed right back as they tumbled through the air. Her arm was slick with blood. Its feathers were painted red.

Sully readied an overpowered concussion spell to tear them apart before they hit the ground, whispering the words and readying the spellforms. But the gryphon had no intention of letting go. It jerked forward and locked her free hand in its beak, screeching and grinding the edges together. Sawing through the bones of her wrist.

Sully felt the grinding more than she felt the pain. Everything hurt too much for any one wound to distract her, but the vibration as tendons and meat were shredded was enough to make her retch. Still spinning. Still burning. Fighting back the urge to puke herself inside out. She cast the concussion spell with the wrong hand. It went off inside the gryphon.

The resulting explosion was too confusing for Sully to take it all in, but the next thing that she remembered, she was lying on her back in a stagnant pond, surrounded by twitching nodules of meat and drifting feathers. The burning had stopped—which was extremely concerning. She tried to push herself up out of the water but a stab of pain ran up the length of her arm even through the numbness. Sully looked down to see how bad it was. Her left hand was gone. Blood was gushing out of the stump like an open faucet. "Oh."

She could hear Tartalo's stomping footsteps approaching. For one stupid moment she splashed around in the water, trying to find her hand. She could feel the eyes of Alecto burrowing into the top of her head. She didn't have time for weakness. "Eyes forward."

She tried very hard not to think about how badly it was going to hurt as she prepared her spell, panting to stave off the encroaching darkness at the edges of her vision. If she passed out, she was dead. She hissed out the last words and clenched her teeth so she didn't bite through her own tongue.

The blue-hot artillery spell could melt steel. In a flash, it blackened the raw flesh and killed the nerves. The darkness swept in again, and it was only the sound of her own screaming that kept Sully awake. When the darkness eased back to the edges of her vision she was drenched in a cold sweat. She didn't think that she could stand. She was shaking too hard. She set off a chain of concussions overhead. If she was lucky, the giant would toddle close enough to one to go deaf as well as blind, but judging by her night so far, she wasn't going to be lucky.

By the time she found her feet Tartalo was almost on top of her. The pain was coming back, inch by inch. Her anger was coming back, too. She launched artillery fire at the giant as it rushed her, and while the first shot missed, the rest met their mark. Fireball after fireball pummeled Tartalo as Sully roared defiance. Within the cage of his blackened ribs she could still see the flames burning. "Die! Die!"

There was no sound but the roaring fire. She filled him up with fire and then poured in some more. He still had the shape of a man and flames licked up out of his empty eye-socket, yet he kept coming.

Blind, deaf, and scorched beyond recognition, the giant lumbered on toward her, so Sully took flight. The moment she left the ground it felt like the world was spinning around her. In a dizzy spiral she slipped out of his reach. As her vision began to clear and her gut stopped churning, Sully caught sight of the mountainous Hydra on the horizon, churning through the treacherous swamp as if it were nothing. Tears streamed down her face in the chill night air. Then Alecto slapped her out of the sky.

There was no water or mud to break her fall this time. Sully cracked off a standing stone and collapsed onto the ground. That was another bad one. She could still wiggle her toes, so the damage wasn't catastrophic, but wiggling her toes was all that she had the energy left to do. The cracked ribs were almost certainly broken now. She needed to breathe. The Fury swept down out of the sky toward her and all she could do was lie there as her death descended like the blade of the guillotine.

Mol Kalath drove into Alecto from above. For a moment they hung above Sully, talons and wickedly hooked claws sending a shower of feathers, blood, and pus down around her. Then they fell, tumbling and rending one another, until they were out of Sully's line of sight. A crash sounded as they landed in the swamp. With some effort Sully managed to drag in a wheeze of breath but it came back out again as a tiny scream. The ribs were definitely broken. It didn't matter. Mol Kalath was buying her time and she needed to use it. She threw herself forward away from the water and made it onto her feet.

A few steps around the outside of the circle, and she had just enough air to cast. She flicked a dart of pure spellfire at one of the standing stones and the whole thing sprang to life. With only that tiny spark of power, the circle was primed for use once more. The flames in Tartalo were dying down and his flesh was starting to coalesce into a dry, sticky mess. Hunks of charred flesh flaked off as he charged across the swamp toward her. As he burst into the circle, Sully snapped it shut. It did nothing to slow the giant, but it had cost Sully nothing and if she had died without trying it, she would have kicked herself.

With all the time in the world she readied another overpowered concussion spell and snapped it off as Tartalo got too close. It didn't launch him straight upward like it had with the Hydra—the human shape just didn't have enough of a flat surface—but he still flew a fair distance. She was buying time.

Sully felt a tug in her guts that had nothing to do with the strips of flesh that were missing. Alecto howled in triumph as she hoisted Mol Kalath's limp body above her head. The demon had never been still before. Even when it had tried, feathers would flutter and reach out toward her and its eyes would always seek her out. Now they were glazed over and the light deep within them was out. "No."

The Fury launched the demon at Sully with a squeal of delight. Woman and demon tumbled across the ground together, Sully clinging to her shadow-twin as tightly as she could. Mol Kalath rebounded off the invisible wall surrounding the circle and they came to a halt. For all the time it took Alecto to stroll over, Sully just lay there with her arms wrapped around the demon. The fingers that she had left were clenched in the soft feathers on Mol Kalath's underside. She couldn't feel the demon breathing, but she didn't know if demons needed to. She couldn't feel a heartbeat, but who even knew if it had a heart. Sully let all her senses roll out of her body and then plunged them into the demon, searching for any hint that it was still alive. Deep down in the darkness, she found a spark and she poured the last remnants of her own depleted magic into that spark without a thought. The demon shuddered beneath her touch, and that tiny spark, doused in fuel, caught alight.

There was no barrier between them now, not even the hesitation to do harm. This wasn't the cruel stripping of power that Sully had forced on other demons, nor was it the clumsy sharing of power that humans could achieve through ritual. She and the demon shared their power because it belonged to both of them. Mol Kalath sprang back to life, and the power flooded into Sully just as readily as it filled the demon.

Alecto strolled contemptuously through the barrier around the circle, as if it wasn't even there. It had started to rain. A fine mist washed the worst of the ichor and blood from the creature's skin. "You need not be whole when we take you. You can be made to suffer as we suffer. If you surrender now, only the wildling must die."

Sully staggered to her feet and stared the Fury down. She was a beautiful creature. The last of her kind. Everything about her was tragic. Mol Kalath rested its weight against her back. Demons were hideous, they were legion, and they had been waging war on mankind for so long that Sully still couldn't believe that the touch of a demon could be anything but repulsive. Yet here she was leaning into it like it was a loving embrace. She raised her hand and began tracing out a spell.

"Are you blind to the futility? We cannot die. All that you can do is delay the inevitable."

Mol Kalath croaked, "THAT IS ALL THAT HUMANS EVER DO."

Sully had never cast this spell before, but she had written and rewritten it so many times that it was as familiar to her as Marie's face. She traced each spellform with a flourish. Anticipation built in her stomach despite the pain gnawing at the edges of her concentration. She poured the pain into her spell with the power. It only seemed right.

Alecto stopped a foot away from Sully's outstretched hand and spread her arms and wings wide, laughter echoing up into the silent night. Sully traced the last line, whispered the last word, and all the magic that she had was ripped out of her.

Dante's Inferno only lasted for an instant before Sully's protections cut it off, but it burned as bright and as hot as the sun for that instant. The circle bound it, and with nowhere for all the fire and fury to go it doubled back in on itself. Heat and light and searing death looped infinitely within the circle in that one moment. A roaring blinding pillar of light that burned away the clouds and made even Sully flinch away. Then it was over.

When the smoke cleared and Sully could see again, there was nothing left in the circle but a crater of molten rock. Sully collapsed onto Mol Kalath, who had dropped to the ground the moment the spell was cast. It let out a grunt but otherwise didn't complain. Both of them were drained to the point of unconsciousness, but neither of them had forgotten that there were enemies all around them, and both of them were too stubborn to pass out while the other one was still going. Eventually Sully mustered enough energy to speak. "Immortal, my ass."

Mol Kalath crackled and rumbled beneath her with amusement.

Tartalo got to them first but the gryphon wasn't far behind, dragging its trailing entrails. All of the haste had sapped out of them and the moment that they met, the scabrous giant crouched to scoop the mutilated bird-cat into his arms. He cradled the gryphon as he plodded out into the crater, groaning softly as the soft stone seared his flesh but pressing on anyway until he reached the epicenter of the blast. He had not spoken before, and though half of his skull was collapsed and smoldering, he managed to groan out a single word in a voice so deep that it made the ragged remains of Sully's dress quiver with the impact. "End?"

Heart aching, Sully forced herself back up onto her feet. "I can't. I need time. My reserves are . . . They're just gone. I need—"

"End?"

Mol Kalath stirred. Already the wounds on its flank were closing. The power within it was starting to swell and even across the empty space between them, Sully could feel it trickling across to her, too. "IT IS ONLY FAIR."

Sully scoffed. "You're a humanitarian now?"

"YOUR WORLD IS FULL OF OLD THINGS THAT NEED TO DIE SO THAT NEW THINGS CAN LIVE. WE CAN SET THEM FREE. WE CAN. SO WE MUST. THERE IS NOBODY ELSE."

"They just spent all night beating the shit out of me and one of them bit my fucking hand off. I'm not really in the mood to do them any favors."

Mol Kalath lumbered closer and nuzzled at her shoulder. Which she was pretty sure was dislocated. Again. "WILL YOU DO IT OUT OF FAVOR FOR ME?"

Sully sighed and let her head fall to rest on the fine feathers between the demon's six eyes. "How did my life turn into this?"

Sully took her time preparing the spell. In part to give herself time to regain her energy, but mostly to tweak it again so that it was less like the original, and less likely to leave her a hollowed-out husk. It was strange that in the midst of all the other pain her headache seemed the worst, but the first casting had taken more out of her than she would like to admit, and repetition always made the patterns that a spell burned into your brain more pronounced. She didn't think that she had lost any memories the first time, but would she remember if she had? She shook the thought away and continued her preparations.

The sun never rose over the swamp, not really, but hints of grayness were now spreading above them, blocked in part by the mountainous heap of the Hydra. Sully hadn't been able to fathom the logistical problem that killing the Hydra represented, but the moment it arrived it had lowered all its heads into the circle and now lay still. Sully cast a glance at the burned stubs of necks over by the shell and shrugged. She supposed that if anyone knew how to kill the Hydra it was probably the Hydra.

The demons began to arrive while she was still in the midst of casting, but with only a few soft words from Mol Kalath in their chittering tongue, they gathered silently around the outside of the circle to watch. Spreading its wings still seemed to pain Mol Kalath, but it stretched them out as wide as it could and pressed itself against Sully's back as she worked. At once power started to flow into her, far more than she would have guessed that her demon could have gathered from the drained space around them. It was only when she glanced back that she realized that Mol Kalath's wings were being held up by a half-dozen more demons. Through it, she could sense them. Through them she could feel the cumulative strength of every other demon that they touched.

When she had first studied demons, she had wondered how wishes were granted. The standard arguments were that another plane provided a better position to make changes, that probability was so skewed in the hells that great acts of magic were easier and that a demon was simply possessed of greater magical power than any mere mortal. No single demon could accomplish the changes that they made, but all of them could when their powers were combined. How such wild and chaotic creatures were capable of strategy and planning had always confused their human enemies, but now it seemed obvious. If they didn't work together, they couldn't work at all.

She took all the power that they offered until her reserves were swollen to bursting and spellfire was flooding out of her stump, her hand and her eyes in a torrent. She paused before she recited the final words of the spell. Looking one last time at the three endlings in the circle, she didn't know what to say, but her demon did. "GOODBYE."

The Inferno was no less impressive on its second casting, and it was completely fresh to the audience of demons that had gathered so there was a rush of gasps and wails from all around her as the pillar of light shot up once more. The fire burned brighter and longer than before thanks to the changes she had made, but they probably hadn't been necessary. When they had blinked away the dark strip in their vision, Sully and her allies peered past the smoke. At the edge of the circle, the many necks of the Hydra lay cauterized. Within the circle there was nothing but lava and a lingering smell of plasma.

This time, when she collapsed, arms and tentacles reached out to catch her and bear her back into Mol Kalath's warm embrace. She didn't know if demons slept, but Mol Kalath lay inert amidst its kin and once she was wrapped in those oily black wings and breathing in the smoky smells of its fine feathers Sully let shock and exhaustion carry her down into a brief respite from the pain.

NoVember 11, 2015

Gormlaith had a lot of opinions. Since the moment that Sully regained consciousness by the hearthside, wrapped up in furs and painstakingly coated in thick sticky bog mud, there had been a constant barrage of opinions on every aspect of her life. A vampire wasn't good enough for her. Was she sure men held no appeal whatsoever? She needed to take better care of herself, she wouldn't have half the scars she was carrying if she had just used the herbs she had been taught. Did she really have to call that nun a bitch when she was twelve? The fancy spells that she had learned at the Imperial College needed two hands to cast. What had she done to her beautiful hair? If she had just left her wrist unburned, they could have grown her a new hand. Sully let the old woman ramble as she stared into the fire and tried her best to let every one of the barbed words slide over her instead of taking hold. The poultice that her mother had wrapped around her left wrist stank of vinegar and cardamom, but she tolerated it because she was quite attached to the idea of not dying from a secondary infection after all that she had been through. Usually in the aftermath of a fight, Sully wanted a drink, or sex, or both simultaneously, but today cold seemed to have seeped into her. Like the Inferno had been inside her all these years, and now that she had let it loose, she had nothing to keep herself alight. She didn't know if she could face the army waiting for her outside, feeling as reduced as she did.

Hiding in her mother's cottage was a temporary solution, but the old witch was adept at keeping all of Sully's other problems at bay by being such an overwhelming nuisance that Sully couldn't focus on anything else. She had been awake for about four hours before she managed to sit up, and it was another hour before she could shoo her mother away long enough to get some clothes on. Everything that she had been wearing in the battle had been consigned to the fire, so she was in another of her mother's scratchy hand-me-downs until she could mooch a uniform or some real clothes from the American Expeditionary Force. The moment that she stepped outside, everyone was going to see her. The demons were insufferable gossips so there was no chance that the whole world didn't already know what she had done the night before, but she didn't know if her medical condition had been widely publicized.

After her naval service and her arrival in New Amsterdam, Sully had seen a lot of beggars missing pieces. Sometimes it was an arm or a leg. Sometimes it was something inside their head that they'd left behind on the battlefield. She would look at them with feigned empathy and drop spare change to them while thinking to herself that it could never have happened to her because she was stronger than they were. She would never let something like that happen, she had her magic, she had her wits, and she was made of sterner stuff than the pathetic beggars with medals pinned on their filthy over-coats. She stared intently at her stump once she was dressed. It was all wrapped up in bandages, not to help it heal, but to keep the con-coction that her mother had slathered on her while she slept from escaping. That was the logical reason, but Sully felt just as certain that the cloth was there to keep her wound out of sight, like it was something distasteful. When she went outside, nobody was going to see *her*, just the stump.

Sully didn't mind being hated. She'd come to expect it early in her life. Ever since the first nun had screamed the word *dyke* in her face. There was a kind of power in being hated—it was almost flattering to know that she was so important to someone that shouldn't have given a damn about her that they devoted so much energy and thought to loathing her. So hate was fine, but she didn't know what she was going to do with pity. It was worrying her. She liked to think that she knew herself pretty well by this point in her life, that she understood the intricacies of her own mind, but the first time she saw pity she didn't know if she was going to break down and cry or burn the face off whoever had dared to look at her that way.

She could just stay in the hut forever. Blackwood was conscious now. Still manacled and terrified looking, but mostly back in his original shape. He would never look at her with pity, just the bittersweet combination of awe and dread that had been pinned to his bruised face since Gormlaith had told him what had happened to his prized bounty hunters. Gormlaith herself would never look on Sully with pity. She wasn't even sure the old hag was capable of it. If she wanted to then, Sully could just hide in here until the British wished the whole war away. She would get her hand back if the world was reset, or she would be blinked out of existence. Either way, she wouldn't have to deal with the discomfort of the next few minutes.

She plucked another cigar out of the box on the mantle and lit it with a practiced flick of the wrist. They still stank to high heaven, but she was starting to get accustomed to the spicy undertones of the tarry tobacco. Shrouded in a cloud of blue smoke, she walked past her mother's back and stepped out into camp with a scowl already prepared.

She didn't make it far before a sullen silence descended over the gathered soldiers. A solid half of them were Magi, easily recognizable by their outdated clothes and the aura of power that hung around them. The actual soldiers of the American army were as ragtag a bunch of strangers as Sully had ever laid eyes on. Native Americans sat side by side with European rebels, passing around rolled-up cigarettes. Red-tanned Republicans laughed at the jokes of Indian volunteers. Tents had been raised across every dry patch of land, and walkways and rafts had been conjured in between them. The swamp still clung to twilight, but it was full of living people now, and it would never be able to go back to being a place of dread.

Ogden burst out of one of the tents and made a beeline for Sully, face pale beneath his bandana. He wrapped her in a bear hug that set every one of her injuries screaming and it was only pure stubbornness that stopped her from biting off his ear. Eventually he seemed to realize that she had gone stiff and let her go. "Apologies Sullivan, but tales of your tribulations precede you."

"Gossipy bitches." Sully muttered.

"The Hydra that you defeated is being harvested for resources as we speak, but I have heard tell that there were other fearsome foes?"

"Three of them. Bounty hunters for the British. They're all dealt with. You just can't find good help these days."

His eyes flickered down to where Sully had her arm cradled against her chest. "Would you like me to take a look at that? Or one of the other Magi?"

Sully sighed. There wasn't much pity there, not really. Underneath the bandana Ogden had some nasty scars of his own; maybe he understood how pity stung. "No, thank you. I had to cauterize it before I bled out and . . . I'm told there's nothing to be done."

He nodded gravely. "The finest magical healers in the world are at your disposal should you change your mind."

"Get me up to speed. What happened while I was fighting monsters and getting kidnapped?"

Ogden glanced around at the nearest soldiers, then led her back toward the oversized tent he had first popped out of. Maps drifted all around the enclosed space, putting Sully's little display with the globe earlier in the week to shame. Troop movements and supply lines were traced in bright colors over the topography, but the one that really caught Sully's attention was the map of Ireland hanging over a fold-out table. She stared at it while Ogden spoke, memorizing garrisons and redcoat emplacements. "The Fae incursion is continuing at the rate we previously discussed, and we are becoming more adept at discovering the wooden decoys that they have left behind. In areas with high concentrations of loyalists to the Empire, the hunt has been seriously impeded by the lack of trust but it has been decided that the magnitude of the situation would be likely to overwhelm the public were it made known."

"It has been decided. By Pratt." Sully grumbled.

"Yes, but I am forced to agree with his assessment. When my people faced this foe, we didn't even know their name. We shared every whisper and rumor, and the result was pure panic. I would rather not live to see the ensuing chaos on a larger scale."

"If we spend all our time lying, how are we any better than the British?"

Ogden's smirk made it to his eyes, crinkling their corners. "Because we are not trying to rewrite all of existence to obliterate people—who happened to have some very valid objections to our system of government—from existence in a mad power grab to conquer the world by allying ourselves with eldritch nightmare creatures from the furthest planes of existence?"

"Okay, they might have lost the moral high ground, but I still don't like it. What's next? Casting taboos on subjects we don't like?" Sully flicked a finger over the map, expanding some parts and fading others into the background.

"Perhaps we can worry about saving ourselves from imminent annihilation, and we'll concern ourselves with transparency after the fighting is done?"

"Yeah, you're right. Soldiers don't deserve to know what they're dying for."

"Sullivan, is there a reason that you are being even more argumentative than usual?"

Sully took a deep breath. "I saw the way that they were looking at me out there. I was worried that they were going to be . . . you know, with my hand . . . but what I saw out there is worse. They're expecting me to save them, Ogden. They're looking at me like I'm going to cast a spell and make it all go away."

"Heavy is the head that bears the crown." Ogden chuckled. "To be fair to them, there is precedent. Every insurmountable crisis that you have faced seems to have—"

"They're going to die, Ogden. Not all of them. Not many of them, if I have my way. But I'm going to have to give the orders and send them off to die. That's how wars work."

Ogden was too polite to look contemptuous, so he merely looked pained. "Not to be too harsh with your delicate sensibilities, but isn't that part of your job description?"

"I didn't want this job. Pratt blackmailed me into it. You should know, you were in the room where it happened."

"I do seem to recall some tension. And some head-butting."

The fond memory of Pratt bleeding brought a little smile to Sully's face. "I've been in an army before. I'm not officer material. I can't make the choices you need to make, not for other people. I've tried but . . ."

"Sullivan, I rather suspect that your fear of harming your soldiers is why the Prime Minister entrusted this task to you. And why your men follow you so willingly. They know that you will not spend their lives without necessity. That you would put yourself between them and the enemy muskets if given the chance."

Sully flicked the map with her finger and it zoomed back out to show the whole world, flattened out and crisscrossed with lines of longitude and latitude. London sat at the center of the map, the whole world revolving around it.

"We need to take the Archive. It all hinges on that. But without our demons I can't see us getting past the city's magical defenses. We are too vulnerable to artillery spells in the air, and street-to-street fighting in unfamiliar territory is like signing your own death warrant."

Ogden cleared his throat. "On that subject . . ."

Sully glanced at him. Ogden spent every moment floating along on a cloud of his own self-importance, so to see him looking awkward was surprising, to say the least. After everything that had happened, Sully had almost forgotten. "Oh, Pratt finally asked you to kill me? Not surprising, really. You saw the soldiers out there, desperate for a hero. Pratt can't have any heroes, especially ones that hate him. Not if he wants to hang onto control of the Americas. Besides, we're about to head out onto the battlefield, easy for accidents to happen there. Have you decided what you want to do?"

He stuffed his hands into the pockets of his greatcoat and looked around the tent to avoid her eye. "When I first arrived back in this world I was a little lost, and more than willing to align myself with this man and all the friends around the world that he brought with him, but having spent some time in his company and seen the under-handed way that he conducts himself, I must admit that the prospect no longer seems quite so appealing. I know that you have no political aspirations, but I wonder if it might not help my own campaign to have the hero of the War of Independence's endorsement. After the fighting is over, of course."

"So what, if I endorse you, you won't try to kill me?"

He flushed. "That wasn't my—I mean—I have some honor—I—I have no intention of doing you any harm, I was merely—" He finally noticed Sully grinning. "Ah, you are making fun. I see."

She held out her hand to him. "Nobody would be happier to see Pratt out on his ass."

He shook it and Sully felt the magic coursing through him, just under his skin. So close that she could just reach out and take it. She pulled her hand away abruptly, then turned back to the map. "We need to secure our position and our supply line before we do any-thing else. That should give us some time to think on our two pressing problems."

"The wish holding back our demonic allies and . . ."

"The Fae abducting all of our bloody civilians."

"Ah, yes."

After a couple of hours, Gormlaith came in with a pot of tea and a pair of clay cups. Sully and Ogden took them, mumbled thanks and then went back to poring over their plans. When she left the tent, she was grinning so broadly that it gave the poor soldier on guard the fright of his life.

When she returned later with bowls of stew, Ogden had collapsed onto a folding chair and maps blown up to show the terrain of each great city in Ireland were orbiting Sully. She was barking out instructions and Ogden was taking notes. Through a shimmering image of Limerick College, Sully caught a glimpse of her mother and stopped speaking so abruptly that Ogden startled to his feet. "Ah, thank you, kind woman. And my thanks once again for allowing us to make camp here on your property. It is most appreciated."

Gormlaith rolled her eyes and handed Sully a stack of papers along with the bowl. "Just doing my part, Magus."

After Sully was certain that the old woman was gone, she handed her bowl of stew off to Ogden and started rifling through the painstaking handwritten notes that she had just inherited. Resistance cells. Weapons caches. Embedded agents. Troop movements. Secret passages. Smugglers dens. She read through the names and the numbers with the strangest sense of déjà vu. This was the army that Gormlaith had always meant for her to lead. These were the people who had spent decades positioning themselves to drive the British out, without ever hearing the call to arms. Sully flicked an ember from her finger and incinerated the plans that she and Ogden had spent the afternoon preparing, then started barking out a new plan so rapidly that he dropped their dinner.

By evening Sully was hoarse and exhausted, but she still stopped by the quartermaster before turning in. She politely declined the offer of a hook for her left arm, but she let him take a quick measurement and then add a stitch to that sleeve to fold over the cuff and keep the damage hidden.

The uniform was unisex, which was to say, it was stiff men's clothing that she was much happier to wear than her mother's old dresses. The details of it screamed of Pratt's personal involvement in the design. That man loved his tailor more than he loved hot meals and it reeked of his sense of drama. Sully probably would have preferred something more camouflaged than the rich navy blue with gold trim, but beggars couldn't be choosers.

She carried it with her to one of the Manhattanite healers, who dealt with the worst of the burns, bruises, contusions and cuts from the day before, leaving fresh scars all over her. There weren't many people in the world who could boast gryphon and Fury claw marks, so she was vaguely proud of her new additions. The healer had undone the bandages around her wrist and confirmed Gormlaith's assessment that regrowth would have been possible if she hadn't sealed the wound. A freezing touch of healing magic finished the process of scarring, chased away the last of the pain, and left Sully with a nice smooth nub at the end of her arm where she used to have a hand. She tried very hard not to think about it and thanked the healer for a job well done.

There wasn't much clean water in the middle of a swamp, but the rain barrel around the back of Gormlaith's house was still half full so she used that to scrub herself as clean as possible. It had been easy when she was a child and even easier as a teenager when she was tall enough to reach inside without the assistance of the peat stack, but now the experience was slow and clumsy. The cold water numbed her fingers and made everything feel distant. The new scars didn't feel real as she scrubbed the mud away. Sully had spent the first decade of adulthood in unisex barracks and the cramped confines of crew quarters on British dreadnoughts. Usually it didn't bother her when men strolled past while she was getting dressed. Something about her reputation and the mess of scars tended to keep them from ogling, and it wasn't like any of them were a threat to her. Yet this time she felt exposed as she fumbled with the stiff new buttons and buckles of her uniform. It was only once the new jacket slipped over her stump that she realized why. She saved her hair for last so that it would stay slicked back for longer before curling.

The overall look seemed to have the desired impact when she walked in on Blackwood, perched on a stool by the hearth. He didn't see his hostage or a silly little girl with a head full of romantic notions. He was face to face with the highest-ranking military officer in the American Alliance. He drew himself up to his full height and nodded gravely. Sully held his stare as she crossed the room and she was ever so slightly gratified to watch him flinch when she got within punching distance. With a jerk of her hand and a twist of low magic, Sully spun a second stool across the floor to stop in front of him and sat down with a grunt. "I want you to tell me how you are summoning the Fae into the Americas."

"No."

Sully blinked. "I'm sorry, did you misunderstand me? Did you think I was asking if you wanted a nice cup of tea?"

"I will not be intimidated by any thug in a uniform. I am a Lord of His Majesty's privy council and I will not tolerate this treatment."

"Oh, I'm sorry, are you feeling threatened?" Sully smirked.

"You beat me within an inch of my life—as you are well aware—and while I imagine that only one side of my face would be struck this time around, I must warn you that the ratification of Irish independence came with several conditions. The first and foremost of which was my fair treatment and safety. You cannot torture the information out of me because it would be a breach of the contract that your mother and I agreed on, forcing your infernal allies back out of this horrible backwater faster than you could blink. So when you ask me a question, I have as much right to decline to answer as any other man. And so I decline. No. I shall not help you to interfere with my life's work any more than you already have. My arrangement with the Fair Folk stands. My wishes shall be fulfilled and the world shall take shape as it is meant to. No amount of foot stomping and petulance on your part will change that. All of this is just a temporary delay before an eternity of victory. You shall not take that from me."

Sully's smile hadn't faded, but it had taken on a very brittle appearance. "You aren't going to win. I can promise you that much. I'm going to leave in the morning, I'm going to go wage a little war across this beautiful island and then hop over to jolly old England next. And you are going to be stuck here with my mother. Now she might not look like much anymore, but old Gormlaith O'Sullivan has a mean streak in her about a mile wide. If it looks like I'm going to lose, she isn't going to care about treaties or safe passage. She isn't going to care about honor and gentlemen's arrangements. She is just going to flay the flesh from your bones with hellfire and then go have herself another cup of tea. Either I win this war, and you get to go home to a broken empire, or I lose this war, and you lose everything."

"I will be restored to my former glory once you are defeated." His stiff upper lip tremored.

Sully smirked. "That isn't how it works though, is it? I had a long time to think about all the things you told me to mess with my head while I was waiting for your interrogator to come back and I've realized why I don't give a shit. They weren't me—those other Sullys that you wiped out of existence—I'm me. And you're you. If some other bigwig wishes all of this away while you are out here instead of in your magic library of eternal boredom, you're going to blink out of existence too. Sure, there might be somebody wearing your face and name tag, wandering around doing paperwork in the world after the wish, but it won't be you anymore. You'll be dead and gone."

"I—"

Sully cut him off before he could start. "Why don't you sleep on it? I realize that betraying the Empire that has done nothing but use you for your whole life is a big decision. We can talk in the morning."

She tossed her stool back into a corner full of bric-a-brac and strolled back out to find a tent. She'd already spent more time back in Gormlaith's house than she had ever planned to in this lifetime and now that she wasn't feeling so vulnerable, she was a little concerned that the next of her mother's opinions was going to be met with her blowing the walls off of the place.

NOVEMBER 15, 2015

The redcoats attacked just before the gray thing that could be called dawn. Sully was stirred from a dream of beaks grinding on bones by a whistle going up from the sentries. It started to the north of the camp, then the next sentry picked it up at a slightly higher pitch, then the next, then the next, so that by the time it got back to the first one it felt like they were encircled by one long continuous harmony. Sully was up and into her new boots so fast that it scared the Magus opposite her awake too. She had just enough time to snap "Raid!" before the artillery started to rain down on them. A huge serpent made from crackling green lightning crashed down into the camp, making anyone its sparks discharged into start retching until a Magus caught it in a glowing sphere and launched it straight up into the sky to illuminate the battlefield.

More spells were raining down, but now that the American forces were roused, veils and screens were being conjured up to catch the worst of them. Sully realized that she didn't have an assigned position on the perimeter line a moment before she ran toward it. The Magi had torn up a trench of the sodden earth and thrown it straight at the charging British before ducking down inside. The soldiers without magic slipped into that trench with a comfort that came from a great deal of practice. Sully wondered how many of those trenches had been ripped out of the turf of upstate New Amsterdam before this troop had shipped out. Their Gatling guns started to chatter, a steady percussion underneath the more dramatic overtures of the spells being flung back and forth.

Sully spun on the spot, letting her ears do the heavy lifting of understanding the battle in progress. There was gunfire all around and the roar of magic along with it. The British were attacking them on all sides, giving them no way out. They obviously planned to crush the expeditionary force in one blow. Sully grinned. Being underestimated was always a treat.

Most of the Magi were still close to the center of the camp, preparing spells too complex to risk interruption, so Sully left them and Ogden to their own devices and started to return fire on the artillery positions. It was easy enough to follow the angles of attack back from where they impacted on the translucent dome above her and suddenly out there in the dark expanse beyond the lights of camp there was light as her white fire lanced down, shattering defenses and blinding the enemy casters as they tried to adjust their aim. Sully was far from thorough, but she didn't have to kill or blind every one of them. She had an army for that. All that she needed to do was buy enough time for the Magi to do something spectacular.

With the element of surprise lost, redcoats began traveling by magic right into the middle of camp, appearing amidst the tents with tiny thunderclaps that led Sully straight to them. The ones that she caught by surprise went down with just a single spell, but the lucky few who appeared facing her had a chance. One went for a saber, which ended his chances pretty abruptly as a dart of flame went right through his gut. The next one actually got a spell off. A crackling purple dart that Sully caught in a spellfire-wreathed hand and flung right back at him, turning him into a lichen.

One appeared inside a tent. That one had enough time to snap up some defenses before Sully arrived, and then things got interesting. Sully's first blast was deflected and the flaming whip that followed it up got entangled in some sort of arcane squid that the redcoat called out of thin air. Dispelling her own magic and snapping its strange glassy tentacles with little blasts of ice, Sully ducked behind the questionable cover of another tent and prepared her vengeance. White fire snapped out in a line, parallel to the ground, and whatever shields the redcoat had wrapped around himself didn't do much more than contain his liquid remains once the fire had passed through them. She gave that gory puddle a contemptuous salute before the next round of thunderclaps sent her off again.

Sully was efficient in her brutality. She husbanded her strength, but even as she paced herself, it became clear that the well of her strength was going to run dry long before the British reinforcements stopped coming. She whistled once, shrill, in between casting vicious little darts of roiling black smoke to choke the redcoats who crossed her path.

She could feel Mol Kalath nearby. It was flying with the other demons and snatching spells out of the sky to add to its mass. This was like a feast for the magic-starved demons and they were gorging happily as they protected the camp from the worst of the bombardment. Mol Kalath swooped low over Sully and she raised her hand and let its tail feathers discharge raw magic back into her depleted reserves. She blew her demon a kiss before engulfing a trio of unlucky redcoats in a torrent of flames. She could get used to this.

A cluster of the redcoats had managed to pull together within the camp, near to the latrines. Fewer than ten of them, as far as Sully could make out through the opaque shields they had thrown up. They started to bombard the perimeter at a steady pace. Sully could almost hear the regular beat of the drum from basic training, the steady pacing of suppressing fire.

Since the fighting had started, there had been a regular staccato of gunfire, but now it ground to a halt as the soldiers took cover. Mud slumped into the trenches, burying men alive. The rush of water carried the noxious spells out to touch the few who still had the wherewithal to crawl away.

Flashes of light. First irregular, then a strobing nightmare that made it look like the world was moving in slow motion. One after another, the layers of the redcoats' shields were stripped away by the lashes of white fire coiling out of Sully's hands, but there were too many of them. The redcoats didn't even slow their bombardment. Sully threw shields up to intercept their spells. Again, she was too slow to catch them all. Once the perimeter was gone, the redcoats out there in the swamp could sweep in. The Magi would never have a chance to cast whatever monstrosity they were concocting.

Sully opened her mouth to cast once more, the Inferno on the tip of her tongue. Then she paused. She didn't have to win this war alone. Her whistle didn't reach Mol Kalath up in the clouds, but there were plenty of demons who were closer. The one who landed bodily on the redcoat's shields and absorbed them with a gulp looked like the misbegotten issue of a hairless bear and a crocodile, with a moth's dusty wings hammering away on its back trying to keep something so impossibly huge in the air. When the demon took off, the redcoats only had time to catch a glimpse of Sully's grin before a whip of flame tore through their ranks at waist height. The bisected corpses toppled to the ground, bloodless and cauterized. Sully cackled. This was what war was meant to be. This was glorious.

Reserves nearly spent again, Sully reached out to draw in more magic from the air, only to find it missing, already consumed by the great tangle of magic in the middle of camp. The Magi's spells cascaded out across the battlefield, each one hitting the next and sending it on with more force than the last, like dominoes of raw power. A mist rose up from the swamp and clung to the British, soaking into their uniforms, seeping into their gear. Lightning rushed out across the field, leaping from redcoat to redcoat and leaving everyone in that uniform who hadn't shielded themselves blackened and dead. Those that had shielded themselves had it worse. Those the lightning clung to and danced over. If they moved, it shocked them, and if any of their allies came too close, it leapt out to strike them down. Sully was impressed by the cruelty of it.

Silence fell over the battlefield, the mists muffling any sound so that all the cheers and chatter from her soldiers seemed to be coming from another room. Sully staggered to the nearest trench and started dispelling what she could of the damage until her magic ran dry and she had to snatch up a shovel to help pull the last of the buried gunners out. It was tiring work and the stump at the end of her left arm started to ache as she used it to lever the shovel. The Magi were celebrating behind her and Ogden was amongst them, whooping at their victory. Sully kept working until she was certain that the still-buried men were dead and beyond rescue.

The mist took half an hour to die down after that. Then the regular soldiers that had survived the trenches climbed back down into them, waded through the mud, and came up on the far side with grim expressions on their faces and bayonets screwed to their guns. It didn't take them long to finish off any redcoats that were left standing. They were back to camp in time for breakfast, but most of them looked like they had lost their appetites.

Mol Kalath fluttered down to land beside Sully where she stood staring out into the swamps. It had doubled in size overnight. "THEY FIELDED ONLY FIVE OF THE ONES YOU CALL MAGI. MY KIN MADE A MEAL OF THEM BEFORE I COULD INTERVENE."

Sully shrugged. "Good job, Magus eaters, I guess?"

Mol Kalath cocked its head to one side. "YOU APPROVE?"

"I wouldn't have eaten them, personally. But they'd have been just as dead if I'd done it my way."

It blinked all of its eyes at her and cooed. "YOU LOOK WELL, SHADOW-TWIN."

"I'm feeling more like myself again." Sully grinned, then slowly the smile slipped off her face and her brows drew down. Mol Kalath leaned in a little closer then jerked back in alarm when Sully bellowed, "Sentries, sound off!"

The whistles went off again, one after the other, and Sully felt the hairs on the back of her neck standing up. She grabbed at Mol Kalath and whispered, "Did you feel that?"

"WHAT?"

"The circle."

She yelled again. "Sound off!"

This time she watched Mol Kalath. Watched its feathers shiver as it felt the circle being drawn around it with sound.

She pointed to the nearest edge of camp and snapped, "Try it."

Mol Kalath took flight and Sully yelled to her sentries once more. "Sound off and keep it going!"

She ran beneath the demon as it flew, until she was close enough to the nearest sentry to see the perplexed look on his face and the blood oozing from the wound on his cheek. Her demon hit the invisible barrier above them and flapped frantically to right itself. Sully grinned. "That'll do, sentries. Good job!"

She caught Mol Kalath on a buffeting cloud and eased it to the ground. It lay there, the deep rumble of its laughter rolling out through the churned mud below it. "A CIRCLE MADE OF SOUND."

"A circle we can't see!"

She crashed into Ogden as she rushed into the map tent and sent the far bigger man staggering back. "I've solved it."

He was flustered for a moment, but then he drifted over to watch as she re-centered the maps on the Americas. She patted the pockets of her uniform absentmindedly then held out her hand without looking back. "Phone."

Ogden pursed his scarred lips under the bandana but handed his prized cell phone over without complaint. She dialed rapidly, then put it on speaker and set it down on the table.

On the ninth ring, Raavi answered. "Hello, this is Doctor Sharma."

"Holy shit, is that how you answer the phone when you don't know it's me?"

"Sully, my dear? How are you? The last that I heard, you were missing and presumed dead."

"Sorry to disappoint, I'm still breathing, despite the best efforts of practically everyone I meet."

He let out a little snort. "To what do I owe the pleasure of this call?"

"Uh, I actually just need you to turn on the radio and shut up for a few minutes."

"You really are a horrendous bitch, you know that?"

She smiled. "It's come up before, yes."

There was a loud clunk as he dropped the phone, but a moment later there was a crackle of static that resolved itself into a series of numbers, being read out in a cultured English accent. Now that she knew what she was listening to, Sully could recognize the monotone voice of a Magus. As the numbers were read out, Sully found the corresponding co-ordinates on the map and marked it with a spot of spellfire. With each number, she added another spot and before five minutes were out, those dots were getting close enough that the spellfire was licking out to join them together. Anyone could see that it made a circle that surrounded a good portion of the Americas, but only someone who knew about the abductions and the stocks would know the significance of the circle's position. Ogden let out a groan when he saw it, which prompted Raavi to pick up his phone. "What the hell was that, Sully? Was that a man? Have you switched teams on me? Am I playing you tunes to set the mood?"

"Shut up, Raavi. I just solved your stupid number station."

"Oh! Oh! Tell me. I can be the coolest kid on all my conspiracy theory websites. That's like being the *least* cool kid everywhere else. I could be on the coolness spectrum!"

"Probably classified information."

"That's even better! You have to tell me. I helped you, Sully. You owe me for turning on the radio and shutting up. You know how much I hate shutting up."

"Thanks for your help, Raavi. I'll catch you later."

"No. Sully, no. Don't hang up on me you absolute bi—"

She handed the phone back to a bemused Ogden. "Friend of yours?"

"Yeah, he is, actually." Sully's smile was so genuine that Ogden was taken aback.

"We need to call Pratt. He is going to need to get a technologist to help shut down those radio signals. I remember something from the navy. Some sort of blocker or jammer that they used when we were fighting the Mongols in the forests. The tech is out there, he just needs to get it up and running before the Fae grab anyone else."

She paused. "Can you get me another phone? I've got another quick call to make while you talk to his Highness."

In less than a minute: "Hey, darlin'."

Sully smiled softly. "You answer every call like that? Do I need to get jealous?"

"I think your claim's safe. Just don't have many callers." Marie should have laughed. Deep and rich as butter. It should have run right down the back of Sully's neck and made her purr. Instead, she could picture Marie sitting hunched over on her parents' sofa, face pinched, trying to be positive for Sully. "To what do I owe the pleasure of this call?"

"Never had a girl to write home to when I was off to war the last time. Guess I'm making up for lost time."

"I ain't too proud to admit I was worrying about you. Never thought I'd see you in the arms of another woman again. Especially not some naked angel with pointy teeth and tiny tits."

Sully chuckled. "You know you're the only girl for me."

There was a long pause. "Well, darlin', just for my peace of mind . . . You killed her, right?"

"Nothing left but ashes."

"That's what I like to hear." There was a gentle huff of breath on the other end of the line. Maybe a sigh. "How's that war going, darlin'? You coming home to me soon?"

"Soon as I can. Listen, there are some things I need to tell you in case I don't get a chance later. Your mother, I'll do what I can to get her back. She isn't the only one who's been taken and I don't think the chances are good of her coming back in one piece. I need you to be ready for that."

Marie wasn't crying when she whispered, "All right."

Sully took a deep breath. "If something goes wrong, if I'm too hurt to get back to you right away, talk to Ceejay at the Bureau. He'll help

you get out before Pratt remembers about you. He'll get you somewhere safe."

"That ain't going to happen, darlin'."

"Of course not. But just in case, there's some money in a safe in the
bedroom. The combination is your birthday. That will see you set up
somewhere, give you a month or two to find your feet."

"I ain't going to need it, darlin'."

"Of course not. But it makes me feel better to know you'd be taken
care of."

Marie's voice grew softer. "You're the one who's got to take care of
me. Money and plans ain't going to help none if you don't come back
in one piece."

Sully stared down at the abrupt ending of her left arm and felt her
eyes burning. "I'll try to get back to you with all the important parts
attached. Can't promise much more."

Sully could hear Ogden coming back, surrounded by a cloud of
attendant Magi. "Listen, I've got to go. I love you."

"Love you too, darlin'. Don't go doing anything stupid."

Sully grinned. "Me? Never."

Sully didn't gamble. There were enough risks in her life that she
didn't feel the need for the artificial rush of squandering her cash on
mathematically solvable games. Even so, she would have been willing to bet that the moment the signal was blocked, the abductions
had stopped. Of course, there was no way to be sure, so she was left
in limbo all day while she and Ogden took turns handing out orders
to the units that they had patched together out of their remaining
troops. Constables and the IBI were still scouring the Americas for
new stocks, but even if they found them, there was no way to know
when the damned things had arrived. It was infuriating. She wanted
to know that she had won. She wanted to know that the Fae weren't
going to get their hands on anyone else.

By sunset she was almost vibrating with pent up energy, and
every discussion turned into a screaming argument. The British
would be in disarray after their failed attack, with nearly every

redcoat in the whole of Ireland spent, and Sully was in favor of pushing that advantage and seizing cities as soon as possible. Ogden had
more conservative plans. They had a solid position here, one that
would be hard to assault, and he intended to use it as a command
center to coordinate the arrival of the troops that their allies around
the world had promised to commit. He was used to the slow pace
of wartime logistics from his own time. Sully was not. She had a
sneaking suspicion that if any of their so-called allies had had any
intention of sending bodies for the meat grinder, then they would
have already arrived. Meanwhile, she knew that she could build up
a militia out of pissed-off Irishmen within a couple of days and have
them trained and ready for use within a week.

Adding to her frustration was the nasty suspicion that this was
all her mother's idea. Every time she caught sight of Gormlaith as
she dithered around, delivering tea and soup to the soldiers, the old
woman gave her an approving nod. That nod was almost enough to
convince Sully that she was on the wrong side. If her mother wanted to
turn left, Sully's gut told her to turn right. It wasn't that the old woman
was manipulative—not any more than the ocean was wet—she would
just calmly and quietly lay out information and the conclusions that
you reached happened to be the same ones that she had come to before
the conversation even started.

When the wave of magic rolled over the camp, the regular soldiers
didn't notice, but every demon and Magus suddenly leapt to attention. The ambient magic had been sapped pretty thoroughly by all of
the spells being flung around the day before and the demons had a
habit of soaking up the rest, but suddenly it felt like the whole world
was recharged. Sully and Ogden stopped bickering and stared at each
other. "What the hell was that?"

Ogden shivered. "It feels like . . . It feels like Manhattan all over
again. The purity of it. Like the source of magic just leapt closer."

"There's no way that's good news."

"None whatsoever."

Seconds later the radio operators came barreling out of their tent screaming for attention, and the few Magi who had been trying to get past the blocks on scrying on London were doing the same. Ogden tried to guide them toward a private conversation in their tent, but Sully stood her ground with them in the middle of the camp. "These men were willing to die for us. They deserve to know what's happening."

"Sullivan, now is not the time for—"

She pointed at the closest radio operator. "What happened?"

He glanced nervously from Sully to the glowering Magus at her back, then mumbled, "I'm not sure."

Sully growled. "You seemed pretty damned sure when you came wailing out of that tent. Now talk."

"London is out of British control. I mean they're fighting something in London. They broke radio silence. They're trying to withdraw all their troops back to England. All of them, from everywhere in the Empire. They're abandoning India. Abandoning Hong Kong. Everything."

One of the Magi interrupted. "There is a portal in the center of London. It was heavily veiled against scrying. Even the name of the building is under a taboo but it has all been stripped away in the rush of power."

"The Archive." Sully nodded.

"Perhaps so. This portal seems to be the source of the sudden influx of magic, but that isn't the only thing that's coming through."

"Deaf ears is what my warnings fell on." Gormlaith croaked from amidst the crowd and every head turned. "The Fair Folk care nothing for trade, they've no honor to keep, they'll just take what they want. Every choice you make has consequences, girl. Didn't I tell you?"

Sully gritted her teeth. "Bring me Blackwood."

Ogden, Gormlaith and Blackwood stood awkwardly in the midst of the press of bodies as a terrified bureaucrat that Ogden had portaled in frantically typed by lantern light beside them. Mol Kalath had been selected to represent the demons, but it seemed more intent on clinging to Sully than on speaking. She was forced to tangle her fingers in its feathers to stop it nudging at her. Even then, she could feel it vibrating beneath her hand. A circle of soldiers and Magi surrounded them, horror painted on their faces. A familiar horror to the Magi who had lived through Manhattan's banishment to the Far Realms and a fresh horror for the soldiers who didn't yet know that there was a whole universe of other planes out there. A whole universe filled with things that wanted them dead or worse.

Sully tried to keep her voice steady, but she could still remember the moments that she had spent with just one of the Fae. She couldn't imagine the horrors that London was experiencing right now. "With their supply of fresh captives cut off, the Fae have broken through the Archive and are invading London. From there they will spread like locusts across the entire world."

Mol Kalath spoke as softly as its anatomy allowed. "WE FLED TO ESCAPE THEIR INCURSIONS, AND THOSE WERE FEW AND FAR BETWEEN. THE FAE HAVE SHAPED OUR SHARED HISTORY. THEY DROVE US FROM OUR HOME WITH NOTHING BUT THE THREAT OF THEIR TOUCH. THEY DROVE US TO SEEK YOU OUT, TO SELL YOU THE BOUNTY OF OUR POWER FOR A CHANCE AT ESCAPE. IF THEY HAVE FOUND A PATH TO YOU, THEN HUMANITY IS DONE."

Gormlaith crooned. "British called up what they can't put down. Always knew they'd kill me. Never knew they'd kill us all."

"My underlings will have attempted to negotiate a new arrangement when the summoning circle around the Americas was interrupted. It is possible that they were not entirely briefed on the correct protocol and on the reason that we do not invite the Fae directly onto our plane. They may have been overpowered and forced to open the portal back to London, but surely the city's defenses will be more than enough to contain—"

Sully cut Blackwood off with a glare. "The British troops on the ground are being pushed out of London, or slaughtered wholesale. The Fae aren't interested in renegotiating. They don't care about deals. They just wanted a way in and now they've got that."

He sank into sullen silence then begrudgingly nodded when he realized nobody else was going to speak. Sully pointed to the secretary. "Papers are getting drawn up. You are going to surrender, and as part of that surrender the mainland of Britain is going to become Irish territory. Not American. Irish. After this situation is dealt with, you can negotiate with the Irish provisional government to have it handed back to you."

Blackwood bristled but he said nothing. Sully grimaced. "There aren't going to be any more wishes. Not now. Not ever. The game of empires is over for all of you. The world we've got now is the only one we're ever going to have, and I'm not going to let you throw it away over a bad dream that is already over." She held out her hand. "If we move now, there is a chance we can contain them before it's too late. They're bottlenecked in the Archive. If we hit them there and close the path, we can end this. What do you say? Want to go down in history as the man who saved the world?"

He stared down for a long time, then lifted his own manacled hands to take a hold of Sully's.

"We shall be keeping our foreign territories and I will expect the negotiations after the fighting is done to acknowledge the sacrifices being made by the British Empire right now. Reparations shall have to be paid to the Empire from all parties, as you are all complicit in creating this situation."

Sully tightened her grip until he winced. "Don't worry. You'll get exactly what you deserve."

A Magus conjured a table and the frantic typing of the legal secretary that Ogden had dragged from New Amsterdam ground to a halt. The treaty she had been preparing was slapped down in front of them. Only a few soldiers were stupid enough to cheer when Blackwood scribbled his signature at the bottom. The war wasn't over. It was just getting started.

Sully uncuffed Blackwood and passed off the manacles to one of the few technologists that the army had managed to recruit. That poor woman was set to the task of breaking them down and melting them into bullets. They wouldn't make many, but any weapon that was guaranteed to kill the Fae was worth investing time in. The whole camp was a flurry of action as Ogden barked out new orders and started the arduous prep work for the portals that would send them into battle.

Sully laid out the basics of their strategy with Blackwood at her elbow, poring over the map of London, overlaid with the amorphous red blob of lost territory updated in real time by the radio operators and scrying Magi. A good quarter of central London—what Blackwood insisted was the original city—was already red. Judging from the reports, the Fae were snatching up civilians and combatants alike. Vanishing back down to their home plane once enough had been gathered. Travel down through the planes toward the source was relatively painless compared to the difficulty of making a dimensional breach in the other direction, or so the Magi conveying the intelligence said. The Fae didn't need to hold the territory; any humans that rushed into it were just making the next round of abductions faster. Faeries were only spreading when the streets that they had claimed were stripped of life. Once the bare bones of a plan were laid out, Sully pushed her way past all the officers and tag-alongs until she was outside. There was a pull deep in her stomach that led her through the crowds until Mol Kalath came into sight. It was lurking in the shadow of Gormlaith's cottage, which had somehow weathered the morning's battle without a scratch.

"GREETINGS, SHADOW-TWIN."

Sully closed the artificial distance that she had been holding between them and did what she had wanted to from the start, rubbing a hand along the side of the demon's beak. Soothing the tremors running through it. "Hey, big bird. How're you doing?"

"I AM WELL, SHADOW-TWIN. I HUNGER FOR THIS BATTLE. I HUNGER FOR SLAUGHTER." Demonic voices did not quaver the way that a human's might, but there was a stiffness in Mol Kalath's guttural growl that was unfamiliar.

"You're shitting yourself?"

The demon cocked its head to one side. "THIS BODY I HAVE FORGED CANNOT—"

"I mean, you're scared."

It puffed up its feathers. "FEAR? WE ARE THE VANGUARD OF HELL. WE FEAR NOTHING."

"You literally fled your own plane of existence to get away from these guys . . ." Sully trailed off.

"THAT WAS NOT FEAR. THAT WAS . . . IT WAS . . ."

"It's all right. I'm not going to tell anyone."

Its feathers smoothed down suddenly, slimming its profile until it was only three times the size of the first time Sully had seen it. "MY KIN WISH TO LEAVE. THEY BELIEVE THAT THE RARE BREACHES THAT THE PALE ONES MAKE INTO OUR HOME HELLS WILL BE EASIER TO ENDURE THAN WHAT IS COMING HERE."

Sully sighed. "They're probably right."

"SOME WISH TO FLEE NOW. OTHERS WISH TO GRANT YOU A WARNING FIRST. A LAST FACTION WISH TO OFFER YOUR KIND SHELTER IN THE HELLS. THOUGH THEY ARE FEW IN NUMBER."

"And what about you?" She tugged at its feathers, turning its eyes to face her.

"I DO NOT RUN."

Sully laughed. "Okay, maybe you are me."

"AS I HAVE ALWAYS SAID."

A group of soldiers rushed by, hauling crates of ammunition to the portal stations that were being set up under Gormlaith's watchful stare. Once they were past, Sully pressed her forehead to Mol Kalath's. Its voice vibrated through her. "DEMONS ARE NOT LIKE YOU. WE ARE ETERNAL. IF WE DO NOT STAND HERE THEN WE WILL ALWAYS BE RUNNING UNTIL THERE IS NOWHERE LEFT TO RUN. WE HAVE ALREADY SPENT AN ETERNITY ALONE WITH THE PALE ONES, JUST WAITING FOR THE TIME WHEN WE

ARE THE ONES THAT THEY TAKE." The demon's shaking stopped abruptly. "NOW, FOR THE FIRST TIME, WE ARE NOT ALONE. WE STAND TOGETHER, IONA. DEMONS AND HUMANS. YOU AND I. WE ARE STRONGER AS ONE."

Sully leaned back. "Think you can convince some of your demon buddies of that?"

Mol Kalath wheezed and crackled with laughter again. "SOME, PERHAPS."

"Then tell the rest that they're free to go. This is a volunteer army."

The demon took a step back to look her up and down. "MERE HOURS BEFORE YOU WADE INTO BATTLE, YOU STILL LET MORALITY GUIDE YOUR COURSE. YOU WOULD LET THE ADVANTAGE OF HAVING A COHORT OF DEMONS AT YOUR BACK PASS YOU BY?"

"There's no advantage in having an army you can't trust. If they don't want to be here, they'll find a way not to be, quick enough, and then my battle plans will have a hole in them big enough to drive a train through."

"YOU TWIST EVERY VIRTUE INTO A SIN. YOU ARE NO CYNIC, IONA. I HAVE SEEN HOW YOU LOOK AT THESE SOL-DIERS. THEY ARE LIKE YOUR CHILDREN."

"Even when you dress them up in uniforms and hand them weap-ons, they're just people." Sully smirked. "Which means they'll fuck up as much as humanly possible and then expect me to pick up after them. I suppose that isn't much different from children."

Ogden cleared his throat behind her. "Sullivan, we are ready to begin."

Mol Kalath took flight and, as Sully watched, it rose up in a great spiral, catching other demons in its wake and croaking out her message. She didn't know how many demons were going to stay, and she didn't have the time to find out. She faced Ogden and almost laughed when she realized that he had slipped on one of the uniform jackets instead of his greatcoat. Between that and the tri-corn hat he had never parted with, he looked like something out of the history books. If the day went their way, then they would all be in the history books, she supposed. Immortalized on paper, never to be rewritten again. She nodded. "I'm ready when you are."

NOVEMBER 15, 2015

They weren't fool enough to portal right into enemy territory. Blackwood had been on the radio firing off messenger spells in every direction since the moment that Sully had left him, so the British should have known that they were coming as allies, but there was no guarantee that there wouldn't be a bloodbath wherever they arrived. Still, Sully liked their odds against some battered and terrified redcoats a lot better than their chances against the Fae, and if the ambush at camp had shown anything, it was that jumping into battle without knowing the lay of the land was a good way to get shot in the back. Sully took Mol Kalath and two of the Magi with her squad, a gnarled Frenchman who had been ancient even before his trip to the Far Realms, and a rotund African woman who had started out life as a baker in old Manhattan. She wasn't sure how their magic would fare against the Fae, given that demons weren't even close to as powerful and could swallow spells like breadcrumbs. If nothing else, these Magi had held out against the Fae on their home turf for a good few centuries in the fortifications of Manhattan. Sully was fairly certain that they wanted a taste of revenge, if nothing else. Sully didn't ask their names and they didn't offer them. It would probably be easier that way. The soldiers looked terrified from the moment they landed in the smog-shrouded streets, but they'd probably fare better than all the witches in the world in the same position. After all, every one of them had a cold iron bullet in their pistol and Sully knew from experience that that particular metal did the job.

Evacuation had already hit this part of town. Knowing how limited their time was going to be, Sully had picked destinations for the portals that were perilously close to the edge of the Fae's new domain without quite encroaching on them, assuming that their intelligence was good. Sully held still and silent for a long moment with her hand resting against Mol Kalath, waiting for orders, before she remembered that she was the one giving them. Frenchie conjured a little map that aligned itself to the street beneath them, and they set off into the heart of London without a backward glance.

Without knowing how acute the Fae's magical detection was, the different squads didn't dare to contact each other, so for all that Sully knew hers were already the only survivors of the offensive. The last time she had passed through London, the sheer mass of living people within it had been almost overwhelming. Now it was desolate in its silence. Every footstep echoed off the towering buildings as they made their way through the valleys of concrete and stone. Sully hoped that the citizens had gotten away, but with every new hint it got less likely. Here was a stone column, warped into a spiral by the touch of some strange magic. There the cobblestones were drifting up to float in the air. In one street there was no air at all, and they had to rapidly backtrack out of the vacuum and find another way around before they all suffocated. That had led them to traipse through one of the abandoned houses.

The table was set and there was food blackening and smoking in pots atop the oven that they passed as they made their way to the back door. Mol Kalath scrambled up and over the building, trying to catch sight of the enemy ahead of time and seeing nothing but more of the endless strangeness that the Fae had left in their wake. A forest of mushrooms had grown up in one of the city's few parks and huge brightly colored lizards were leaping amongst the towering fungi with skin-flap wings. When it was reported back to her, Sully hoped that they were constructs rather than transformed people, but life as a leaping lizard sounded pretty sweet compared to any amount of time in the tender care of the Fae.

They met someone who had tried to fight back a couple of streets over. He or she had been plastered across a car, the pavement and the side of a building, spread over them all, paper thin. They hadn't recognized what the strange overlay was until one of them had stepped on a nipple. When Sully finally spotted a contorted face in the expanse of skin, up by a window, it blinked at her and she had to resist every urge to burn the whole thing away. They couldn't afford to announce their position. Not yet.

Every squad had the same mission, to press into the heart of enemy territory and close the portal in the Archive. Rifts between dimensions were notoriously unstable, you only had to look at the chaotic mess in Kolikata to know that. All it would take was a solid enough hit with a spell, any spell, and the whole thing would probably unravel. Every squad had at least one Magus who was likely to be able to do that, and one demon that would try to eat as much of the magic flung at their squad as it could. Sully had been genuinely surprised how many of the demons had stayed after Mol Kalath's outburst back at camp, but she suspected that like most humans, demons would be brave if they were given the choice.

Frenchie's little map showed them well into the red zone before they caught sight of their first Faerie. It was over so quickly that half of the squad missed it by blinking. A pale head popped up from behind an overturned car. Huge almond-shaped eyes stared back at them. Then it vanished in a flash of light. The Baker hauled a wall up around them from the wire-riddled earth beneath the street and they hunkered down in it like a foxhole, bracing for an attack that didn't come. Long moments ticked by with half-formed spells hanging ready and guns cocked, then Mol Kalath rumbled, "IT HAS GONE."

Sully didn't move. "You sure of that?"

"I CANNOT SENSE ITS PRESENCE AND TIME IS OF THE ESSENCE."

Frenchie snorted. "Why is it that demons always talk in rhyme?"

"WE DO NOT DO SO, ALL OF THE TIME."

One of the squaddies started sniggering at that and the crushing tension that had held them all pinned in place broke. Rolling her eyes, the Baker pushed their little bunker back down into the ground and they set off again.

Sully strode ahead of the group. "We've got to assume that they know we are coming now. Stealth probably isn't viable, so let's pick up the pace."

Mol Kalath had to hop along with a flutter of its wings to keep up with Sully. "IF WE ARE TRULY ABANDONING STEALTH, THEN WHY DO WE NOT TAKE FLIGHT?"

Sully counted off the reasons on her fingers. "Only four of us can fly. The soldiers are probably going to have better odds against the Fae than us so we need to stay together. There is no cover in the sky. They might know we are here but they don't have our exact position. Any more questions?"

"NO, GENERAL SULLIVAN."

Sully whacked the demon with the back of her hand and smiled. "No back talk either."

That was when the Fae attacked.

Sully didn't even recognize that a spell had been cast until time ground to a halt around them. She turned to throw up a shield, but it was like she was moving through molasses. Mol Kalath was their savior. It flung its wings out wide, a meager shield against the beam of coruscating golden light that rushed out from a side street to envelop them. Those standing in the demon's shadow were saved. The Baker. Sully. Four of the gunners. The rest didn't have a chance. For a moment they stood there like statues, then they began to unravel, layer after layer of their bodies coiling off like when Gormlaith used to peel off apple skins in one tapering piece.

The demon let out a screech of agony, toppling forward. Mol Kalath was growing fast, but it seemed that there were limits to how much magic even a demon could swallow down before the spell asserted itself anyway. Feathers drifted away from it, swirling up into the sky one by one. Droplets of ichor began to spot the cobbled street beneath them and Sully's protections finally cast, snapping her out of the timeslip. She stayed low beneath the demon and listened carefully for any sound beyond the hysterical panting of the Baker and the soft hiss as their team blew away. A footstep. Almost too soft to hear, despite the echoes of the empty streets. Then another. Coming closer with a gait too ungainly to be human. Sully cast as close to silently as she could, layering on defenses and finally infusing herself with flight, almost as an afterthought.

She shot straight up into the air. The Fair One stood only a few feet away, hunched over, low and reptilian, to prod at what Sully would guess had been Frenchie. She didn't have time to be afraid now. A dart of pure white fire leapt straight down, aimed right between the huge black eyes that stared up at her. For a moment it looked like it was going to strike true, but the Fae flickered out of the spell's path and it bounced harmlessly off of the ground.

Sully launched into a barrage, letting her flying spell cut out so that she tumbled down toward the monster alongside the lightning, fire, and razor-edged nothingness that she was flinging wildly down. Not only at the Fae but at the whole street around it. She shattered the very earth it had walked. She left it with nowhere to blink away to.

"Clever girl." She didn't have to turn to realize it was hanging in the air behind her. On instinct she hammered an elbow back and was gratified when the creature folded around the blow. The soldiers opened fire. There were only four Gatling rifles left, with the rest rendered down to metal shavings on the ground but if Sully thought that her spells had left nowhere to run, they were nothing compared to the sheets of bullets that now filled the air. Her old contingency spell fired off, turning the storm of bullets away from her. In the moment she was protected she hit the ground and flung herself prone.

The chattering of the guns echoed off down the streets around them when the shooting stopped. Sully lifted her head up reluctantly. The Fae didn't bleed, so there was no satisfaction to be found in a gory mess, but its rubbery body lay perfectly still on the street, riddled with so many holes that Sully could see right through it. "Somebody put a cold iron bullet in it. Finish it off."

One of the soldiers had made the mistake of looking down at his companions and was now vomiting noisily. Another had fallen to his knees and the closest squaddie was trying to haul him back up. The last was frantically trying to reload her rifle with a new drum so that she could go back to firing until there was nothing left of the thing on the cobbles. Sully gave that one a smack around the head that stopped the reloading process, then held out her hand. "Pistol."

One of their few precious cold iron bullets spent, right between its eyes. It was only after Sully had handed the pistol back that the perfect circles all over the Fair One's rubbery surface stopped creeping shut. Sully spat on it. "Let's not get caught out again. Shall we?"

She wound her way through the remains of her soldiers until she reached Mol Kalath and the Baker. "What's the prognosis, doc?"

The Baker looked up from the demon's back with a blank look on her face. Enough trauma gave you that dead mask to wear. Sully was pretty sure her own face was an almost perfect replica of that absence of expression right now. "I have seen demons heal from worse. It just needs to shed some mass. It can take them a few hours, but they will recover from nearly anything."

Sully nodded and tried very hard not to look at the oozing mess of Mol Kalath's back. She ducked under its wing and whispered. "Can you heal this?"

"I NEED TIME. SHELTER. COVER. IN CASE . . . MORE OF THEM."

Sully cast a quick glance around then grabbed onto Mol Kalath's wing. With a nod, the Baker took the other one. Both women infused themselves with strength.

Sully snapped out orders as she started to drag the demon along. "One volunteer to take point. One to harvest ammo from our dead friends. Two volunteers to help lift my friend here. Fuck, you're heavy for a bird."

"NOT A BIRD," it mumbled.

"I'm not touching a demon."

Sully stopped to look—it was the one who had thrown up, of course it was. "That demon just stopped you from turning into sausage meat, so you can either help us carry it or you can scout ahead to make sure we don't come under fire. You've got about a half second to decide before I kick your ass so hard that I've got to open your mouth to polish my boot."

Pukey looked from Sully to the glare of the other soldiers, then ducked under Mol Kalath to lift its back legs off the ground.

They made it to a shop and when the door proved to be both locked and too small, Sully set off a concussion and took out the window. They were in a high-end boutique, which meant that there was plenty of fabric to heap up into a makeshift nest for the demon. Mol Kalath slumped down onto the heap gratefully, then its eyes closed. Sully slapped a barrier up over the front of the shop, then dug out a kettle from the tiny breakroom in the back. Sully had never considered herself British, but they had a tradition for hard times that seemed to have been adopted across the colonies. She made everyone a cup of tea while they waited for their demon to pull itself back together. The Baker stayed at the front of the store, layering on more protections. Pukey and the girl who'd tried to keep on shooting huddled around their mugs as though the tea was the last beacon of hope in a wicked world. The other two were making themselves useful dividing up gear and the remaining cold iron rounds evenly among the squad.

Sully could feel every passing second like a pendulum slicing more and more of their chances away. The longer that they took to close the portal, the more of the Fae would have taken up residence. She started to pace. Pukey's eyes following her back and forth. Eventually, he couldn't keep his mouth shut any longer. "How come you're friends with demons? You ain't from Manhattan."

Sully could have snapped at him or yelled about insubordination or picked any of a million other ways to avoid the topic, but with Mol Kalath lying so close, bleeding for them, it seemed cruel to pretend she didn't care, so she shrugged. "They're people, same as us. They just come from somewhere different."

"They're demons, not your funny Oriental neighbor. I mean, look at it. They're monsters."

Sully pushed her first, poisonous words back down and kept her cool. "There's no shortage of monsters out there if you want to go looking. I've run into a few of them myself over the years. But big bird over there has pulled my ass out of the fire more times than I can count. Because it was the right thing to do. Because of honor, or friendship, or one of those other words that we think mean human. Demons are good people. They've just been fighting those things out there for so long that they got desperate."

The Baker nodded. "We lived with them for centuries and they never did us any harm. Even when they could have."

There was a rumble from the middle of the shop and Mol Kalath lifted its head. Feathers had regrown, and ichor had halted. "I AM NOT A BIRD."

Dawn had broken while they took shelter inside. They left the shop through the back and Sully let her barrier stand as a misdirection until they were almost a mile away. This close to the portal there was no shortage of magic drifting all around them to restore her reserves, so it hardly felt wasteful. According to the little map that the Baker had conjured up, they were only about ten minutes away from the epicenter of the chaos. The buildings here were older, less sleek and more conservative. Patches of marble glinted here and there, but so did stranger things that the Fae had left behind. A fountain of blood had grown up out of a dead body on the ground, a contorted skeleton twisted into a spire and basin that a beating heart kept refilling as it drained. Some of the glass in the nearby windows had turned into liquid, held in place only by a surface tension that the slightest breeze might disrupt. Every time one sloshed down into the street, guns were trained on the empty window. Bubbles of molten glass drifted around in the sky above them, dispersing rainbows through their prismatic curves. It would have been almost whimsical if the hollowed-out city wasn't so terrifying.

The fact that they had made it so far without facing a coordinated defense made Sully deeply nervous. Either the Fae were so confident in their abilities that they didn't feel that formal defenses of the incursion point were necessary—which seemed in character with what Sully had seen of them and probably accurate given that one of the bastards had taken almost her whole squad with a single attack—or Sully and her squad had been lucky up until now. The second option frightened Sully much more. Luck was the kind of lover who would lay you to bed with kisses at night and wake you up for a breakfast of your own liver in the morning. She caught herself walking closer to Mol Kalath than was necessary. When she realized that the rest of the squad were doing the same, she very deliberately strode a few paces ahead. Cowardice could get them killed just as surely as brashness.

She grumbled, "Spread out, will you? I don't want to lose you all in one shot."

They seemed reluctant to leave the sanctuary of the demon, but they followed orders. At the end of the row of houses, they paused to consult the map. There were only two streets left before they hit the Archive and there was a patch of greenery between them. A public garden wouldn't offer much cover, but a straight run through it would get them right to the doorstep of the nondescript building without any more delays. Under Sully's watchful eye and with some trepidation, the Baker cast a scrying spell. Sully stared into the shimmering orb of liquid metal and counted. "Nine of them between here and there. Mostly clustered at the entrance."

Pukey looked green again. The Baker was shaking her head sadly. Mol Kalath's feathers were slicked down and the other three looked ready to run the moment somebody raised their voice. The girl mumbled. "We can't . . . You can't think we're going to . . ."

Sully cut her off. "What do we know about the enemy?"

The squad glanced at Sully nervously before their eyes snapped away again, scanning for any hint of danger. The Baker scowled. "They are so powerful that just one of them can wipe all of us out without trying?"

Sully nodded. "You're right. They don't seem to be working together at all. Every one I've met is overconfident in its abilities."

The Baker looked more furious with each passing moment. "Overconfident? That thing melted half of our squad before . . ."

Sully snapped. "Before we killed it. Remember that part. We killed it. We won."

"AT WHAT COST?" Mol Kalath nudged against her.

"The price that you've got to pay to win wars." Sully flexed her fingers. "Now what else do we know?"

After a moment of silence, Pukey and the girl both spoke at once.

"They move fast."

"They port around."

Sully treated them to a smile. "So focusing our fire isn't the best plan. Scattershot."

They fell silent again, so Sully pressed on. "You know what I've noticed? They can't take a punch. I hit that thing once and it folded up. They're too reliant on their magic. If you can lay hands on them . . ."

The quiet one who had harvested the bullets from his dead friends finally spoke up. "What? You want us to charge in and bayonet them?"

"No, but if you can hit them, you should. Just don't let *them* lay hands on *you*." Sully checked that her saber was loose in its scabbard. With only the one hand she wouldn't be able to cast if she drew it, but it was nice to know it was there.

"Why not?" The girl whispered.

"They can stitch you together or melt you apart if they touch you, and I wouldn't bet they'll be doing a lot of healing today." Pukey took a couple of steps away and retched against the side of the building. Sully pretended that it wasn't happening. "Listen, once we are inside the building, they lose their mobility. Your guns will cut them down. We just need to clear a path and get inside."

The girl was speaking so quietly that they all had to lean in to hear her. "Can't we wait? Hit them with the other teams when they arrive?"

"The more time they have, the worse our odds get. They're bottlenecked coming through the Archive, but every minute gives them more reinforcements and increases the chances we're spotted. We need to go now." She looked around at their terrified faces. Even Mol Kalath wouldn't meet her gaze. "You've all got friends and family somewhere out there in the world? They haven't got guns or training or spells. If the Fae get to them, they aren't just going to die, they're going to get tortured for years until they can't remember a time when there was anything but pain. We're the only thing between the monsters and the people. It's scary as hell. It hurts. You lose bits of yourself. But you still stand up and put yourself between people and harm because nobody else is going to."

There was a soft clap from the back of the group that ended abruptly when guns were trained on Ogden and he put his hands up. His team was missing its demon and its other Magus, but most of the soldiers seemed to be intact. Ogden slowly lowered his arms. "What an inspiring speech, Sullivan. Do you have a plan to go along with it?"

Sully grinned. "I just might."

No plan survived contact with the enemy. As the Baker opened the portal that was going to get the troops across the intervening territory, a spindly arm reached out of it and killed her. It was barely the lightest brush of the Fae's fingers, but the woman fell apart like she had been unzipped down a seam. Bones, blood and organs tumbled out in a wet rush. Only the collapsing of the portal stopped the creature coming through. In that moment others would have hesitated, but this wasn't Sully's first time going to war. She bellowed, "Stay under the screens but don't stop running until you're inside. On three, we move."

She cast a barrier overhead. "One."

It was joined by angled shields of more complexity a little further out. "Two."

Ogden snatched control of her barrier, layering on more and more complex protections. Sully started scribbling out spell fragments that drifted in a slow orbit around her. "Three."

Mol Kalath smashed into her and Sully tumbled up over its head to land spread-eagled over its back. The soldiers and Ogden sprinted forward. At the far end of the street spellfire flared up. Another team was making its attack. Luck. Damned luck again. With one painful yank on the demon's feathers, Sully sat up on its back and started casting concussions.

Some of the Fae had drifted off to face the rattling guns down the street but there were still more than enough standing guard. One wiped away their barriers with a flick of its wrist as if they'd never been cast. Then the dying started. The soldiers with Ogden had been briefed on tactics, but they quickly reverted to their training. They were trying to aim shots at bodies that had already vanished. The first time that one of the Fae sprang into being amongst them there wasn't even time for them to respond before it had blinked away again. There had been a soldier where it appeared, and now there was just a tattered wet sheet of skin tumbling to the ground. Sully was flinging out curses so fast that her throat was starting to ache, but none of them could make contact. She was even more useless than Ogden's squad. Ogden was throwing up shields to deflect the worst of the Fae's spells, but they were being torn down just as quickly. Sully launched a barrage of white fire out at the Fae to strip away any magical defenses, but it splashed across the street without making contact with anything at all.

For humans, magic took time and ritual. For the demons, it was about channeling the raw power of the cosmos. But for the Fae it came as readily as a thought. They could reach out with their will and snatch the spells away. Turn them aside or contort them into something new. Sully saw one catch a bolt of Ogden's lightning and toss it back as a jagged-edged sickle of black ice to neatly bisect one of the soldiers in a crimson spray. If they'd had a moment to think, the Fae could have just remade the world without bullets or enemies in it, so Sully had to make sure that they never had that moment. She was far from idle as they made their desperate charge, but she was painfully aware that her spells weren't going to turn the tide. The best she could hope for was to distract them long enough for the mission to be completed.

Sully saw only one of the Fae fall, and that was just because a soldier misfired into a space where it happened to appear. Damned luck. By the time that other weapons were trained on the spot the pale tangle of gangly limbs on the ground had already healed itself and vanished again.

There were only six soldiers left, running along beside Mol Kalath. Ogden had taken flight to lay down covering fire now that his shields had proven completely useless, and he was giving the Fae a run for their money. Every spell that they launched at him skimmed by harmlessly and every time one of them leapt into the air beside him they found he had already darted out of reach. Up ahead, three of the Fae were still lounging around the doorway to the Archive, making no move to stop the intruders. Sully gritted her teeth. They weren't even scared. They should have been.

Mol Kalath's bounding steps faltered as Sully sucked the power out of the demon in a rush. There was no circle here to bind the Inferno in—no way to know how far it would travel in the moment that it was lit or if it would rush back at her—but Sully didn't give a damn. She was going to make the bastards burn. She was going to make them pay. Mol Kalath's fury boiled up into her with its power like the righteous anger of people ground under the heel of oppression for too long. Generations upon generations living in dread, coming to a head here. The demon leapt forward one final step ahead of the three screaming soldiers who were still charging and Sully let it all out.

White light, brighter than the smog-dimmed sun above them, flared out from her outstretched hand. For a moment there was silence, then the fire died and the roar washed over them. The soldiers toppled over backward. Ogden was slapped across the sky to batter against the buildings on the far side of the road. Only the black beast beneath her stopped Sully from being flung to the road too. It had hunched down and locked its claws into the cobbles. Smoke rushed out toward them, almost lost in the huge black spot that the Inferno had left in their vision.

The Fae up ahead were gone and so were the upper levels of the building, sheared clean off the surface of the earth by the impossible heat, leaving only a blueprint of the walls in glowing molten stone.

Raw magic rushed up through the elevator shaft, drawn by the vacuum inside Sully and her demon. She ran her hand absentmindedly across its feathers and tried to remember its name. They bounded forward again and Sully at least had the wherewithal to scream back over her shoulder, "Charge!"

Three Fae stood behind Sully, their fingers embedded in the corpses splayed in the streets. Reshaping them into abstract statues of gory sinew and graven bone. Six huge almond-shaped eyes, black as midnight, stared right into her as pain and memory flooded back through her mind, carrying a wave of terror along for the ride. She was alone with them again.

Mol Kalath did not slow, even as the burned-out husk of the building seared its feet and scorched its feathers. It carried them forward to the brink of the precipice. Then Sully twisted to raise her surviving middle finger to the Fae before she vanished out of sight into the warm comforting darkness of the elevator shaft.

Demon and woman clung to each other as they spun down through the pitch blackness. It was a more comforting embrace than Sully had ever found with her conquests, her girlfriends, or even her own mother. It occurred to her that she'd completely forgotten to say goodbye to Gormlaith before she went off to war, but that seemed entirely appropriate given their history. She drew in a deep sulfurous breath through Mol Kalath's feathers and let strength and power flow back into her from the endless font beneath them. Her flying spell caught them before they hit the ground. There were no guards down here in this beige corridor, but Sully supposed that made sense. The Fae wouldn't use elevators when they could travel at the speed of thought. The moment they were through the portal, the Fae could just burst up into the city. There could be a million or more of them already through. Even if she managed to close the portal, there were so many Fae in London that the world as humans knew it was already over. It would be a new dark age, with people and demons alike fleeing from the hunters. *"Mankind will learn fear again. They will remember what it means to be prey. The natural order of things shall be restored."*

Sully hissed, "Shut the fuck up."

They reached the next shaft after a few staggering steps and Sully cast a quick concussion to dislodge the elevator and send it screeching down into the depths.

"You have already lost. Better to submit now. Better to give in and hope for mercy."

"Get out of my head. It's already crowded enough in here." Sully flew down in the wake of the elevator, letting the sparks of its fracturing brakes light their way.

Mol Kalath bellowed from behind her. "THEY KNOW NO MERCY, IONA. DO NOT BELIEVE THEIR—"

"How stupid do you think I am? Of course they're lying," she scoffed.

"But still there is the temptation to submit. It is rooted in all of you. You spend all your lives in fear of the coming storm, but when the thunder rolls you fall to your knees in supplication. Perhaps this time the lightning will not strike. Perhaps this time your doom will pass you by. Submit to me. Submit and chance may be on your side."

She rolled her eyes. "Oh, god. It is the whitest version of Pratt. Who knew you could so love the sound of your own voice when you don't even have a mouth?"

They landed on top of the elevator and with a flash of blue fire, Sully stripped the metalwork away.

"This is your final opportunity. Submit."

Sully stepped out into the hallway and smiled. "Go fuck yourself."

A single Faerie stood at the end of the corridor. Its arms were held wide, its gristly fingers flexing. Sully's stomach turned over at the sight of it, but she kept going. Mol Kalath was shuddering behind her, its fear vibrating through the floor to reach her. She'd been afraid of these things for a few days. The demons had been scared of them since the dawn of time. That was a dread with some momentum behind it. The pale thing took a step forward and it was all Sully could do to keep moving.

The fluorescent bulbs above them flickered and the pale monster darted forward. Sully launched an orb of flames the size of a watermelon down the corridor toward it, searing the varnish off the floor in a long sticky line. The Faerie darted around it with casual indifference, but proximity detonated the spell and the resulting explosion wasn't so easy to dodge.

The Faerie might still have been alive in the cloud of acrid smoke up ahead, but Sully doubted it. She smiled back at Mol Kalath and then froze. Three Faeries were holding on to the demon. Sinking their fingers into the oily black feathers and siphoning the magic away. Sucking the life out of the demon. "*Submit.*"

Sully let the spellfire die in her hand. "Stop."

"*Submit to me and your pet can live. We have no specimens of different species ready paired. You are a curiosity.*"

"So you've never seen what we can do?"

"*You are the first paired specimens that I have—*"

Mol Kalath barked out, "SULLY. NO."

She closed her eyes.

Mol Kalath was there in her mind, its reserves of power a glowing presence so palpable she could reach out and touch it. There was no question that she could draw on its power, just as readily as it could draw on hers. They'd never tried it over a distance of more than a few inches, but Sully was willing to bet she could suck that well of power dry from where she was standing if she wanted to. That wasn't the plan. She let her senses roll out over the demon, felt the places where the alien, encroaching presence of the Faeries were intruding into the still waters of the demon's power. She was connected to Mol Kalath the way that the demons had joined together to support her out by the stone circle. The Faerie hissed into her mind. "*What are you doing?*"

It took no effort to feel her way out from the points where they were connected to where their reserves of magic lay. Mol Kalath groaned as they tightened their grip on it. "SULLY. YOU MUST ESCAPE."

Sully just smiled. "We don't run."

She drew on the Faeries' power through Mol Kalath, yanking it out through the demon so hard and so fast that none of them had a chance to respond. The demon's reserves filled to bursting in a moment, then the overflow made the leap across the room to Sully, an invisible torrent of power that knocked her off her feet. Her own depleted reserves filled up. Spellfire overflowed out of her hand. Gushed out of the stump of her arm. Boiled out of her eyes in towering columns of light. Still there was more, an impossible amount of power.

Sully threw up her hand and forced it out. A tidal wave of raw red spellfire swept along the corridor, careening off of the walls. Everything that Sully had dumped right out of her as even more poured in from the other side. She had forgotten why she had started this, forgotten everything except the sweet burning of the power coursing through her. She was nothing but a living conduit.

She didn't notice when the Fae collapsed in on themselves and crumbled apart. She barely even noticed that Mol Kalath was withering too until it crawled across the space between them and dropped itself bodily on top of her, startling her back to awareness. The corridor up ahead was covered in a kaleidoscope of colored ash. The corridor behind them was filled with the dusty remains of the Fae that had stood in their way. She gasped for air as Mol Kalath funneled magic back into the both of them.

Eventually they were steady enough to rise back up onto their feet. The demon croaked, "NEVER DO THAT AGAIN."

Sully sank her singed, shaking fingers into its feathers. "Wasn't planning on it."

They walked along the rest of the corridor leaning against each other and crunching through the crystallized magic on the floor as they went. Sparks trailed behind them, drifting up from each step they took. Shimmers of spellfire still trickled out of Sully's hand, crackling in the charged air. She paid it no mind. This close to the boundless resources of the portal, she could afford to lose it.

The Fae had done some remodeling of the closet where the Archive portal had been stored. It was at the center of a perfect sphere now, carved out of the surrounding rooms. Pale immobile figures hung in the air. The Fae lined the walls on each level, hundreds upon hundreds of them staring down. Mol Kalath bristled with terror.

When Sully opened her mouth to cast, one of the Fae sprang into place beside her and jammed fingers inside to catch hold of her tongue. Sully gagged. Another one appeared and caught a hold of her wrist. More of their grasping hands latched onto her. Encircling her legs. Locking onto her hips. Everywhere that she looked she was surrounded by pallid flesh and she couldn't even scream through the fingers inside her.

Mol Kalath was wailing with anguish behind her as it got the same treatment. The demon lumbered forward, dragging the Fae along behind it for a few steps. Sully bit down hard and the fingers in her mouth came off with no more resistance than raw dough.

She spat them out and screamed out her traveling spell, burning the patterns of the spell into her own mind with no way to get them out. The demon lunged forward one final step, feathers tearing loose in the Faeries' implacable grasp, and made contact.

With a gasp of agony, Sully released her spell and she and her demon were torn out of the rubbery, grasping hands. Everything went white as the magic overwrote even the channels of her senses. There was a distant sensation of falling, then her eyes started to work again. Mol Kalath was flung bodily into the side of a hut in an unfamiliar swamp and fell limp to the ground. She caught only a glimpse of it before the grotesque hands latched onto her once more and dragged her back along the course of her spell to land in a heap.

She dragged in half a ragged breath, then the pain hit her. The human body wasn't meant to travel that way, not at the best of times, and certainly not dragged backward through a collapsing spell. She spat out a mouthful of blood and ignored the tickling as more ran out of her ears and her nose. She wasn't meant to be here. She could remember that. The rest of her memories hurt to touch, so she left them alone for now, smoldering beneath the tracks that the traveling spell had cut into her brain.

"*Will you submit?*"

She barely knew what the words meant, but deep down in her gut, she knew what the right answer was. "No."

She got herself up onto her knees and the nearest of the Fae started to edge forward. She held up her hands. Her name was Sully. They were monsters. Sully killed monsters.

"*It will be easier for you if you submit. We will treat you with kindness. We will take your pain away.*"

"No." She spat out more blood.

The memory of Marie came back to her, and with it a rush of other names and places. Kisses and fights. Screams and cold skin. Another fragment of who she was. More pain.

"*Shall we hurt this one? Will his screaming convince you?*"

Her eyes focused on the man dangling by the scruff of his neck in the monster's grasp. His eyes were bulging with terror. The hat. The bandana. Ogden. Screams. Fear. Knives. More pain.

Sully pushed herself up onto her knees. Her life was slowly returning to her, memory by memory. "Kill him if you want. I was going to do it if you didn't."

"*Such disregard. Why was this one to die?*"

As she said the words, she remembered. "He killed people. Hundreds of people. He's a murderer and Pratt was going to let him walk away, just because he's useful."

Ogden was trying to struggle but with the Fae's fingers lodged in his spine he couldn't do much more than groan. Sully's memories came back to her like a sledgehammer blow. She fell forward and retched up another mouthful of blood.

Kneeling in the center of the circle of Fae, blood pouring out of her and damage she couldn't even comprehend riddling her aching body, Sully came to a realization. "You . . . You're still scared of me."

"Fear is an emotion. Emotion is a trait of lesser species."

"Then why are we still talking? Why were you begging me to give up all the way down here?" Sully gave them a red toothed grin. "You know that if I go down, I'm going down swinging. You know that I'll take some of you with me. You might not be scared like a real person, but you don't want to be the one that catches it, do you?"

Even as ruined as Sully was, she could still call spellfire to her hand without effort. The glow of the portal had illuminated the room with a sterile white light, outlining the Fae with stark shadows, but now those shadows began to dance. They tremored and shook in Sully's presence, even though the monsters themselves were still. *"Will you submit?"*

This close to the portal, Sully's reserves refilled faster than she could burn the power off. The flames in her hand licked higher. "I've got a wish. Just a little one. Not like anything Blackwood and his fools would have asked you for. If you grant it, I'll submit."

"What is your desire?" the Faerie whispered.

"There's a girl. A vampire. Marie. I wish that she has a happy life from now on. Can you do that? Can you make it so she's happy more than she's sad?"

"Granted."

Sully had seen how the demons granted wishes, but that was nothing like the terrible beauty of the Fae's magic. They did not spill out spellfire, they traced perfect white lines of blinding cosmic power to rewrite the laws of probability. The image of that spellform would have haunted Sully for the rest of her life, if she had expected to live longer than the next few minutes. A wave of darkness rushed out from the center of the room when the spell was complete, a void like the absence of all existence. It swept out and washed over everything, leaving nothing in sight changed. The moment that the darkness had passed she nodded and snuffed out her own fire without a second thought.

"Let's get this over with."

NOVEMBER 17, 2015

The Far Realms were a lot like the Archive drawn large. The air tasted of nothing and hung at a temperature so moderate you couldn't even detect it. The sky was the same blinding white as the Fae magic, and the sand beneath her feet as she staggered along was only a shade darker. The white of staring directly into the sun. There were a great many Fae scuttling around, floating by and blinking into sight for only a moment before moving along, but they paled in comparison to the number of humans. Each of them seemed to have been paralyzed, and they drifted in cocoons of force so delicately constructed that Sully could barely sense them. Only their eyes betrayed the fact that they were still alive. Wild and terrified. Every so often one of the Fae would stroll by and a cluster of humans would drift off after them, heading into the empty expanse that rolled out in every direction. Ogden was bound up in much the same way, drifting alongside Sully and the Faerie that had granted her wish. Another of the Fae manifested a loop of chain around her waist and started to drag her along.

The arch of the portal was the only solid object that Sully could see anywhere. It only took a moment for her to understand why. Why would you need buildings when there was nothing to shelter from and you had no possessions? Why would you have objects or art or history when you could satisfy any desire with a thought? It was no wonder these creatures were so alien. They hadn't risked touching Sully to heal her, so it didn't take long before the pure white expanse all around her had become a little gray around the edges. She walked on through the ceaseless shifting sands with only a few small comforts. She had gotten Mol Kalath to safety and it would be able to return to the hells it knew. Ogden was here with her, so he was going to get the kind of punishment for his crimes that she wouldn't have wished on anyone. Marie was going to live a happy life.

Sully wasn't sure about that last one. She didn't know if she could trust that the Fae had done what they had said they'd do, but there weren't many other options left by that point. She wasn't getting away, she couldn't kill them all, and she sure as hell wasn't going to get them to stop by asking nicely. "What is the point of all this? Why are you stealing people?"

The Faerie closest to her was probably the one speaking, but they all sounded alike. "*We have not had access to fresh live samples from your dimensional strata for many of your millennia. Locally grown stock assimilates our traits too swiftly for us to produce statistically significant results.*"

She wished she hadn't asked. Even so, there was nothing to do to stave off unconsciousness from her blood loss except talking. "My wish from earlier, is it really going to come true?"

"*I adjusted the probability as completely as possible in favor of its completion. There are few true impossibilities once you have skewed reality far enough.*"

"Uh, thanks. I guess." Sully looked at the pallid thing as they trudged on.

"*It is unclear to me how well-developed human senses have become. The easiest way to ensure your compliance was to grant your request with the utmost accuracy.*"

"You were scared I'd catch you in a lie?" Sully smirked, and a trickle of blood ran down her chin.

"*Fear is an emotion. Emotions are—*"

"Yeah, yeah, we suck for feeling things, I got the memo."

They trudged on for what felt like hours but could have been minutes. There was a ringing in Sully's ears that wouldn't quiet and even the white sand right in front of her looked gray and hazy. She stumbled one time too many and the Faerie sprang on her. Its hands plunged inside her, shredding her uniform but passing through her skin unscathed. She could feel it inside her. Touching things that hands were not meant to touch. She tried to vomit but a finger traced over the underside of her stomach and halted it before it could happen. The whole process was over so fast that Sully didn't even have time to breathe but when she did, she found that the half-drowned sensation of her collapsed lung was gone too.

When she had enough air to stand up, she wheezed out, "Thanks again."

"*Your damaged body was inefficient for the task at hand.*" It strode on.

There was still nothing in sight, and as far as Sully knew the desert was going to go on forever. The floating bodies and the Faeries drifted on ahead. It wasn't like she was a prisoner at all, really. She could have run whenever she pleased. There was just nowhere to go. A whole world, a whole plane of nothing but sand and light and the Fae. She closed her eyes and let the power flood in. This close to the source of magic there was no longer any point in quantifying it. It was as close to infinite as anything Sully had ever dreamed of and it flushed through her so fast it was as if she wasn't there at all.

She trailed after the procession for a while longer. Letting the plan that she had been so careful to keep from her thoughts resurface. There was nothing that she could do to help the people here. Even on her own plane, the Fae had been so powerful that she wouldn't have been able to free their prisoners, but here all of reality was theirs to control. Clementine and Ogden, all the bystanders who had been sold off to the Fae as payment for their service, they were all as good as dead. Sully was too, but she couldn't bring herself to be upset about that. She'd done all that she could to put her affairs in order.

The Fae were fundamentally selfish creatures—Sully doubted that the concept of self-sacrifice would have even crossed their minds. Humanity was just too alien for them to understand. Even now she couldn't really bring herself to hate them, but she didn't need hate and anger to drive her forward. Not when she had people left behind her that needed protecting.

There was all the time in the world for her to trace out the spell. It was so familiar to her that she didn't even have to think about it. It was almost bizarre to think that she had never cast the original before. When she got to the part where she had amended it so heavily, she stripped out any limitations and went with the version she had first learned. It was near to completion when she noticed the Fae looking at her from the next dune. "*What is the purpose of this? You have lost. Your world has fallen. Nothing that you do now matters.*"

Sully grinned. "The purpose is . . . fuck you."

When the Fae spoke again, it was like thunder in Sully's skull. Hammering down onto her already fragile mind with all the subtlety of a lightning strike. "*Still you do not recognize your own utter insignificance. Compared to me you are nothing. Your existence spans barely a moment of my eternity. Your mastery is so feeble it cannot even stretch beyond the moment of casting.*"

Blood began to flow from Sully's ears once more and another trickle escaped from her nose. The Faerie pressed into her mind with a will like a scalpel blade but still she churned out more and more spellfire, linking the Inferno to her own reserves of magic, repeating the lethal mistake that Dante had first set on paper centuries before with a smile on her face.

"*Even this paltry spell is beneath my notice. You mean to conjure fire? The mightiest flames that you have ever been able to summon are as nothing to me. You think yourself an inferno? You are a guttering candle in the midst of the raging typhoon of my raw might. You will blink out and I will go on.*" Sully laid the final line of spellfire. The spell hung ready to be unleashed. "*Tell me, foolish mortal. What does a candle do in the face of the storm?*"

She met the gaze of the monster and smiled. "It burns brighter."

With her arms spread wide and the infinite power of the Source rushing right through the open channel her body had become, Sully unleashed the Inferno, one last time.

November 18, 2015

London was burning. That was what the few scorched and terrified soldiers who had returned from the attack told their superior officers when they finally arrived in Ireland. Something had gone terribly wrong with the Fae's portal, but before it had collapsed shut, there had been some sort of explosion. One poetic soul who was missing half his face described it as being like the gates of hell falling open. There had been some consultation with the few remaining demons and Magi, but no consensus had been reached on what could have caused it. The damage was expansive. Central London, the part that Blackwood insisted on calling the Old Town, was burned down to the ground. The only good news was that it seemed to have burned the heart out of the curse that afflicted the city too. London had finally stopped growing and the latest half-built constructions on its outer limits had collapsed.

The Fae that had survived the blast had fled in short order, and the few sightings of them so far suggested that they were in poor shape. Without the steady recuperating flow of magic from their home plane, they seemed to be withering rapidly. Pratt had dispatched the few remaining Magi to hunt the Fae down and avenge both their fallen comrades and their beloved leader, Magus Ogden. There were already plans for a statue of him to be built in Manhattan. Pratt decided to wait a week before taking bids on it.

Gormlaith heard all these things and more, shambling around

and handing out cups of tea to the soldiers. None of the soldiers had a clue who she was, beyond being the owner of the beaten-up cottage at the edge of camp, but she had a maternal quality to her that they appreciated. Particularly when it meant a nice cup of something warm while they were on guard duty.

Mol Kalath took up fully half of the cottage, huddled by the fire in a despair so deep that even Gormlaith couldn't penetrate it. Most of the other demons were heading home, back to the lives that they'd left behind. Mol Kalath didn't seem to care. Its mate had visited in the late morning, a huge spike-riddled bear-like thing that couldn't squeeze through the door, but even its guttural wailing hadn't been enough to make the demon move.

The other half of the cottage held Blackwood, who was no longer a prisoner but who had nowhere to go for now. He had plans for after the chaos and the flames had died down to catch a portal back to the outskirts of London and reassert himself as ruler, or at least kingmaker, but for now he was content to listen to Gormlaith's whispered reports and to speculate along with her on their meaning.

Before the end of the day, the Americans broke camp. A group of Magi came to haul away the carcass of the Hydra, which was starting to get a little ripe, so Gormlaith was quietly pleased with herself that she'd harvested the parts she wanted in the middle of the night. The tents and the temporary walkways were all broken down until eventually Gormlaith's swamp returned to its state of cold damp misery, with the addition of a great many boot prints and almost as many graves. Gormlaith trailed around after they were gone, picking up every shiny scrap that she could see amidst the scrub grass. There was some kindling and string that she'd have had to do without. Some metal pegs that she could repurpose into something useful. The portal points had been the most fruitful. Ritual components that she would never have been able to lay hands on in her life were just laid out for the taking.

By nightfall the silence outside of the cottage's walls had become oppressive. There was an unpleasant intimacy to being together now that everyone else was gone. It was enough to have Blackwood abandon his plans. There was a little house in the Scottish Borders that he was fairly certain was empty, so he bid Gormlaith farewell and vanished to wait out the next few days in solitude. If Gormlaith gave a damn about any one of those things, she showed no sign of it. Instead she settled in to read an ancient and crumbling book on the history of the Fair Folk and more specifically on the opening of portals to the Far Realms. After an hour, she produced a scrap of paper and started scribbling fragments of a formula. It didn't take long before the demon was hanging over her shoulder and rumbling comments of its own.

FEBRUARY 12, 2015

By now it was almost a habit for Gormlaith to go take a stroll past the stones at midnight. The demon skulked around them at all hours, never flying far enough away for the circle to be truly out of sight. The big black bastard probably should have been an annoyance to Gormlaith, but now with her purpose withered away and her only daughter gone, it was just nice to have some company, even if the conversation was still sparse.

When she arrived this night, Mol Kalath was sitting up on its hindquarters, staring into the circle, as if it might light up at any moment. It didn't look away from its vigil, but it held out a wing to keep the worst of the rain off the old woman as she waited beside it. "I CAN FEEL HER."

Gormlaith rolled her eyes. "You say that all the time."

"THIS TIME IT IS MORE TRUE THAN THE OTHERS. THIS TIME IT IS LIKE SHE IS ONLY A ROOM AWAY. A WISH DRAWS HER BACK, I CAN FEEL THE SHAPE OF IT JUST BEYOND THE WALLS OF THIS PLANE. ANY DEMON COULD TELL YOU THE SAME. SHE IS COMING BACK."

"Well, I haven't many more of your lot to consult with now, do I? You must be the last one in the word by now, and nobody's answering my summons." Gormlaith blew on her hands and rubbed them together.

"THEY HAVE NO NEED TO. THE DANGER IS PAST. THE FAE ARE GONE."

She grumbled. "That don't help me get any bloody answers though, does it?"

"SHE COMES. LOOK TO THE CIRCLE."

At the center of the circle there was a tiny spark of flame. It couldn't have been much bigger than the light of a candle, but in the pouring rain and pitch darkness it shone out. Gormlaith took a step toward it but the demon stopped her with a bark. "WAIT."

The fire erupted, first into a blaze, then into a pillar of light. Demon and crone stared up as it seared the clouds away and then blinked out, all in an instant.

The moment the fire was gone, they rushed forward, Mol Kalath bowling Gormlaith over in its excitement. The ground was too hot to touch, but it danced over the flame-smoothed stone to reach the blackened heap at its center. Gormlaith had only just tripped and stumbled down into the circle when the heap started to scream. The sound was piercing in the sudden silence of the night. A mindless wail of pure anguish, more animal than human. It sent steel shooting right up the old woman's back. That was her baby crying.

She rushed forward and knocked Mol Kalath aside with a gust of wind before falling to her knees by Sully's side. The thing on the ground was blackened all over but as it wailed, that charcoal coating cracked and glimpses of wet red flesh could be seen underneath. Here and there was a glimpse of white. Bone or tooth. The few places that looked human were so blistered and raw that Gormlaith couldn't understand how Sully was still alive. The screams got worse when they tried to move her, until she was nestled on Mol Kalath's back and fell so silent that Gormlaith had to scramble up and make sure she was still breathing.

Back in the cottage, she surveyed the damage as Sully's lidless eyes stared out at her from the ruined mask of a face. Uncomprehending. "We'll be needing a healer. This is well past herbs and mud. Go, demon. Fetch help."

Mol Kalath fled into the night and launched itself into the

tempest, grateful for the thunder because it drove away the memory of the screams.

FEBRUARY 18, 2016

Visitors had come after the healer from Manhattan had done all that she could. It was impossible to keep stories from spreading, even for Pratt, and he couldn't have any legends growing up around his lost general, not when things were finally settling down again. With no small reluctance he took a flight over to Ireland with an entourage of lackeys and a few of Sully's friends who had been clamoring to come and see her—two colleagues from the IBI and the girlfriend who had provided such useful leverage, but was now, tragically, leaving the country to pursue opportunities elsewhere.

He made certain that he had the first audience with Sullivan so that he would have the most time to spin anything that she was likely to say before she repeated it to anyone else. Ideally, he would have made the trip by himself, but Chijioke Okoro, who insisted on the ridiculous abbreviation of Ceejay, had managed to make many friends throughout the American administration, many of the same ones who had favored Sullivan in her day. Pratt couldn't afford to alienate that faction at this juncture. Not when their martyr might be about to come swinging back into the fray once more. There had been a great deal of conflicting information about Sully and her current state, so when Pratt ducked into the smoky cottage, he really didn't know what to expect.

She was sitting by the fire under a heap of furs looking at least a decade younger than when he'd last seen her. Her hair was little more than a red fuzz, regrowth from after the healing was completed and no more. Her skin had a puckered pinkish appearance that he would have found disturbing if he hadn't been distracted by the fact that all the scars and freckles that had given her face its character appeared to be gone. He nodded to her politely and perched himself on the stool that seemed to have been set there for his use, even if his backside did overhang it ever so slightly. The old woman whom he had been informed was Sullivan's mother was lurking in the back corner of the house. She had been glowering at him since they had first arrived, and he had decided to pretend she wasn't there until she became necessary. "Good evening, Miss Sullivan. How are you?"

"Good evening, Mr. Pratt." Her voice was still rough and ragged at the edges, but the undercurrent of malice that he was so used to hearing, the fury that had made her so easy to manipulate, seemed to be gone.

"Your mother will have told you who I am?"

"You're the Prime Minister of America. I used to work for you. I was the general of your army."

"That is correct. Very well done. We also used to be rather good friends before all of this war business kicked off."

She smiled at him, then winced when it pulled too hard on her new skin. "You seem very nice, but I can't remember you. I'm sorry."

He stared at her for a long moment, trying to work out what her angle was. "You cannot recall anything about me or our time together?"

"Sometimes . . . sometimes I get little pieces. A girl smiling or a bit of song. Most of the big stuff hasn't come back yet. Mother says it is burn-out. When somebody uses magic for too long or too hard they can hurt themselves. Lose parts of who they were."

It was like he had just hit the jackpot. This Sully was the war hero everyone was clamoring for, the savior of the Americas and the human race, and she was a blank slate. He could have her say anything at all, and she wouldn't even know that she was lying.

"I am very sorry to hear that has happened to you, Ms. Sullivan.

I was very fond of the woman that you became, but I am certain that with time I will come to be very close with the new version of you as well."

She stared at him for a little bit longer, a tiny frown just starting to form. "I remember eating something with you, we were in some sort of restaurant, I think. It was spicy."

He smiled. "Whenever I passed through town, I would always try to make dinner arrangements with you because you were such delightful company. More often than not you were busy but—"

Gormlaith coughed loudly and they both jumped. She pointed to Pratt, then nodded to the door. He smiled at Sully again. Just as genuine looking as the first time. "If you will excuse me for a moment, I think your mother worries that I am going to tire you out before you have the chance to see your other guests."

Ceejay and Raavi sneaked in while Gormlaith chased a back-pedaling Pratt around the side of the building. She spat right next to his foot. "You're to leave her be."

"Madam, I can assure you that I have no intention of—"

"I said you're to leave her be. No parades. No news. No anything. Just let them forget her. She's a chance at a life of her own now that all this is over, I'll not have you taking that from her. You know how she was before. You know who she was. There's no telling what'll come back, but I'd wager you want her as far off as you can get her if it does. Am I right?"

He considered that for a moment then conceded the point with a nod. "Your daughter was a wonderful person, Mrs. Sullivan, but she could be a little abrasive, and in her tender state, perhaps it would be best if she remained in the loving care that only you could provide."

Gormlaith's mouth tightened into a thin line amidst the wrinkles. "And a pension for her?"

"Of course. She was injured in the line of duty, after all," he added benevolently.

"Then I'll keep her disappeared for you."

He was about to hold out a hand to shake but he paused. "And if she should regain some portion of her memories, I can rely on you to ensure her . . . complacency?"

"I'm her mother. Nobody else has hooks in her like me," Gormlaith cackled.

Sully had not taken well to the booming voice of Ceejay or the way that Raavi kept trying to touch her. She'd thrown both of them across the room with a wave of her hand and a pulse of low magic and now they weren't entirely sure if they were having a conversation or a hostage negotiation.

Ceejay had come back to sit on the stool beside her, but Raavi was hovering near the door. "I'm very, very sorry," he said. "I didn't realize that you were so . . . sensitive."

Ceejay laughed. "If only you had brought your sister along, she would have had no trouble getting her hands under Sully's blankets."

Sully let out a little snort that might have been a laugh. It was nice to get some suspicions confirmed. "You can come back over. Just don't prod at me. I've had enough of doctors."

"Right, sorry. Force of habit. Usually when you knock lumps out of yourself, it is me that you call on to get stitched up."

"I got hurt a lot?"

Ceejay cackled. "You had a collection of scars that you liked to show off at the bar. Particularly when we went out with the secretaries for ladies' night." He guffawed. "You were like a shark dropped in a barrel of fish. It was amazing. Before you met us, you were in the navy and I think you must have had a girl in every port and a scar to match. You had a claw mark on your face from some snake-man that you fought in Laos. That was your favorite."

Sully looked down at the bare skin of her arms. "Guess I'll have to start over."

Raavi pointed to the smooth stump of her arm. "That's a good one to get you going. I hear you had that bitten off by a gryphon."

The grinding of beak on bones. The thunder of the concussion. Sully stopped breathing for a moment as it came back. Another tiny sliver of who she had been. She tried to cover it with a laugh but the other too glanced at each other nervously. "Aren't they extinct?"

Ceejay threw back his head and laughed. "They are now."

Her mother grumbled back into the room to shoo them out as the storm outside came on in earnest. "That's enough visitors now. You'll exhaust her. Off with you."

Marie came in after the clamor of the other visitors had passed and only the distant sound of Gormlaith lambasting them could still be heard. She perched herself carefully on the stool, smoothed her dress over her legs and finally pulled herself together enough to speak.

"Hello, darlin'."

Sully turned to stare into the fire.

"Sully? It's me. Marie."

Sully didn't look at her.

"I know you've forgotten a lot of things. Your momma made that much clear, at least." Marie sighed. "You weren't wrong about her, by the way. I could've gone my whole life without hearing her hissing at me."

Sully snuggled down under the furs and let out a little sigh.

"Are you listening to me, darlin'?"

She glanced over at Marie and that little frown returned.

"Do you know me, at all? Don't you remember me?"

Sully shrugged, then turned back to the fire.

"You were going to marry me, Sully. We were going to have a big wedding in Imperial Park. I was going to walk down the aisle with a parasol and all my bitchy theater friends were gonna come and throw rice."

Sully yawned and closed her eyes.

"And now you don't know who I am no more. You don't even—" Marie cut herself off with a strangled sob. Sully just lay there as she cried. Not saying a word when before she would have had her arms wrapped around Marie before a single tear could fall. When Marie pulled herself together enough to speak, Sully still hadn't moved a muscle.

"I loved you, Sully. More than anybody I ever loved in all my life. When you come back to yourself, you're gonna come back to me. No matter what poison your momma's spittin' about me. I know you're gonna come back."

She slipped down from her seat and leaned over to plant a gentle kiss on Sully's cheek. Sully turned just before she got there, and their lips brushed against each other. Marie stared down into Sully's eyes and there was nothing there but confusion. It was more than Marie could stand. She ran out of the house without another word. Her tears were lost in the torrential rain.

Sully jerked upright with all of her senses on edge. There was a strange perfume hanging in the air and she was certain that something had just touched her lips. She ran her tongue across them, and there was a hint of salt there that she couldn't explain. Closing her eyes, she let her stronger senses roll out through the house and out. Here was the familiar weight of her mother and the demon. There was the cluster of one man with magic and two without. She strained, but that was all that she could feel. When she opened her eyes again, she turned away from the fire and peered into the deep shadows that dominated her mother's home. She whispered, "Is someone there?"

Marie nearly crashed right into Gormlaith on the path. The hag was grinning as rivulets of water traced the terrible topography of her face. "Told you. Didn't I? I told you she'd forgotten about you. She always deserved better than your kind. Even when you was living, you was trash. She's going to have a life for herself now. Don't need any ticks latched on her legs, slowing her down."

The moonlight flashed off Marie's fangs as she hissed at the old woman. "Do you even know how much she hated you? She couldn't even speak about you without feeling sick. Does she remember that? Shall I go and tell her?"

Gormlaith cackled. "Who is she going to listen to, her mother or a stranger?"

The old woman barged past Marie without a care in the world, then called back over her shoulder. "I wouldn't be trying to come back if I were you. There's charms you can lay down against bloodsuckers and I'll be laying them."

"I wouldn't come back here if it was the last shit-heap on the planet. My darlin' will come and find me. She always does. You'll see."

Gormlaith's laughter faded off into the rain, and Marie was left alone again.

She started trailing along the path toward firmer land and the cars, following the dull glow of warmth still left in the others' footprints. Her pink tears washed away in the rain just as quickly as she cried them. She was almost to the edge of the swamp when something huge and dark burst out of the shallows to loom over her. Mol Kalath shook its wings to rid itself of the worst of the bog-slime, then crouched low enough that Marie could smell the brimstone in the air around it. She had never seen a demon up close before. It terrified her, but she faintly remembered something Sully had said about vampires being hard for them to see. She edged a little further along the path, but the bird-thing let out a low rumbling croak that stopped her in her tracks. "SHE IS COMING BACK."

Marie whispered. "She is. She is coming back."

"SAFE TRAVELS, COLD ONE. SHE WILL COME FOR YOU SOON ENOUGH."

She managed another couple of stumbling steps away before she turned back again. "Thank you."

Mol Kalath took flight, spiraling up into the storm, gaining speed and height with each pull of its wings. When it broke through the clouds it could see the dullest glow of the sunrise in the east, barely brighter than the night sky but clear enough to a demon's senses. It whispered, "SHE IS COMING BACK."